"I Want You,

he said, his face inches from her own. "And you want me."

His lips brushed hers and, grasping his wrists, she cried, "No, don't!"

Then her grip loosened as a cascade of emotions drowned any objections. She ran her fingers through his hair, giving up the uneven struggle.

"You're so beautiful. I knew the minute I saw you that you were going to be mine. I want it all from you."

Samantha opened her eyes slowly, the import of his words hammering at her brain. It wasn't physical attraction; it was business, pure and simple. *I want it all from you!* He wanted her, yes—and he wanted Morgan Construction!

TRACY SINCLAIR
has traveled extensively throughout the continental United States as well as Alaska, the Hawaiian Islands, and Canada. She currently resides in San Francisco.

Dear Reader,

Silhouette Special Editions are an exciting new line of contemporary romances from Silhouette Books. Special Editions are written specifically for our readers who want a story with heightened romantic tension.

Special Editions have all the elements you've enjoyed in Silhouette Romances and *more*. These stories concentrate on romance in a longer, more realistic and sophisticated way, and they feature greater sensual detail.

I hope you enjoy this book and all the wonderful romances from Silhouette. We welcome any suggestions or comments and invite you to write to us at the address below.

Karen Solem
Editor-in-Chief
Silhouette Books
P.O. Box 769
New York, N. Y. 10019

TRACY SINCLAIR
Castles in the Air

Silhouette Special Edition

Published by Silhouette Books New York

America's Publisher of Contemporary Romance

SILHOUETTE BOOKS, a Simon & Schuster Division of
GULF & WESTERN CORPORATION
1230 Avenue of the Americas, New York, N.Y. 10020

ISBN: 0-671-53568-4

First Silhouette Books printing January, 1983

10 9 8 7 6 5 4 3 2 1

Map by Ray Lundgren

Other Silhouette Books by Tracy Sinclair

Paradise Island
Holiday in Jamaica
Never Give Your Heart
Mixed Blessing
Flight to Romance
Designed for Love

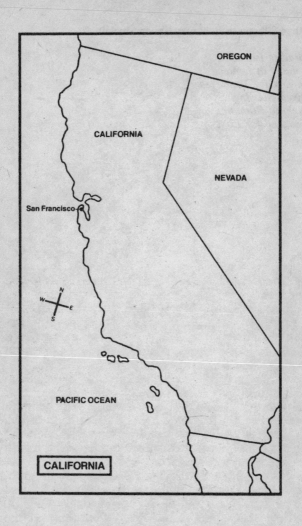

OREGON

CALIFORNIA

NEVADA

San Francisco

PACIFIC OCEAN

CALIFORNIA

Chapter One

I'm sorry to interrupt, Sam, but could I talk to you for a minute?" Pete Grogan asked tentatively.

Samantha Morgan looked up from the column of figures in front of her. Any respite from the disastrous profit-and-loss sheet she was working on would ordinarily be welcome, except that Pete's expression indicated he was the bearer of more ill tidings.

She managed a smile, however. "Sure, Pete. What's up?"

"I'm afraid I have some bad news," he said, confirming her fears. "Johnny Matlock is quitting."

"Oh, no!" She ran slender fingers through her short, glossy black curls. "He's our best trim man."

Pete shrugged. "I know."

"But we have that Jackson Street house to finish, and Mrs. Drucker is the fussiest woman in San Francisco. Every nail has to be practically lined up with a slide rule." She looked doubtfully at the column of figures on the desk. "If it's a question of money, maybe we could manage a few more dollars, but—"

Pete's head shake cut off her halting words. "We could never match the offer he got from Sutherland Construction."

Samantha gritted her teeth. Mike Sutherland again! Her deep blue eyes flashed sparks of fire. "He can't keep doing this to us! For months, he's been raiding our company, luring away our best men. I'm going to bring him up before the Building Commission!"

"And charge him with what? It isn't against the law to offer a man more money. That's called free enterprise," Pete said wryly.

"But why always us? That man—" she almost choked with anger. "He's deliberately trying to put me out of business."

Pete cleared off an edge of the desk so he could settle one hip on it. "Maybe you ought to think about his offer, Sam."

"Never! Even if I would consider selling Morgan Construction, it would never be to him," she cried passionately.

"You can't be emotional in business," he said gently. "You have to admit his offer was certainly generous."

Pete was more than just her foreman, he was her trusted friend. She had always valued his opinion, but right now, Samantha was beyond reason. "Nothing about that man is fair. He's a rotten, male chauvinist creep! Because my father died, he thinks I'm incapable of running the business alone. Well, I worked alongside of Dad and I can carry on now that he's gone."

"You're an architect, Sam," Pete said patiently, "and a fine one, too. But that's different from taking on the whole operation of a construction company."

Her shoulders slumped. "I know it isn't fair to you, Pete. You've had to assume more than your share of responsibility, but I'm learning."

"I'm not thinking of myself. It's you I'm worried about. While Rufus was alive, I didn't say a word—it wasn't my business. But he's gone now, and it's time you started leading your own life. You're a young woman; you shouldn't be tied to a career you let your father choose for you in the first place."

"Dad didn't pressure me," she said defensively. "It was what I wanted too."

His eyes were shrewd. "Was it?"

Samantha thought about the Fine Arts course she was enrolled in before she switched to architecture. It had been very stimulating, but her father was correct when he said that serious artists almost never made a living. He pointed out, very rightly, that she could utilize her talents in a much more constructive manner.

"It's been very challenging working here," she insisted. "I'm really very lucky. And nobody can say I took advantage of being related to the boss. I've always tried to be just one of the guys."

Pete looked at her slender figure and sighed. Even in jeans and a plaid shirt buttoned up to the neck, there was a feminine quality about Samantha that refused to remain hidden. "Your father should have had a boy," he remarked somberly.

"Well, if he had to settle for two daughters, at least he got one of each kind." Samantha grinned. "Brooke, the fluffy little southern belle, and me, the big, capable one."

Is that how she saw herself, Pete wondered? It only went to show what you could accomplish if you treated a girl like a boy for twenty-five years.

The phone rang and Pete slid off the desk, raising a hand in farewell. "Think about what I said, Sam."

9

The call brought more bad news. "I'm sorry about our date tonight, Samantha, but I have to work," a male voice informed her.

"Oh, Donald, can't you get out of it?" She looked down at the odious balance sheet on the cluttered desk. "I was looking forward to getting away from it all tonight."

"I'm sorry, dear, but it's tax season, remember?"

How could she forget? Donald Crane was a certified public accountant with a busy San Francisco firm. In the three years they had gone out together, that seemed to be his major topic of conversation. Remorse smote Samantha at the errant thought, and she quickly said, "I understand. It's just that I'm disappointed, that's all."

"I am too, baby, but I'll make it up to you. We'll go out to dinner tomorrow night instead."

"I can't, Donald. Brooke is staying overnight and I promised to go to that foreign film at the Orpheum with her."

"I was planning on taking you to that myself," he said stiffly.

Samantha sighed. Donald hated movies with subtitles and would never have thought of taking her to one if Brooke hadn't suggested it first. This jealousy of her sister was unreasonable. "I don't think you would enjoy it," she pointed out.

"Neither will you. You're only going because Brooke wants you to. I can't understand why you let your whole family walk all over you."

Samantha tapped her pencil impatiently. Why couldn't Donald and Brooke get along? His antipathy for her sister was long-standing—and returned with interest. The nicest thing Brooke called him was Donald Duck.

Samantha reflected, not for the first time, that it

was a good thing she had taken her own apartment in the city. At least that way, the two didn't meet very often. Not that Donald was the reason for the move. It had been wrenching to leave the lovely home in the suburbs where her mother and sister continued to live. Yet after her father died and she had to be at work by seven o'clock, it was just too far from San Francisco to be practical.

"Samantha?" Donald's voice recalled her sharply. "When am I going to see you?"

A shadow fell across the desk and she looked up to see Johnny Matlock standing tentatively in the doorway. "I can't talk about it now, Donald. Call me again."

After she hung up, the young man came forward with obvious embarrassment. "I guess Pete told you I'm leaving."

"Yes, and I'm sorry to see you go, Johnny. I wish I could change your mind."

He attempted a smile. "You've heard about those offers you can't refuse."

"Mike Sutherland is good at those," she said bitterly. "Well, I hope he appreciates what a good man he's getting." Johnny still hovered uncertainly, so she added, "I'll make out your check. You can pick it up this afternoon."

He waved an awkward hand. "No hurry, Sam."

When he failed to leave, she looked at him curiously. "Is there something else, Johnny?"

"I just wanted to say . . . I mean . . . I didn't influence Burt. I wouldn't want you to think I tried to do anything behind your back."

There was only one Burt with the company—Burt Shaunessy, their roofer. "Burt? You mean he's leaving too?"

"I'm not sure. I only know he went to see some-

11

body at Sutherland's. If they made him an offer, I didn't want you to think I had anything to do with it."

She stood up. "Okay, Johnny, thanks for telling me."

Taking one look at her smoldering eyes, he beat a hasty retreat.

Without waiting until he was out the door, Samantha yanked open the drawer that held the phone directory. After hastily riffling the pages, she savagely punched out a number, drumming her fingers on the desk as she waited.

A dulcet voice announced, "Sutherland Construction Company. Can I help you?"

"I want to talk to Mike Sutherland," Samantha announced in murderous tones.

A short, frustrating conversation later elicited the information that he wasn't in the office. His secretary refused to divulge his whereabouts, saying that he was out on the job, only refusing to tell which one.

Samantha's eyes narrowed in concentration. The most likely place was the multimillion dollar insurance building he was erecting in San Francisco's financial district. That one was a plum even for a firm as big as Sutherland's. It would merit close supervision.

A short time later, her small red car screeched to a stop in front of the block-long construction site. A tall board fence with peepholes for sidewalk superintendents completely surrounded it, leaving only a wide entrance for trucks to go in and out. All the observation posts were filled with people fascinated by the giant hole in the ground and the bizarre machinery that looked like mammoth, mechanized dinosaurs.

Ordinarily, Samantha would have shared their

fascination, except that today she was a woman with a single purpose. Striding determinedly through the opening, she spied a construction shack across the yard. She was making for it angrily when a hand grasped her arm, spinning her around.

"Where do you think you're going?"

She looked up, and then up some more, at a tall, bronzed giant who towered over her. An orange metal helmet covered his hair except for one dark lock which fell across his broad forehead. There were laughter lines at the corners of his gray eyes, but the humor they indicated wasn't apparent now. He was regarding her coldly, the wide, generous mouth thinned with displeasure.

Samantha glared back. Under any other circumstances, this was the kind of man who would definitely rate a second look, but his rude tone of voice struck a match to her smoldering anger. "Take your hands off me," she commanded.

"As soon as I escort you out of here," he said, pulling her toward the exit.

She wrenched her arm away. "Trust Mike Sutherland to keep a bouncer around the place. Don't you have anything better to do than harass defenseless women?"

He looked at her curiously. "What do you know about Mike Sutherland?"

"More than I want to! Now, will you get out of my way?"

"So you can do what? There's heavy machinery out there, lady—and I use the term advisedly." He looked her up and down in a way that made her squirm. "You can get hurt."

"What am I supposed to do, faint with fright?" she asked, pushing by him contemptuously.

A long arm pulled her back. "In case you haven't noticed, this is a hard-hat area." Without relinquishing his punishing grip on her arm, he reached down and picked up a helmet from a cluster on the ground, plunking it on her head with a thump that made her ears ring.

Rage swept through Samantha. Tearing off the offending headgear, she threw it as hard as she could. It hit the ground with a clatter, rolling in an erratic path like a drunken orange. "That's what you can do with your hard hat," she stormed.

He started toward her, a sparkle of pure fury flashing from his gray eyes. Even though she was sustained by righteous indignation, Samantha blinked, taking an involuntary step backward. Her challenge had awakened something primitively male in this powerful giant.

To her relief, he checked his progress just inches away, contenting himself with a glare that would have given pause to a charging elephant. Recovering swiftly, Samantha returned his glare. The gray eyes narrowed dangerously.

Raising his arm, he pointed toward the construction shack. "In there," he bit out through clenched teeth.

Samantha lifted her chin defiantly. "If you think I'm going anywhere with you, you're sadly mistaken."

"Would you like me to carry you?" he inquired, almost pleasantly.

For just a moment, she considered defying him. Then discretion took over. There was no doubt that he was capable of carrying out his threat. The muscles in those brawny arms and broad shoulders rippled in anticipation.

Tilting her nose in the air haughtily, Samantha preceded him toward the shack, trying to give the impression that it had been her own idea, yet painfully aware of the rather alarming male following close on her heels.

After he had slammed the door shut, he turned to confront her, his sheer bulk seeming to fill the small room. "I think it's time we had a little talk," he stated.

"What's the matter, are you tired of trying to intimidate me? I wonder how brave you are with someone your own size."

With hands splayed over narrow hips, he rasped, "Who the hell are you and what are you doing here?"

"Not that it's any of your business, but I came to see your boss. When I tell him what a good watchdog you are, he'll probably give you a raise," she taunted.

He took a deep breath, controlling himself with an obvious effort. "When you say, my boss, I assume you mean Mike Sutherland?"

"Who else?"

"Correct me if I'm wrong, but I gather you don't care for the man."

"That's the understatement of the year!"

"Could I ask what caused this outpouring of dislike?"

"Abomination describes it more accurately," she cried.

"That's rather a strong word." He smiled and the transformation was startling, suffusing his craggy face with charm. "I always understood he was a very likable fellow."

"Sure, if you like unprincipled men without a spark of decency," she said bitterly.

"What did he ever do to you?" he asked curiously.

"I don't wish to discuss it," she said stiffly. "Would you just tell me if he's here on the job?"

"Yes, he's here."

"Well . . . can I see him?"

One dark eyebrow raised sardonically. "Who shall I say is calling?"

Samantha drew a deep breath. "Tell him Sam Morgan wants to talk to him, and I'm not leaving until I do."

The effect this produced was unexpected. His mouth actually dropped open. *"You* are Sam Morgan?"

"I assume you've heard of me," she said coolly. "It's very flattering, although I wouldn't think a small company like mine was worthy of so much notice."

He seemed at a loss, something Samantha felt didn't happen too often. "I can't believe you're Sam Morgan."

"Believe it," she said shortly. "What's the matter, did you think I was older, fatter, thinner—what?"

"I thought you were a man," he said simply.

"I guess it's a natural mistake," she conceded.

"That isn't your real name, surely?"

"Well, actually, it's Samantha, but my father always called me Sam, and everyone in the business followed along." She looked at him sharply. "What difference does it make? Mike Sutherland knows I'm a woman."

"I can assure you, he doesn't."

"I'm equally certain that he does," she said angrily. "It's the reason he is so sure he can put me out of business. Your boss thinks a mere woman isn't capable of running a construction company. But just to make sure, he's hiring all my best men away, offering them salaries he knows I can't meet. That's your wonderful, likable Mike Sutherland!"

"I understood he offered to buy you out," he said slowly.

"And that makes everything all right? Suppose I don't *want* to sell?"

"That's your privilege of course."

"Not if he keeps tipping the scales in his favor."

"I don't think . . . uh, Mike . . . understood the problem."

"Oh, he understood all right! As soon as Dad died, he closed in for the kill."

"That's not exactly fair. After all, your father was negotiating a deal with Sutherland's before he died. He was planning to retire."

"That's a lie!"

"He didn't tell you?"

"Of course not, because it isn't true. Dad would never sell out—Morgan Construction was his life!"

But even as she said it, little things came back to Samantha. How tired Rufus had seemed at times, and the way he said he was getting too old for the rat race. She had jollied him out of it, thinking he was depressed by high interest rates and the squeeze on the small builder in today's tight economy. Was he secretly yearning for the free time he never seemed to have? No! It was just another trick of Mike Sutherland's, one she mustn't let herself believe.

"He wanted out," this man said gently. "I don't know why he didn't tell you. Maybe he was just waiting for the right time."

"I don't believe you!"

"Why is it so difficult to accept? He worked hard all his life. Didn't he deserve a little leisure?"

"Yes, but . . ." Samantha sank slowly down on a chair. There was no reason in the world to believe this man—except for the quiet assurance in his voice. "Why wouldn't he have discussed it with me?"

"I can't tell you that. All I know is that I offered him a fair deal and he was receptive."

The words took a moment to penetrate her

numbed brain. Then, *"You* offered him a deal?" She looked at him in complete outrage. "Who are you?"

White teeth flashed in the tanned face. "The abominable Mike Sutherland, at your service."

"You . . . you . . ." She was sputtering with rage. "You tricked me! You knew who I was all along. You let me say all those things just so you could make a fool of me!"

"I assure you, I had no idea who you were when you charged in here." He looked her up and down, amusement curling his firm mouth. "I never expected Sam Morgan to turn out to be a hundred-and-five-pound wildcat."

She ignored that with a great effort. "I *told* you I came here to see Mike Sutherland."

"That's right, you did. What was it you wanted to see me about?"

His calm dismissal of this whole charade infuriated Samantha. Gritting her teeth, she said, "I want you to stop raiding my company. "I'm warning you—stay away from my men."

He folded his arms, looking at her impassively. "Or you'll do what?"

The worst of it was, there was nothing she *could* do. They both knew that. It was galling, but Samantha tried to curb her temper and appeal to him reasonably. "Why are you doing this to me? My company is no threat to yours. What satisfaction will you get out of ruining me?"

"I don't suppose you would believe me if I told you that was never my intention?"

"How can I when you're luring away all my best men?"

"This is going to be hard for you to swallow, but I didn't approach them. They came to me."

"No! Why would they do that? They loved my father. They all worked for him for years."

There was compassion in Mike Sutherland's eyes as the import of her own words reached Samantha. They trusted Rufus, but that confidence didn't extend to his daughter.

"Times have changed," Mike said gently. "High interest rates are pricing the small builder out of the market. You can't really blame your men for worrying about their jobs. How many new houses have you built lately?"

"We could get by on remodel work," she said defensively. "Okay, so people aren't building new houses, but they're fixing up the ones they have. I could make it if you didn't take all my craftsmen."

He shook his head. "Give it up, Samantha. Sell out to me."

"How about the people who have stayed? The ones who depend on me?" she cried. "How about my foreman, Pete Grogan? He's been with Morgan's for eighteen years."

"I'd be happy to get Pete. He can have a job here anytime he wants—for a lot more money than you're paying him. He's too loyal to leave you, but if you were really concerned about him, you'd let him go." He looked at her troubled face and his eyes softened. "I'll even find a place for you."

"Thanks for nothing!"

His lips twitched with amusement. "I thought it was very generous of me, considering your lack of experience."

"What?" The word quivered with outrage. "I'll have you know I've worked in this business for four years!"

"For your father," he said dryly. "What's the matter, Samantha, are you afraid you can't cut it in the big outside world?"

His male assumption of superiority was maddening. She wanted to pound on that rock-hard chest, but something about him, maybe his sheer size, stopped her. "I went to work for my father because he needed me. That doesn't mean I couldn't have gotten a job somewhere else."

"Being Daddy's girl made that unnecessary though, didn't it?" he asked cynically.

"Are you saying I'm not competent?"

"I don't know. Why not come to work for me and we'll both find out."

"I wouldn't work for you if there wasn't another job in San Francisco—no, make that the world!"

"Spoken like your typical, emotional female."

Before Samantha could respond, they were interrupted by a workman who stuck his head in the door. "There's some trouble with that pneumatic drill they just delivered, Mike. I think you'd better take a look."

"I'll be right there." Turning to Samantha, he said, "As fascinating at this conversation is, it will have to wait. We'll finish our discussion over dinner tonight."

"I wouldn't—"

"I know—if I were the last man on earth," he mocked, anticipating her declaration. "Don't worry, there's nothing personal in the invitation." His gray eyes swept over her with a totally male look, pausing at the swell of her breasts under the thin cotton shirt. "You're a little underdeveloped for a real man's tastes."

He left before she could make a reply, but in any case, Samantha couldn't have done so. No man had ever looked at her in quite that way, and it left her oddly shaken. She had never met a man so virile, so overpoweringly masculine. Even though she detested him, his appraising glance had made her pulse beat faster. It was almost as though he could see through the studiously boyish attire to the female attributes she was at great pains to conceal. Damn the man anyway! Without even admiring her, he made her feel like a woman, and that was something she could do without.

As soon as she got back to the office, Samantha sought out Pete. Wasting no time, she put the question to him bluntly. "Did my father ever talk to you about selling Morgan Construction?"

From the way his eyes shifted, she had her answer even before he replied. "He was going to tell you, Sam. He just never got a chance."

"You know better than that. We were together every day," she cried. "Why would he keep a thing like that from me?"

"Maybe he felt guilty," Pete mumbled. "Since he got you to come into the business and all. Maybe he felt like he was running out on you."

"I can hardly believe all this." Samantha's expression was dazed. "How about mother and Brooke—the country club and all the rest? How did he expect to keep up that standard of living if he quit work?"

"He probably planned to invest the money from the sale of the business. You could do the same thing, Sam. Keeping up that big house for them in Hillsborough must be breaking your back, not to mention Brooke's tuition at Stanford."

If Pete only knew the panicky hours she spent worrying about it in the middle of the night! But no one must know that. She took a deep breath. "I can manage."

"Why, when there's no need? Sell out to Sutherland, and get out from under."

"No!" The idea of it filled her with panic. "How do I know what you've told me is the truth? I have only his word for it and yours." Ignoring the hurt look in Pete's eyes, she rushed on. "Dad would have discussed something that important with me. He wouldn't have just gone ahead and—" Her voice broke. Turning swiftly, she almost ran toward the office.

Pete watched her go, shaking his head sadly.

It was a long afternoon for Samantha. The fact that she hadn't had her father's confidence, no matter what the reason, was a bitter pill. If he had truly meant to sell, that is. It all came down to that. Or was it just a gigantic plot against her? No, she mustn't become paranoid. Still—Mike Sutherland was Machiavellian enough to do anything to get his own way. She could almost feel the cobwebby brush of his web being spun about her.

By the time she reached home that evening, Samantha's head was aching. All she wanted to do was take a long, hot bubble bath and crawl into bed. The sound of loud rock music coming from the apartment put an end to that plan. It had to be Brooke. She had a key and often popped in unannounced. Why tonight, though, Samantha groaned inwardly?

"Hi, Sammy, you're late." Brooke waved from the couch where she was curled up with a fashion magazine. "I hope you're not busy this evening. I couldn't wait to see that movie."

"Something better came along for tomorrow night like a heavy date, is that it?" Samantha smiled, turning down the hi-fi. "It's all right, I have nothing planned. Slumping down in a chair, she kicked off her shoes.

Her sister's answering grin was shamefaced, telling Samantha she had guessed right. "You look beat. Hard day?" Brooke asked.

"You might say that."

"A nice hot shower will fix you up. It always does me when my muscles are sore from tennis."

Samantha rested her head on her hand. "It did me too when I was nineteen."

"And now that you're twenty-five, you're an old lady?"

They smiled affectionately at each other. It was always a shock to strangers when they discovered the two were sisters. They couldn't have been more different. Brooke's long, straight hair was blond like their mother's. She was small like her also, although her figure was already voluptuously curved. Only their deep blue eyes were the same, but even here there was a difference.

"Why did you have to inherit those thick black lashes that never need mascara?" Brooke used to complain. "Not to mention those perfectly arched brows."

"Maybe because I take after Dad and you take after Mother," Samantha had answered with amusement. "I don't know what you're complaining about. If you attracted any more men, we wouldn't be able to get in the front door."

There was genuine affection between the two. Brooke said now, "If you're too tired, Sammy, we don't have to go tonight."

"No, I'll be fine. It might be just what I need. Besides"—she grinned—"I told Donald we were going and he's apt to quiz me on it."

"Donald again! What you see in that turkey is beyond me," Brooke exclaimed with exasperation. "Honestly, Sammy, when I think of all the guys that were crazy about you. That darling Stan Rasmussen for one, and Mel Bennett and—"

"Stop!" Samantha laughingly told her. "You're making me sound like Helen of Troy."

"Well, it's true. There are any number of men dying to take you out. How can you settle for a nerd like Donald?"

"He's really very sweet when you get to know him," Samantha said defensively.

"Hogwash! He's a fussy old maid."

"Donald isn't old. He's only thirty-five, although I suppose that does sound ancient to you."

"Not at all. Most men are really interesting at that age, but Donald acts *sixty*-five. He's about as romantic as a wet sponge." Brooke looked at her sister sharply. "I'll bet he's never even made a pass at you."

"I don't consider that a liability," Samantha said stiffly.

"Aha! I was right!" Brooke's eyes narrowed appraisingly. "What is it with you, Sammy, are you afraid of sex? Is that why you stick to old dull and dismal?"

"I'm not frigid if that's what you're implying."

Unaccountably, an image of Mike Sutherland surfaced. After their furious encounter, Samantha could have sworn that all she had noticed about him were the smoldering gray eyes and pugnacious jawline. Yet somewhere in her subconscious, that blatant masculinity of his must have registered. Samantha realized that she could give a perfect physical description of him—the flat stomach and slim hips that tapered down from broad shoulders, the muscular forearms, even the big hands with their long, well-shaped fingers. A strange flutter made her stomach muscles tighten, and she shifted uneasily.

Fortunately, Brooke was too annoyed to notice. "If Donald is so wonderful, how come he hasn't asked you to marry him?"

"How do you know he hasn't?"

Brooke was aghast. "Sammy, you wouldn't?"

"Not right now," Samantha assured her. "I have too much on my mind at the moment to even think of marriage, but maybe someday. After all, what would be so bad? Donald has a good job and a bright future. We have a lot of the same interests and we get along reasonably well."

"That sounds like a reason for joining a health club with someone, not marrying him. Are you trying to convince me, or yourself?" Brooke asked dryly.

The doorbell saved Samantha from the necessity of answering.

"I'll get it," her sister offered.

Brooke's criticism had disturbed Samantha more than she was willing to admit, probably because of this upsetting day. But was she right? Was she, Samantha, hanging on to Donald because he was safe and didn't put any pressure on her? It was true that bells didn't ring when he kissed her, she had to admit. Was that really important though? Wasn't it better for two people to respect each other? Love was something that developed slowly over a period of time. Only youngsters like Brooke expected sparks to fly the first time they met a man. It would be nice, she thought wistfully, but it just didn't happen that way.

She was so involved in introspection that she didn't hear the murmur of voices in the foyer or register the undercurrent in Brooke's voice when she announced, "Look what I found."

Glancing up in bemusement, Samantha was electrified. Towering over her diminutive sister, and looking impossibly handsome in a charcoal suit set off by a white silk shirt, was Mike Sutherland! "What are you doing here?" she asked rudely.

25

"Don't question a gift horse, Sammy," Brooke murmured, eyeing the rugged face with admiration.

He cast an appreciative eye over her curvaceous body. "I can't believe you two are sisters."

A small pang assailed Samantha at the familiar comment, although it didn't usually bother her. "What do you want?" she demanded, frowning ferociously.

He was not intimidated. "I believe we had a date for dinner."

"We had no such thing!"

Brooke was watching them both with interest. "If you don't want him, can I have him, Sammy?"

Mike threw back his head and laughed. "Under any other circumstances, it would be a pleasure. Unfortunately, I have something to discuss with your sister."

The "unfortunately" stabbed Samantha like a knife. "I can't imagine what that would be," she said icily.

"How about Morgan Construction for starters?"

Samantha's heart plunged as a quizzical frown appeared on her sister's clear brow. There was no reason for Brooke to be upset. If and when the time came to throw in the towel, that would be soon enough to tell her mother and sister. Neither of them had ever worked a day in her life, so even a hint that the business might be in trouble, would be frightening.

Casting wildly about, Samantha said, "I'm afraid the job is no longer open, Mr. Sutherland."

He started to speak, then stopped as her eyes silently pleaded with him. Glancing from Samantha to her sister, a look of comprehension crossed his face. "We can at least have dinner and talk about it." He gave her a sardonic smile. "You owe me that much."

"I don't know what the job is," Brooke said, "but you'd be a fool to let him get away."

"Go in the other room, Brooke," Samantha said desperately. "I want to talk to Mr. Sutherland alone for a minute."

"We can talk over dinner." He consulted his watch. "It's getting late and you still have to dress. You do intend to change, don't you?"

Samantha's cheeks flamed as his derisive eyes swept over her. "I'm a working woman, Mr. Sutherland. I'm afraid this is all my wardrobe runs to," she declared defiantly.

"Who are you kidding?" Brooke hooted. "Go put on that darling dress you bought for Mimi's wedding." Giving Samantha a push toward the bedroom, she flicked her eyelashes at Mike. "I'll keep Mr. Sutherland entertained while you get ready."

Samantha paused irresolutely. It was pure blackmail, but if she didn't go to dinner with him, Mike would surely spill the beans. The implacable look on his face warned her of that. He was perfectly aware of her subterfuge, and willing to exploit it for his own ends. Suddenly, there was a straw to cling to, and Samantha grasped it. "I can't go to dinner with you. I just remembered, I promised to take Brooke to the movies."

"Oh, Sammy, don't be dumb!" Brooke exclaimed disgustedly. "I can call any number of people."

The smile on Mike's face told Samantha she was beaten.

The dress she chose was a blue silk the color of her eyes. It had a demure neckline and a simple cut, yet looking at herself now, Samantha was doubtful. The narrow skirt hugged her slim hips and a slit up one side displayed a flashing glimpse of long legs when she walked. It had been selected in a fit of pique at the way Mike's eyes had flicked over her in that disparaging manner. And the way he had expressed amused disbelief that she and the luscious Brooke were sisters. She'd show him! But now, she was having second thoughts.

The tall, slender girl looking back at her from the mirror was a stranger. Instead of a mop of unruly black curls, her hair was brushed into a shining halo around her head. Even the eyes gazing out of the sooty black lashes were different, their customary blue darkened now to violet by the strange excitement coursing through her veins.

A thrill of something very like fear traveled up Samantha's spine as she turned toward the closet. It was all the fault of this silly dress! She should have worn something sensible like the long-sleeved brown wool.

The door opened and Brooke stuck her head inside. "Oh, good, you're all ready." Opening it wide, she called over her shoulder, "You're in for a treat, Mike."

Samantha had only a moment to register the fact that her sister was already on first-name terms with this odious man before he sauntered over to the doorway. His eyes roamed over her from head to toe, noticing the way the silken fabric clung to her slim figure, emphasizing the curves underneath.

The look on his face was totally male. "So I see. The transformation is astounding."

His amused surprise was insulting. "I've changed clothes, Mr. Sutherland—nothing else," she informed him.

"We'll see," he murmured.

"Have a good time and don't hurry home," Brooke said brightly. "I'll write out the plot of the movie for you, Sammy. In case Deadly Donald really does ask questions." When Mike's eyebrows rose questioningly, she gave him a mischievous grin.

"Donald is the competition, but my money is on you."

Casting an exasperated look at Brooke, Samantha exclaimed, "There are times when I can see a distinct advantage in being an only child."

It didn't help matters that Mike joined her sister in laughter.

Chapter Two

Samantha sat stiffly in the bucket seat of the sport-white Ferrari, her rigid posture betraying uneasiness. Mike's presence was altogether too close for comfort, his overwhelming size and the confidence he exuded making her feel very vulnerable. That was arrant nonsense, she tried to assure herself. He couldn't force her into anything, could he? But that tall, rangy body so near her own was making her nerve ends quiver.

"I don't know why you insisted on dinner," she said resentfully. "We could have said everything we have to say to each other in my living room."

"I gathered you didn't want your sister to find out about our little business dealings."

"There aren't going to be any. I wish you'd get that through your head," she cried passionately. "That's why I didn't want Brooke to know anything about it. Or my mother either."

"You mean they don't know about the precarious state of the company?"

"Listen to me, Mike Sutherland, Morgan Construction isn't going to go under no matter what you do," she said grimly.

He raised an eyebrow. "Wishful thinking, little girl."

"And don't call me little girl," she flared. "I have a perfectly adequate name."

"Which brings up an interesting point. Why does everyone call you Sam or Sammy? Samantha is a lovely name." His gray eyes warmed as they slid over her. "You look like a Samantha tonight."

She squirmed uncomfortably under his penetrating regard. "I told you about that," she said shortly. "My father called me Sam from the day I was born. Understandably, the nickname stuck to me."

"That's not all that did," Mike said slowly. "I'm beginning to understand a lot of things. You've taken over more than your father's business, haven't you?"

"What do you mean?"

"You're the head of the household now—the unofficial oldest 'son.'"

"You're as bad as Pete." She sighed disgustedly. "Just because Dad called me by a boy's name, you assume he treated me like one. My father and I had a very warm relationship."

"That doesn't answer my question. Are you supporting your mother and sister?"

"Don't you think that's a rather personal question?" she asked stiffly.

"Not under the circumstances. Why aren't they at work helping out? Why are you shouldering this burden all alone?"

The idea of either of her relatives at the construction yard was laughable. Samantha could just see Cecily, her petite blond mother, tripping around in high heels, her long, polished fingernails meticulously flicking specks of dust from her designer clothes. She would probably fill the office with African violets and put up organdy curtains. As for Brooke, she would be more interested in the lean young men they hired.

"Samantha?" He was waiting for an answer.

"You don't know them so you wouldn't understand. Besides, it doesn't concern you." She glanced out of the car window, closing the subject. "Where are we going?"

"To dinner. Wasn't that the agreement?" He grinned.

There was no agreement. It was coercion and he knew it! "I hope this won't take long," she said distantly. "I have to get home early."

"What's the matter? Do you have a late date with Donald?"

For some odd reason, she didn't want this man to know anything about Donald. Samantha could cheerfully have wrung Brooke's pretty neck. The best thing to do was ignore the question. "At the risk of repeating myself, where are we going?"

"Well, if you had persisted in wearing those scruffy jeans, I would have taken you to a diner on the waterfront. But since you dressed so nicely for me, I guess you expect to go some place fancy," he teased.

"The diner will be just dandy," she told him coldly. "I only put on a dress to satisfy Brooke."

"Mm, and such a nice one too," he murmured.

They pulled up at a long, low modern building before Samantha could reply. A parking attendant opened her door, and she saw that they were at a private supper club she'd heard of but never been to. Donald wasn't a member.

Taking her reluctant arm, Mike ushered her inside where he was greeted by name. The lighting was muted and there was music playing for several couples who circled a small dance floor. They were shown immediately to a choice leather booth against the wall.

After they had ordered drinks, Mike lit a cigarette, squinting through the smoke. "I believe we were talking about Donald."

"No, *you* were," she remarked pointedly. "I see no reason to discuss my friends with a perfect stranger."

"Thank you for the 'perfect.' " He grinned. "Is he someone special?"

"He—" Unaccountably, she stopped. Why didn't she come right out and say, yes, Donald is *very* special? Was it because at the moment, she was having difficulty remembering what he looked like? How nonsensical! This man had the ability to scramble her brains, his dominant male personality making her uncertain about even the fixed poles of her life. "We're going to get married someday," she said firmly.

"Someday? That sounds rather indefinite." His voice mirrored the amusement on his strong face.

"I just meant we haven't set a day."

"Or even a year." He grinned.

"Why is that so hard to understand?" she asked defensively. "We both have responsibilities. Donald is trying to get ahead in his accounting firm, and I have to be sure Morgan's is on its feet before I can begin to think of marriage. I couldn't expect him to support my whole family." Why was she explaining in such detail to Mike Sutherland of all people? She didn't have to justify herself to him. "After all, there isn't any hurry," she finished coldly.

"Isn't there?" His eyes fastened on her full mouth before traveling downward. "If I were engaged to you, I could think of several compelling reasons for getting married."

A flood of warmth swept over her, making her tremble with anger at his unmistakable meaning. He had no right to imply that Donald was somehow lacking in virility. She couldn't let that pass. Veiling her eyes, Samantha gave a musical laugh. "How very old-fashioned of you, Mr. Sutherland."

His narrowed gaze surveyed her appraisingly. "So, you're playing house together, is that it?"

She was immediately sorry for her flash of temper. His supreme male arrogance was certainly irritating, but was that any reason to give the impression that she was sleeping with Donald?

Her blush deepened, making her grateful for the dim lighting. "Really, Mr. Sutherland, that does overstep the bounds of propriety."

Unexpectedly, his big hand cupped the back of her head. Drawing her close, his firm mouth covered hers. Samantha stiffened with shock, pushing against his hard chest, futilely, as it turned out. He held her easily, the fingers of one hand tangling in her dark curls while his other hand wandered caressingly over her back. The sensuous feeling sent a ripple down her spine that he couldn't miss, and the demanding pressure of his mouth lessened.

As though sensing her vulnerability, he relented. His lips were gentle now, teasing hers open so he could deepen the kiss. This had an even more devastating effect. The slow, seductive exploration of her mouth caused a fire storm of sensations that seemed to be centered in her midsection. Without being aware of it, Samantha stopped struggling, giving in to the unaccustomed demands her body was making. She was so lost in the whirlpool of emotions he had generated that when he removed his arms, she looked at him blindly, not understanding how he could stop.

Mike surveyed her dazzled face mockingly. "That was because I'm tired of being addressed as Mr. Sutherland. You can scarcely call a man "mister" after you've kissed him, can you?"

Samantha's heart was racing like a long-distance runner, while he seemed completely unaffected. Worse than that, her reaction *amused* him! She took a deep breath to quiet her uneven breathing. When she could trust herself to speak, indignation accompanied the words. "I didn't kiss you—you kissed me. That's an entirely different thing, Mr.—" She stopped, aware by the determined look on his face that she was inviting more of the same. "All right, you win."

"Not till I hear you say it."

She hesitated, but he was adamant. "Mike," she said softly.

A long forefinger ran down her tilted nose. "I like the way that sounds. Now admit it, isn't Mike a more manly name than Donald?"

Surprising even herself, she laughed. "I don't think you've ever had to worry about your manhood."

He tilted her face up, inspecting the lovely features with bemused eyes. "Do you know, that's the first time I've ever heard you laugh?"

Suddenly Samantha felt remorse. It wasn't like her to be as churlish as she had been with Mike. Even though he had given her great provocation, she hadn't handled it in a very adult manner. She couldn't quite bring herself to apologize though.

"We haven't met under the greatest circumstances," was the best she could manage.

"And whose fault was that? Who spit at me like an angry kitten the first time we laid eyes on each other? No, don't answer that, I don't want to risk a recurrence." He laughed. "I have a much better idea. Let's dance."

Samantha preceded him onto the small floor with mixed emotions. She loved to dance, although she got little chance; Donald complained about crowds. Yet every time she had physical contact with Mike, it disturbed her in one way or another.

She held herself stiffly apart when he took her in his arms, but he made short work of that. Folding her close, he moved effortlessly in time to the music. Mike was a superb dancer, with a grace that was surprising in such a large man. Soon Samantha found herself relaxing, her body molding to his in a fluid line. Neither of them said anything, content to drift to the slow rhythm of the music.

Gradually her head settled on his shoulder as a feeling of utter contentment enveloped her. After the problems and worries of the recent weeks, she felt as though she had found a haven. This hard chest and the strong arms surrounding her could protect her from anything.

Mike nuzzled her hair aside, whispering in her ear, "You dance very well, my little construction worker."

The words brought her back to normal. A haven indeed. This man was her enemy! He was going to destroy her if he could. How could she be so unwary as to let her guard down? She managed to put a small distance between them—at least enough so his muscled thighs didn't brush against her with every step. The warmth of his body still penetrated hers, though; there was nothing she could do about that, or about the heady aroma of English soap mixed with tobacco and something indefinable that would ever after remind her of him.

She responded to his compliment grudgingly. "It's because you're such a good dancer yourself."

"Anything worth doing is worth doing well," he said smugly. "You must sample my other talents."

She drew in her breath sharply. "Never in a million years!"

He feigned surprise. "Don't you like to eat?"

"Of course I do. What has that to do with anything?"

"I was referring to my talents as a chef." His eyes gleamed with mockery. "I'm a very good cook."

"Oh." Her cheeks flamed scarlet and she quickly dipped her head to hide the fact, knowing all the while it was useless. This man was a devil. He seemed not only to know her thoughts, but to anticipate them.

"I'll cook dinner for you one night at my place," he said.

"No, I . . . um . . . I don't go to men's apartments."

"Not even Donald's?" he teased. Before she could frame an angry retort, he asked, "What makes you think I live in an apartment?"

"I can't imagine you inhabiting anything less than a penthouse on Nob Hill," she said nastily.

The music changed to something frenzied and by common consent, Mike guided her back to the table. "As a matter of fact, my parents do have one," he said when they were seated. "I stayed on at the old homestead after they moved out."

"You live in a house all alone?" she asked, surprised out of her pique.

His mouth formed a sardonic curve. "More or less."

"I see," she said stiffly.

"I'll show it to you someday. I think you'd like it. Five bedrooms are a little much for a bachelor, but I'm used to the old place."

"What on earth do you do with five bedrooms?" she exclaimed, wishing she could recall the words as soon as they were out of her mouth. Why did she keep feeding him these suggestive lines?

Except for a mocking gleam in his eyes, Mike let it pass. "I intend to fill them up with children."

A curious sense of depression assailed Samantha. She hadn't known he was engaged. It was to be expected though. The wonder was how such an eligible bachelor remained one for so long. Mike must be at least thirty-eight or -nine.

A woman passed their table, did a double take, and then stopped. "Mike! How are you, darling? It's been ages."

He stood politely, a warm smile on his face. "Sylvia, it's good to see you."

The exquisite redhead put a caressing hand on his arm. "You haven't actually seen me lately, darling."

Mike laughed and murmured something too low for Samantha to hear. She was glad of it because the intimate look that passed between them told her all she needed to know. Mike turned to introduce the two women, who acknowledged the introduction politely and insincerely while appraising each other with the thoroughness only women can achieve. As Samantha inspected the beautiful face framed by long, glamorous hair, the elegant clothes on the svelte body, a feeling of inadequacy enveloped her. Obviously this was Mike's kind of woman—the glittering, shallow kind that Samantha couldn't abide. Why it should matter, she couldn't imagine. Maybe because she was starting to like him a little bit—well, not exactly *like* him, maybe respect was a better word.

After a few generalities, the redhead left, with a pointed suggestion for Mike. "I heard how involved you've gotten yourself these days, but if you can ever get away, give me a call."

A mere engagement evidently meant nothing to Sylvia. To make matters worse, she heard Mike agreeing to do just that.

He raised a derisive eyebrow at her angry face. "You look like you just bit into a sour pickle. What's wrong, didn't you like Sylvia?"

"I can't see that it matters. We're supposed to be here talking business," she told him in clipped tones. "I suggest we get on with it."

"Not on an empty stomach," he said firmly. "I'm completely intractable when I'm hungry."

"How can I tell the difference?" She sighed.

He cupped her cheek gently, the long fingers sliding around to the delicate place behind her ear. "Poor little Samantha, don't worry. We'll get your life straightened out for you."

"I was doing fine until you came into it," she cried.

"Were you?" he murmured, tracing the shape of her full lower lip.

She jerked away from his seductive fingers, feeling her pulses start to race. "Yes, I was! And if you'll just leave me alone, I'll do all right again."

"I don't think I can do that," he remarked thoughtfully.

"You mean you really won't stop raiding my company?" It was a blow. He had seemed so much more approachable tonight that she had started to hope everything might work out.

Their food arrived at that moment. "Eat your dinner, Samantha," he remarked absently.

Mike steadfastly refused to discuss business while they ate. Instead, he regaled her with stories of exotic food he had sampled in far-off places like Egypt and Peru.

"It sounds like you've been all over the world," she commented, her imagination caught in spite of herself.

He shrugged. "Construction work takes you everywhere. One year I worked on a bridge in Lima, another time it was a dam near Cairo. The easiest job was the high rises in Barcelona."

"How could you have handled that much responsibility?" she gasped. "You must have been very young."

"I don't think you understand, sweet Samantha," he said gently. "I wasn't the contractor on those jobs. I worked on them—as a laborer."

"But you're rich," she blurted out. "Your mother and father with the penthouse . . . I just assumed that your father . . ."

"Started the business," he finished for her. "No, you're looking at a self-made man. It's true that my family has money. My father is one of the leading surgeons in this part of the country. He wanted me to follow in his footsteps, but unlike you, I chose my own career." Samantha was too fascinated to be angry. "My parents both thought I was crazy to rattle around the world doing physical labor," Mike continued. "If I was set on building things, Dad couldn't understand why I didn't let him set me up with a company right here in 'civilized' San Francisco." His lips curved with amusement before becoming serious again. "He couldn't understand that a boss who doesn't know how to do every step of a job himself is a man sitting on a shaky throne."

"You mean to say you actually know how to work all those monster machines?" she breathed.

"You betcha." He grinned like a little boy. "Everything from dynamiting for a foundation to throwing the final switch that turns on the power."

She was slightly dazed. "I should think mere buildings would seem like small potatoes after bridges and dams—even block-long office buildings."

"Not at all. Seeing something you've helped build with your own hands rise out of the earth and tower into the sky gives you a feeling of accomplishment that's indescribable. It's probably the closest thing a man can get to giving birth."

"I never thought of it like that before."

"Don't you feel that way when you see your plans materialize into a house?" he asked.

"It's not the same thing," she said slowly. "I've never really done anything on my own until now." She looked down, carefully straightening a teaspoon. "And I'm not doing a very spectacular job of it."

His warm hand gripped her nervous fingers. "It isn't a job for a woman, Samantha."

The moment of self-searching passed, leaving her defensive again. "That's just the arrogant male in you talking. Times have changed. There are women riveters now, and women pilots, and—"

"Okay, I can see you as a pilot, but I can't picture you using a jackhammer." He smiled. Lifting her wrist, he circled it with his fingers. "Face it, kitten, you just don't have the equipment."

"All right, I'll admit I couldn't put up an office building, let alone a bridge. But my sights aren't set that high. All I want to do is build a nice little house or two, remodel a kitchen or a bathroom, add on a room here and there. Is that too much to ask?"

"Not if that's what turns you on," he said negligently.

She could tell he was contemptuous of such small pickings. "We can't all be tycoons," she cried. "You don't even do that kind of work, Mike. Why can't you let me have it?"

"I'm not stopping you."

"You are if you take all my best men."

"Let me get this straight, Samantha. Are you asking for special consideration because you're a woman?"

"You know I'm not!" she said indignantly.

"In that case, you're just going to have to be competitive. If you want to run with the big boys, you have to learn to keep up."

"I've always paid union wages," she protested. "But you pay more—including bonuses."

He shrugged. "I need the best."

"And I don't?" Her eyes sparkled angrily. "Well, let me tell you, Mike Sutherland, our work speaks for itself! Morgan Construction has always been synonymous with quality."

"Sure. Because Pete Grogan is a fine craftsman— as your father was also. They supervised every job and could serve as a backup if anything went wrong. What would happen if Pete left you?"

The idea was too terrible to contemplate. "He wouldn't do that," she maintained stoutly.

"Okay, he's loyal," Mike conceded. "But suppose he had an accident—or died? Could you step in and take over?"

She set her chin stubbornly. "I could sure give it a heck of a try."

"I admire your spirit, if not your common sense." Mike sighed. "I just hope mother, and sister Brooke, can find jobs when the time comes that they have to."

The thought sent chills down Samantha's spine. "They won't ever have to! I'll always find a way to take care of them the way Dad would expect me to."

Mike's mouth set grimly beneath his cold, gray eyes. "I always respected your father, although I didn't know him very well. But right now, I could wring his neck for what he's done to you."

"You have no right to say that! Why is it so reprehensible to want to take care of my family? You're determined to make me out to be some kind of martyr, which just isn't true."

"Isn't it? How about your own life? Your marriage to the estimable Donald? Or is he willing to wait until you're a dried-up spinster, too old to have babies? He sounds like a real jewel," Mike said, shaking his head disgustedly.

"I wish you would kindly leave Donald out of this," she said hotly. "He has nothing to do with it at all."

Mike's firm mouth relaxed in a grin. "I doubt whether he'd like hearing that."

"It isn't any of your business if I get married or not."

"So now it's *if*?" His eyebrows rose. "I'm glad to hear you're having second thoughts. The man isn't good enough for you."

"You don't even know him."

"I was always lucky," he said mockingly.

Realizing that she had let herself be led away from the subject, Samantha was impatient. "You don't give a tinker's damn about Donald or me. You're just trying to avoid the issue."

His eyes were enigmatic. "Let's say you're half right. But you're the one who is refusing to face facts, my dear. If I stopped hiring your men tomorrow—even if I could give you back the ones you've lost—you'd still be in trouble. You're operating on a shoestring." Her startled eyes flew to his face, and he said, "I know a lot more about you than you think. You're already in financial straits—what happens if somebody is slow paying, or if an act of God like a rainstorm before the roof is on, causes you to lose money on a job? You have no cash backup. Sooner or later, your precarious little house of cards is going to collapse. Sit there and try to tough it out and you'll wind up with nothing."

What Mike said was true. Ignoring the facts wouldn't make them go away. She bent her head to master the tears of defeat which she considered a sign of weakness.

His big hand stroked the glossy curls gently. "I'm sorry, kitten. I wish I didn't have to be the one to make you face it."

She nodded wordlessly, wanting to hate him, yet realizing that she believed those quiet words.

"Sell out to me, Samantha. Lay down the burden."

"I'll think about it," she murmured.

Hearing the words spoken aloud made it seem almost irrevocable. Suddenly she was filled with a crushing depression. "I'd like to go home now, Mike, if you don't mind."

He was immediately understanding. "Of course, honey, I'll get the check."

They didn't talk on the ride home. Samantha looked out of the window, wondering how the moon could shine and all the stars be in their accustomed places. This was her götterdämmerung. The end of all her futile struggles. A finger of fear ran up her back. Where would she go now? The construction yard was all she had ever known.

Mike left her alone to wrestle with her private devils, but when they drew up in front of her apartment house, he said, "How about making me some coffee? We didn't have any."

"If you like," she said indifferently.

The apartment was dark. When Samantha switched on the lamps, the first thing she saw was a piece of paper lying in the middle of the living-room floor so it couldn't be missed. It was a note from Brooke, saying she had decided not to stay over after all. With all the traumatic things that had happened that evening, Samantha had completely forgotten about her sister. It was fortunate that Brooke's plans had changed. She doubted if she could have hidden her troubles from those perceptive eyes.

Mike followed Samantha into the tiny kitchen, his bulk making it seem even smaller. "Can I help?" he asked.

She gave him a wan smile. "I know you're a mighty chef, but it doesn't take two to make coffee."

After she had filled the coffeemaker, he came up in back of her. His big hands massaged the tense muscles of her shoulders and neck with incredible gentleness. "Cheer up, kitten, it won't be so bad. There's a bright new day awaiting you."

At the first touch, she stiffened, expecting the worst. When his hands didn't stray from her shoulders, Samantha found herself gradually relaxing. The kneading motions were so soothing that she closed her eyes, letting her tired mind go blank.

With the release from tension, she leaned back against his comforting chest, only becoming aware of it when his arms went around her waist. Before she could move away, he kissed the delicate spot behind her right ear. "Feeling better?" he murmured.

His hands had lulled her, now his warm mouth brought her back to pulsing life. Slipping out of his arms, she said, "Yes, I . . . I'm fine."

"You will be," he said confidently. "We're going to be an unbeatable team."

Surely, he hadn't been serious when he offered her a job? "I couldn't work for you," she said in astonishment.

"Why not?"

She backed against the sink in an effort to get away from his disturbing presence. It didn't help. Mike followed her, standing so close their knees touched as he penned her in with widespread arms, his hands resting flat on the counter.

"I just couldn't that's all."

"A typical female answer which I don't accept. You'll have to do better than that."

The only way she could get away was to risk having his arms close around her, a prospect that made her heart beat even faster. Samantha knew she was going to have to tell him the truth. Her eyelashes fluttered on her flushed cheeks as she said, "I don't want charity. You're only offering me a job because you feel sorry for me."

He tipped her chin up, forcing her to look at him. There was a flickering light in his eyes and his voice was husky as he said, "You awaken a lot of emotions in me, Samantha, but not one of them is pity."

Her mouth felt suddenly dry. "I . . . I don't believe you."

"Will this convince you?" His mouth closed over hers before she could turn her head, the lips warm and seeking.

He held her only with his lips, not restraining her in any other way. She could have pushed out of the circle of his arms, should have done so, but she felt strangely weak. He was draining her willpower the way he plundered her mouth. The slow drugging kisses were transporting her to a dreamworld where the only reality was this giant towering over her.

Of her own volition, Samantha moved closer to him, inhaling his special aroma. Her hands clung to his wide shoulders, feeling the ripple of muscles as his arms closed around her.

Holding her cradled against his chest, he began a tender exploration of her face, blazing a trail of kisses from her feathery eyebrows down to her trembling mouth. Her lips parted willingly to let him continue, and she shivered as his tongue invaded the warm moistness.

His intense masculinity subjugated her totally. She was beyond thinking, beyond caring. Something she had never experienced before was igniting her whole being, carrying her higher and higher to an unknown, ecstatic destination. Her hands made little fluttery motions, touching him with timid caresses until he kissed her fingers and thrust them inside his silk shirt. The intimate contact sent a quiver through her, the warmth of his skin scorching her palm where it rested on the hair-roughened chest.

Samantha was unaware of her back zipper sliding down until his mouth touched her bare shoulder, reacting on her aroused senses like a branding iron. She quivered anew when he cupped her breast, slowly teasing away the covering fabric until he could touch the creamy skin.

She was lost in a sea of sensation, so divorced from reality that when he swept her up in his arms, she clung to him without question.

"Making love in a kitchen is like making love in a car," he murmured in low, throaty amusement.

He had carried her into the bedroom before the shocking words penetrated. They acted like a jet of cold water, bringing her abruptly to her senses.

"No!" she cried, struggling out of his arms.

Her frenzied effort took him by surprise and he let her go. She landed in a heap on the bed, scrambling immediately for the other side. But there was no escape. That side of the bed was placed against the wall, and Mike guarded the other side.

In wordless panic, she curled up against the headboard. "Don't come near me," she panted.

To her consternation, he took no heed of her warning. He sat down on the edge of the narrow bed, resting his weight on the arm that spanned her shrinking body, although he didn't touch her. "You know you don't mean that, Samantha," he said in a low, soothing voice.

"Yes, I do!" His hands were at her waist, sliding slowly up her rib cage. She clutched at them desperately. "Stay away from me."

"That wasn't how you felt a minute ago." He nipped delicately at her earlobe.

Her palms were braced desperately against his chest as she twisted her head away from his seductive mouth. "It was all a mistake. I gave you the wrong impression in the restaurant. I've never . . . I haven't . . ."

There was understanding and tenderness in the gray eyes that held hers. "Ever been with a man," he finished for her. "I know, sweetheart."

"How did you know that?" Surprise made her rigid arms relax.

He took advantage of it to draw her close. "There were a lot of indications." He chuckled, running his nails lightly up her spine. When she squirmed protestingly, he transferred his attentions to the nape of her neck, seeking out the vulnerable spot there with unerring precision. "Your unbridled response to my lovemaking was the clincher, I suppose." He smiled.

Samantha felt as though she were blushing over every inch of her body. The shame was accompanied by fierce indignation. With his experience and male magnetism, this man could make a marble statue respond! "I suppose you think I'm a pushover! That I fall into bed with every man who walks in this apartment."

"Just the opposite, my little tiger cat." He laughed. "I could tell you'd never been kissed like that—or touched in that way. I took unfair advantage of you, but I had to find out."

She couldn't look at him. "Well, now you know. You've had your little fun, so will you please leave?"

He framed her face in his palms, his mouth just inches from her own. "I want you, Samantha, and you want me."

His lips brushed hers with a touch that was like a feather. She started to tremble, holding him off with a desperation born of fear—fear of the raging fire that was threatening to burn out of control if he continued his onslaught. She closed her eyes as his hands moved seductively over her body, sliding the dress over her arms and down to her waist. But when his long fingers deftly unfastened the front-closing, lacy bra, Samantha was galvanized.

Grasping his wrists, she cried, "No, don't! I can't!"

"Don't be frightened, darling. I'll be very gentle with you, I promise." He bent his head to bestow a kiss on the shadowed valley between her breasts, his warm mouth sliding across to the rosy peak which he touched lightly with his tongue.

Her grip on his wrists loosened as a cascade of emotions drowned out any objections her conscious mind might make. Arching her body toward his, she ran her fingers through his thick, dark hair, giving up the uneven struggle.

With her surrender, he gave a low cry, capturing her mouth in triumph while his hands continued the devastating exploration his lips and tongue had started.

"You're so beautiful, my darling. I knew the first time I saw you that you were going to be mine," he murmured restlessly. "I want it all from you."

Samantha opened her eyes slowly, the import of his unguarded words hammering at her numb brain. In his triumphant passion, Mike had revealed the real reason for this seduction. It wasn't physical attraction—it was business, pure and simple. *I want it all from you!* Morgan Construction—plus a roll in the hay, she thought bitterly. The degradation almost made her ill.

Mike lifted his head when she flinched away from him. "What is it, kitten?"

The false concern on his face infuriated her. "You can drop the act, Mr. Sutherland. The cat"—her mouth twisted with self-mockery—"or should I say the *kitten,* is out of the bag."

He levered himself off of her. "What are you talking about?"

She used the moment of freedom to twist her body away, curling into a corner, as far away from him as she could get. Her eyes spit hatred. "I'm sure it isn't like you to make a mistake, but you're a very physical man, aren't you? Even *you* can get carried away in the heat of the moment."

Slowly drawing himself up to a sitting position, Mike looked at her with narrowed eyes. "Will you tell me what the hell you're talking about?"

"There is no need to get abusive, Mr. Sutherland. Just get out of my—"

"Call me that one more time and you'll regret it," he cut in grimly.

"I already do! I regret the day I ever met you. I regret the fact that we're on the same planet together!" Her shrill voice carried a hint of hysteria.

Mike's eyes softened as he looked at her trembling body and the shimmer of tears in the wide violet eyes. "I'm sorry, honey, I didn't mean to frighten you. I guess it was too soon, but I wanted you so much. I'm afraid I just got carried away."

"Don't insult my intelligence," she stormed. "The great Mike Sutherland, the *experienced* Mike Sutherland, getting carried away? That's a laugh! You knew exactly what you were doing. You didn't have to go to those lengths though. I was already wavering. But that wasn't good enough for you, was it? You wanted to pin the deal down, make sure that I'd sell out to you."

"Are you out of your mind?" he asked incredulously.

"I was for a little while. You made sure of that, didn't you? Nothing like introducing a timid little virgin to sex. A competent man who doesn't mind putting in a little overtime can get just about anything he wants—including her father's life's work."

His hands bit into her arms like steel spikes. "Do you think I give a damn about your piddling little company?" he demanded.

"Enough to go to great lengths to obtain it!" she flung at him.

His eyes were icy as they surveyed her flushed face. Getting to his feet, he looked down at her with contempt. "Don't flatter yourself, Miss Morgan, it was all in a night's work." Hooking his jacket over his shoulder by one finger, he sauntered to the door, turning for a parting shot. "That's life. You win some, you lose some."

Chapter Three

Samantha was in her office early the next morning, looking as though she hadn't slept all night, which in fact, she hadn't. After Mike's traumatic leave-taking, she had remained curled up in a tight little ball, too miserable even to cry.

How could she have been such a fool? That was the refrain that played over and over in her head. How could she have let him breach her defenses when she knew ahead of time what his objective was? It was no good telling herself that he had vast expertise in the seduction department, while she couldn't claim to be more than a novice.

A shiver ran through her as she remembered the sensuous feel of his long fingers on her body, the arousing caresses that had left her mindless with rapture. She should have known better than to let him get that close in the first place. After seeing the kind of women he ran around with, how could she imagine he would ever be interested in her except for an ulterior motive?

And to think she almost played into his hands! If it hadn't been for that unguarded remark, he would indeed have owned her, body, soul—and construction yard. Well, thank heavens no harm was actually done—unless you counted the complete destruction of her self-respect. At least she hadn't turned the company over to him. And never would! She would see Mike Sutherland in the farthest reaches of hell before she let him get one finger on Morgan Construction!

When morning came, Samantha dragged herself wearily off the bed, her mind as tired as her body. The problems facing her were almost insurmountable. She was in a battle with a ruthless giant who held all the cards. Was there any way she could survive? She set her teeth grimly. Somehow, there *must* be!

Pete came into her office in the middle of the afternoon. Looking at her closely, he said, "You look terrible, Sam. Are you coming down with something?"

"No, I'm just getting over it," she said shortly.

"That's good." He paused uncertainly. "I hope you can take some bad news."

"What now?" she groaned.

"One of our trucks broke down again, way out in Novato this time. I have to go pick Marty up, and that means I won't be able to check on the Bromley job." He hesitated. "We've been having trouble with the grading, I hope Jerry can handle it."

Mike's contention that a boss should be able to step in at every stage of construction echoed in Samantha's ears. She ought to be able to take over for Pete, but the trouble was, she didn't know the first thing about grading. Pushing the troubling thought out of her mind, Samantha said grimly, "He better handle it, that's what I'm paying him for."

"Yes, well . . ." Pete looked doubtfully at her. "I won't be back today, Sam. It's forty miles to Novato, as you know. After I get the truck taken care of, I'll check on any jobs we have out that way, and then pack it in."

"Okay, Pete, see you in the morning."

Samantha spent the rest of the afternoon doing paperwork, which she hated. It had the effect of depressing her even further. When the phone rang about five-thirty, she reached out a languid arm, but the call dispelled her apathy. A Mrs. Farley Remington wanted to talk about an extensive remodel job on her house on Chestnut Street.

The address placed it in Pacific Heights, one of the most prestigious areas of San Francisco. It was a neighborhood of old mansions, some dating back to the turn of the century, but all kept up in a manner befitting their six- and seven-figure price tags. Not that many were ever for sale. This was old San Francisco money, the huge homes being passed down through families.

Some were venerable Victorians, others classic Greek or French Normandy in style, while a few had modern fronts. They were set close together in this city of limited space, the glorious view over the bay and the Golden Gate Bridge more than making up for the proximity of their neighbors. In addition, they had that rarity in city life, spacious backyards, big enough in some cases for gazebos.

A job of the magnitude Mrs. Remington described would be a shot in the arm for Morgan Construction's ailing finances. It wouldn't hurt their prestige either. Ripples of excitement went through Samantha as she listened to this prospective client.

"We're leaving for Europe in a week, so we would like someone from your firm to look at the house immediately."

"I understand, Mrs. Remington. Would nine o'clock tomorrow morning be satisfactory?"

"No, you *don't* understand," the lady said querulously. "I meant right now. My husband will be home in half an hour and we'd like to discuss it tonight."

Tonight! Wouldn't you know it? "Well, we've had kind of an emergency," Samantha explained haltingly. "My foreman won't be back today, so—"

"Young lady, I do not wish to speak to a foreman." The patrician tones were disdainful. "If my home does not merit better attention than that, perhaps I have made a mistake."

"No, wait, Mrs. Remington," Samantha cried desperately. "You're quite right. I intended to come myself, I just thought it might facilitate matters if my foreman was present at the same time."

"I don't understand this at all. To whom am I speaking?"

"Samantha Morgan. I'm head of Morgan Construction."

"I didn't realize . . ." The woman's voice trailed off. "You sound very young."

"I assure you that Morgan's is an old, established company," Samantha said with dignity. "I guarantee that we can do a fine job for you."

The new client didn't share her confidence. It took a lot of reassurance before she agreed to see Samantha at the designated hour. Why did Pete have to be unavailable at this particular time, Samantha wondered despairingly? Well, it couldn't be helped. She would just have to project such an air of confidence that the Remingtons would be bowled over by her professionalism.

That proved to be easier said than done. Mr. Remington was a tall, portly, white-haired man with a probing manner. He was chairman of the board of a large mining company, and had not reached those heights on his trusting personality. Fortunately Samantha's answers to his pointed questions satisfied him, but Mrs. Remington was another matter.

She was a large woman with a perpetually suspicious look on her rather homely face. "I will never understand why we need an entirely new kitchen," she said disapprovingly, "but Maggie—that's our cook—is turning absolutely mutinous. Honestly, servants these days! First a color TV for her room and now this."

Samantha smothered a smile. She could tell that Mrs. Remington longed for a return of the old days when servants were kept in "China rooms." At the turn of the century when thousands of Chinese were brought in to do cooking and laundry in the railroad camps that were opening up the West, some of them made their way to San Francisco. Many found work in the great houses of the wealthy where they cleaned the huge rooms filled with polished, heavy furniture and glistening chandeliers. Their own accommodations were tiny, cell-like rooms in the basement, hence the designation, "China rooms."

Samantha remembered her indignation on seeing one of the last remaining ones. They were mostly gone now, remodeled into decent-sized quarters or playrooms. Just as the old servants were gone. The Chinese in present-day San Francisco accounted for a goodly amount of the bankers, lawyers, and doctors.

Her wandering attention was recalled by her client's complaining voice. "I shudder to think of all the mess it's going to cause—not to mention the expense. But as long as we're going to Europe for a month, it seemed like a good time to put in that sauna Mr. Remington has his heart set on." She turned disapproving eyes on her husband. "Not that you'll ever use it once you have it."

This was evidently something he had heard many times before, and he ignored it the way he would a troublesome stockholder. "I presume all your men are bondable?" he asked Samantha.

"Oh, yes, you needn't worry on that score," she assured him.

"We have a great many very valuable pieces," Mrs. Remington informed her loftily.

Samantha felt drained as she walked down the brick path a long time later. She had gotten the job, but the pleasure it should have caused was dampened by the ordeal she had been through. Both Remingtons had exacted their toll in different ways.

Her mind was so occupied with the problem that she jumped when a horn tooted in the gathering dusk. A familiar white sports car was nosing into the curb. Mike Sutherland! That's all she needed right now, Samantha thought grimly.

She walked steadily toward her small Mustang, ignoring his presence completely. But Mike refused to take the hint. Getting out of the low, racy car, he sauntered over, trapping her before she could open the door.

"Fancy seeing you here," he drawled.

"Every day can't be perfect," she snapped, reaching for the door handle.

His hand got there a second before hers. "What's the hurry? On your way to meet the patient Donald?"

"Where I'm going has nothing to do with you."

"I was just trying to show polite interest," he said mildly.

"Don't change your whole personality for me.

57

What are you doing here anyway?" Her eyes narrowed. It was too much of a coincidence that he just *happened* by. "I've heard of lawyers chasing ambulances, but surely you're not so hard up for work that you have to follow *me* around."

"What do you mean?"

It seemed to Samantha that his innocence was exaggerated. "You found out somehow that I was coming here to look at a job, didn't you? What were you going to do, underbid me?" Her eyes were violet with rage.

"My dear Samantha, I believe you're getting paranoid. That little company is going to be your undoing yet."

She clenched her fists, rigid with anger. "Don't patronize me, Mike Sutherland—and don't try to fast-talk me either! I know your methods. If you can see to it that I don't get any work, I'll have to fold, right? Well, you're too late this time," she finished triumphantly. "I already got the job."

"I'm delighted to hear it."

"Oh, certainly! That's why you turned up here so fortuitously."

He looked at her dispassionately. "I turned up here because I live next door."

Her eyes flew to the house he indicated, a lovely English Tudor of mellowed brick with many-paned windows of sparkling glass. "You live *there?*" she asked incredulously.

His amusement threatened to turn to outright laughter. "I'm aware that you thought I crawled into a cave every night, but I must plead guilty."

A deep blush stained her cheeks bright strawberry-pink. What a fool she must look after that impassioned speech! "Well, how was I to know?" she mumbled.

"I seem to remember telling you I kept the old family digs."

That was the whole trouble. She had pictured it as something ancient and outdated. It should have occurred to her that if he lived there, it would have to be a mansion.

"Come on in. I'll show you around," he offered.

"No, thank you, I have to get home," she said primly.

All she wanted to do was get away from this aggravating man who had the knack of keeping her completely off balance. There was never a moment when he didn't provoke some kind of reaction, violent—or otherwise.

Pete was delighted to hear about the Remington job. Maybe this would change their luck. If they could satisfy these difficult people, perhaps they would recommend Morgan's to their friends. The key to remodel business was referrals. And this wasn't some dinky little laundry-room job. Enough houses like the Remington's could pull Morgan Construction out of the doldrums.

Samantha drew up the plans with extra care, conferring with Pete at every step. Together they figured material, labor, and overhead. Nothing was left to chance. And at the start, everything went according to plan. The old kitchen was gutted, their best men finished other projects in time to start the Remington job, and the sauna moved from the drawing board to its beginning in the house. Then things began to go wrong.

At first it was only minor annoyances, like material being delivered late or a man not showing up for work. Then it became serious. A call from Al Bartolli, the job boss, was the opening gun.

"Somebody better get over here," he said. "Those cabinets we ordered from Wydmeer don't fit."

"I can't believe it," Samantha cried. "We used him even though he's more expensive than anyone else because his work is the best."

She could almost see Al's shrug over the phone. "They don't fit," he said simply. "Come see for yourself."

Samantha's tires screeched to a halt in front of the Remington house a short time later. Those cabinets couldn't be wrong. They had been specially made and the work would never be finished in time if they had to be redone. Not to mention the extra expense involved!

Standing in the shambles of the kitchen a few minutes later, Samantha felt her heart sink.

"You see, I told you," Al said. "It's only an inch and a quarter, but there's no way we can fit them in."

"Can't you cut them down?" she pleaded.

The foreman shook his head. "Not with that fancy trim. Even if we took some off of both sides, that curlicue molding would be thicker on the top and the bottom. It would throw it all off scale." He looked at the cabinets disgustedly. "What did she want all that junk on there for anyhow?"

Samantha had thought the same thing when Mrs. Remington showed her a picture of an old Victorian kitchen, demanding an exact duplication of the cabinets. They weren't functional, it added to the cost, and they weren't even attractive, but Mrs. Remington had been adamant.

"Oh, Al, I don't know what to say." Samantha faltered.

"Having trouble?" a deep, male voice inquired.

Samantha swung around, her troubled eyes meeting Mike Sutherland's. "What are you doing here?" she demanded.

"Just professional curiosity," he smiled.

"This happens to be private property," she told him stiffly. "You're trespassing."

"That sounds a little harsh. After all, I am a neighbor."

"It doesn't give you the right to come snooping on me."

Ignoring her, he started to prowl around the kitchen, snickering when his eyes lit on the offending cabinets. "What seems to be the trouble?" he asked the foreman.

Samantha gasped. The nerve of the man! Coming in here like he owned the place and asking questions even. But Al was already explaining the problem, turning it over to Mike to solve. That was too much for her. Walking up to the two men, she tried to insinuate herself between them.

Giving her an impatient glance, Mike put his hands on her arms, picking her up bodily and setting her away. "Later, Samantha," he said, "I'm busy now."

She was too choked with rage to do anything except make some strangled sounds, which they ignored.

Mike was rapping with his knuckles on the wall. "There's a stud here, but it's back far enough so it won't be in the way. You can cut a pocket in the sheet rock and slide them in. A scribe strip will cover the raw edge."

"Yeah, that would work," Al said with rising admiration.

"Be sure you mask off that stud before you make your first cut," Mike warned. He turned to Samantha. "Wydmeer should stand the extra expense of going into the wall. Don't let him get away with it," he told her crisply.

"You mean they'll fit now?" she asked with rising hope.

"Like a glove," Al told her happily. "Thanks to Mr. Sutherland here."

Mike's eyebrows rose. "You know who I am?"

"Everybody in the business knows you, Mr. Sutherland. It's a pleasure to work for you."

"You're not working for me," Mike said wryly. "You're working for the stainless-steel butterfly here." He put his arm around her shoulders, propelling her out of the room before she could respond.

In the front hall, she pulled away from him. "I guess I should thank you," she said stiffly.

"Not if it's going to ruin your day." He chuckled.

She ignored that with an effort. "It was good of you to help. I . . . it would have caused a serious problem."

"There's usually a solution to everything if you just know where to look," he said easily.

"Why did you do it, Mike? What's in it for you?"

His face hardened. "Do you think I'm going to send you a consulting bill?" When she hesitated, his mouth curled cruelly. "Don't worry, you'll pay. We both know I never do anything without an ulterior motive, don't we?"

She scuffed her toe on the entry floor like a little girl. "I didn't mean that the way it sounded."

"Didn't you, Samantha?"

She couldn't look at him, not wanting to see the coldness in those gray eyes that had once looked at her so differently. "Well, maybe I—you have to admit it's not in your best interests," she said defensively.

"Don't be so sure. Perhaps it's an object lesson."

He was gone before she could answer, having

driven home his point. Samantha was only too well aware of what that was. Today was ample proof of Mike's contention that the boss should know more than his men. It wasn't fair though. Pete could probably have done the same thing if he had been available. But he wasn't, a small voice whispered, and she didn't possess the same skill.

So what? Samantha tossed her head, the gratitude she had initially felt evaporating rapidly. It was another of Mike's devious tricks, designed to wear her down. There was no goodwill in what he did today, just one more step in his campaign. Well, it wouldn't work! If he thought she was going to go all softhearted and feminine, he was in for a rude awakening. Mike Sutherland would never get his grubby hands on Morgan Construction, she promised herself again.

For a few days after that, everything ran smoothly. Unfortunately, it wasn't destined to last. The weather turned bad, causing a problem on a job where they were pouring concrete. Samantha and Pete had their hands so full that they didn't give much thought to the Remington house, especially since everything there seemed under control for once. That confidence was shredded by a phone call from Mike.

"What the hell is the matter with Pete Grogan?" was his opening blast.

"What are you talking about?" Samantha asked wonderingly.

"Do you know it's starting to rain?"

"It's good of you to call with a weather report," she said acidly, "but I usually get mine from the evening news."

Mike swore impatiently. "I don't know why I bother. The only reason I can think of is that I'm a pushover for lost causes."

"If you're recruiting for your fan club, I must regretfully decline. Did you call for any reason other than to annoy me, Mr. Sutherland?" Samantha inquired sweetly.

"I called to tell you—" he shouted, then checked himself until he could get his anger under control. When he continued, it was in a dangerously mild tone. "I called to discuss the Remington job, *Miss* Morgan."

"Something that doesn't concern you in any way," she said loftily.

"True," he conceded. "Including the fact that they ordered a sauna not a swimming pool."

"What do you mean?" she asked, jarred out of her complacency.

"Correct me if I'm wrong. You cut through the roof for a vent. It isn't covered. It's starting to rain." The sentences were short and clipped, as though he were talking to a backward child. "By morning, you'll have several inches of water in there."

"Oh, no, it can't be! How do you know?"

"I live next door, remember? Which is a blessing." He sighed. "At least I don't have to go all the way across town to check on your inept work. Get some plasticene on there immediately, Samantha." He hung up before she could reply.

Samantha streaked out of the office to locate Pete. When she gave him the information Mike had relayed, Pete smote himself on the forehead with the heel of his hand. "How could I have forgotten about that? What an idiot I am! But don't worry, Sam. Everything will be all right, thanks to Mike."

She walked slowly back to the office, Pete's words ringing in her ears. "Thanks to Mike." Every time she turned around, one of her men was giving thanks to Mike. She was grateful to him, of course—or was she? Why couldn't he stay out of her life and let her sink or swim? If she was as inept as he seemed to think, maybe she really wasn't fit to run the business.

As soon as the traitorous thought entered her mind, she rejected it. That was just the kind of insidious thinking he was trying to foster!

Samantha was tense and jumpy the rest of the day. Usually the time flew by, but today, she couldn't wait to get out of the office. She dressed carefully for her date with Donald that night, perhaps to make up for the fact that she wasn't looking forward to it. What was the matter with her lately? She had always had a pleasant time with Donald. Was that the trouble? Was she now contrasting it with the excitement of being with Mike?

She stopped with the hairbrush in midair, staring at her startled face in the mirror. Where had that thought come from? It was utterly ridiculous. The emotion he aroused wasn't excitement, it was pure loathing. She hated Mike Sutherland with every ounce of her being!

Her greeting to Donald was warmer than usual, bringing a look of pleased surprise to his face. "Mm, that was nice. Maybe we should just stay in tonight."

"Whatever you like," she told him, smiling seductively through a determined effort.

"No," he said regretfully. "I have tickets to the theater and they aren't refundable."

After the play, they went to a small bar for a drink. It had been an entertaining musical, yet part of Samantha's mind had been on her business problems. Perhaps it would help to discuss them with Donald. He had a logical mind, maybe he could counsel her. While she was weighing the advisability, he gave her an opening.

"You seem kind of preoccupied tonight, dear. Is anything wrong?" he asked.

"Not exactly. It's just . . . well, I've had an offer to sell the business."

"Really? For how much?" he asked. She named a figure that made him whistle. "I don't see what the problem is. Grab it quick before they change their minds."

"It was my father's business, Donald," she protested. "He built it from nothing, and he expected me to carry on."

"Don't be ridiculous, Samantha," he said impatiently. "This is no time for sentiment. Do you know how much you can earn on that kind of money in today's market?"

Donald warmed to the subject, taking a pencil and a notebook out of his inside pocket. His eyes sparkled as he wrote down figures to illustrate his point, unaware that Samantha didn't share his enthusiasm.

A feeling of revulsion filled her as she watched the avidity with which he totaled the numbers. Without realizing it, Donald had made up her mind for her. There had to be more to life than money. Everyone was pulling her in different directions, each for his own reasons, but she wouldn't be a pawn in anyone's game. Morgan Construction was going to stay in the family where it belonged.

The next few days weren't the pleasantest Samantha had ever spent. Her date with Donald ended disastrously, the Remington job which she had counted on so heavily was threatening to lose money through countless delays, and Brooke's grades were slipping. Well, at least Mike was leaving her alone, Samantha thought, wondering why that didn't make her happier.

She was sitting at her desk when the phone rang at five-thirty. Just lately, all it brought was bad news. Looking at it distastefully, she had a strong inclination to ignore it, knowing all the while that she couldn't.

The sound of Mike's voice sent a shiver of something very like pleasure through her veins, even though it was grim as it so often was recently. "Samantha? Well, you've done it again."

"Wha . . . what's the matter?" she asked fearfully.

"My houseboy just called. One of your bumbleheaded nincompoops cut the lines. I have no electricity."

"How . . . how do you know it was one of my men?" she asked, trying to work up some righteous indignation. It was difficult when she knew in her heart he was probably right.

"Because he came over to say he was going to shut the power off for half an hour. That was two hours ago and your crew is gone."

"Oh, is that all?" She was relieved. "He probably just forgot to turn it back on; it's simple."

There was the sound of heavy breathing at the other end. "No, it's *not* simple. What he did was flip the breaker switches without checking to see that everything was working. I'll wager a year's profits that's what happened."

"You don't know that," she protested.

"No, and for your sake, I hope you're right instead of me. Just get your man over there to check it out—now!"

"But it's after five-thirty," she cried.

"What's the matter, did he turn into a pumpkin? I thought that didn't happen until midnight," he remarked sarcastically.

She was too upset to take offense. "Everyone is gone for the day. If I call them back, I'll have to pay overtime."

"That's not my concern," he said coldly.

"But Mike, couldn't you . . . couldn't you sort of check first? If it is only a switch . . ."

"Why the devil should I?"

He was right. Why should he? It was just one more of the endless disasters plaguing her lately. Struggling to keep the tears out of her voice, she said quietly, "I'll have someone out there as soon as possible."

There was silence at the other end of the phone. Then Mike gave a mighty sigh. "Meet me at the house with the key. I'll fix it."

"No, it's my responsibility. I'll take care of it."

"You're trying my patience sorely, Samantha." She could almost see him running his fingers through his thick dark hair. "Will you stop arguing and get over here?"

"I don't need charity, Mr. Sutherland. I may have had a run of bad luck recently, but I'm a business woman, I can take it in my stride."

"You're a featherbrained little idiot, that's what you are. You need a husband or a keeper, I don't know which."

"I'm well aware of your opinion of me," she said icily, "but that isn't getting your electricity turned on. If you will get off the phone so I can call one of my men, I will do so."

"If it's a sliced cable as I suspect, it will take one of *your* men a couple of hours to fix it," he said insultingly. "That's double time, plus traveling allowance of course. Do you know how much that's going to cost you?"

She did rapid calculations and gulped. "Yes," she said in a small voice.

"I'm offering once more—but I warn you, this is the last time. Are you going to meet me at the house?"

Samantha gave in. "Yes," she murmured.

After he hung up, abruptly as always, she sat with the receiver in her hand. How much longer was she going to let Mike Sutherland bail her out? For that matter, how much longer would he be willing to? She should have insisted on sending her own man. It would have been just one more cost added to an already disastrous job. Was it really to save money that she had agreed to meet Mike at the house? Or was there another more complicated reason? Like the fact that she hadn't seen or talked to him in days?

Before she could explore the troubling implications of that thought, Samantha reached quickly for her car keys.

Chapter Four

Mike was waiting on the porch of the Remington house, a box of tools at his feet, when Samantha arrived.

"I'm glad to see that you're prompt anyway," was his peremptory greeting.

She followed him meekly inside, standing prudently silent while he made his inspection.

Tracing a line of wires from a control box, Mike gave a growl of annoyance. "Just as I thought. Come here and take a look at this."

Samantha advanced cautiously, stopping a few feet from Mike. In his present mood, it seemed safe to keep her distance. An impatient arm snaked around her waist, drawing her against his long body.

"Do you see that?" He pointed to two pieces of wire that had been neatly severed. "The cable's been cut, like I told you."

Samantha was terribly conscious of his arm around her, the male angles of his body emphasizing the softness of her own. "I . . . I guess you were right."

He cocked a satiric eyebrow at her. "Did you really doubt it?" To her great relief, he released her, bending to rummage around in the toolbox. "Here, hold the flashlight while I splice these together."

His movements were deft, the large hands incredibly dexterous as they manipulated the fine wires. The light trembled slightly as Samantha's eyes went to his strong face, sweeping over the thick, sun-tipped eyelashes and the high cheekbones before lingering on the wide firm mouth. A poignant thought flashed through her mind—if only they weren't enemies.

"There, that ought to do it," Mike said with satisfaction. "I'd better check out the rest of the job though, as long as I'm here."

"I'm sure that isn't necessary," Samantha protested. "I don't want to take up any more of your time."

"It's easier to anticipate any blunders your men are making than to have to come back later to clean them up." Ignoring the indignant words Samantha was prepared to utter, Mike prowled around, nothing escaping his sharp eyes. Kneeling down next to the stove, he gave a short exclamation. "What the devil is wrong with your foreman, leaving exposed wires untaped? Do you know you could start a fire this way?"

Samantha looked down at the tangled coil on the floor, noting the tiny copper wires that bristled from the protective rubber tubing in several places. "I . . . we have a subcontractor on the job. It must have been his fault."

"What difference does that make? Your foreman should have caught it, that's what he's for. Hand me that coil of friction tape," Mike said disgustedly.

Fortunately there were no other major problems.

Not until he had made sure of it, though, did Mike pack up his tools.

"I don't know how to thank you." Samantha faltered, after he had locked the door and given her the key.

"Don't you?" He grinned wickedly. "I can think of a way."

"I'm afraid your idea of payment is excessive," she said coldly.

His feigned innocence was belied by the dancing mischief in his gray eyes. "A drink at my house? That's what I had in mind."

"And what else?" she asked skeptically.

"Oh, I guess I could scare up some cheese and crackers." He took her arm, leading her across the broad lawn. "As an architect, aren't you interested in seeing my house? It's quite old."

Samantha told herself that was the reason she allowed herself to be persuaded. She really did want to see where Mike lived.

The house was a complete surprise. She had been prepared for something blatantly modern, the kind of bachelor's pad depicted in the slick men's magazines. Instead she discovered a tasteful, quietly luxurious home furnished in an eclectic mixture of priceless antiques and comfortable modern pieces. In the living room, a large Chinese screen decorated with figures done in jade and mother of pearl was of museum quality. The glowing Persian rug on the floor was of equal value.

"I'll show you around later if you like," Mike said as Samantha paused on the threshold of the handsome room, her dazzled eyes darting from one exquisite piece to another. "Right now, I think a drink is in order."

He guided her into a den with a curving bar along one side. The color scheme was restful beiges and browns with mellow paneled walls and comfortable-looking, tweedy couches and chairs scattered around.

Samantha couldn't keep the surprise out of her voice. "Your home is just beautiful!"

His amusement was evident. "I'm sure you were expecting a lot of chrome and glass, with some of Picasso's naughtier sketches on the wall."

The revealing color in her cheeks told him he was right, but she tried to deny it. "Certainly not. Why would you say a thing like that?"

"Because ever since we met, you've been trying to force me into a stereotype—the rapacious tycoon, the womanizing playboy. Why can't you just see me as a man?"

Samantha's long eyelashes dropped to veil her expression. If there was one thing she was quiveringly aware of, it was that Mike Sutherland was a man! Every time she was near him, her emotions reacted in an alarming way.

"You have to admit you're rather overpowering," she said faintly.

"You mustn't be afraid of me, little Samantha," he said gently, cupping her cheek in his palm.

Her chin came up. "I didn't say I was afraid of you."

"No, you don't allow yourself any weaknesses do you?" he asked wryly. He went behind the bar. "What would you like to drink?"

"Whatever you're having will be fine," she said, grateful that he didn't pursue the subject.

After Mike had mixed the drinks and handed her one, he carried his over to the couch. "Sit down and make yourself comfortable," he invited.

Samantha perched on one of the high bar stools, but he beckoned to her. "Not there. Come sit next to me."

To refuse was to make it seem important, so she did as he said, carefully seating herself at the opposite end of the couch. "This is a very nice room," she said primly.

"I'm glad you like it." He smiled.

There was a short silence while her nerves tightened like a fishing line being reeled in. Samantha was poised for flight, although he made no move to shorten the distance between them. She had an awful feeling that Mike was aware of her tension— and amused by it.

She set her glass down. "You promised to show me the rest of the house."

"There's no hurry," he said lazily.

"I'm afraid there is." She got to her feet jerkily. "I . . . I can't stay long."

"In that case." Mike stood up with the lazy grace of a large jungle cat. "We'll start with the master bedroom and see how far we get."

Her startled eyes flew to his face, the indignant words dying at the teasing look she saw there. "If you're hoping to get a reaction out of me, I don't intend to oblige," she said coolly.

He laced his fingers with hers, her small palm almost disappearing in his large one. "Don't issue challenges, kitten, or I'll be forced to prove just how much I can make you react."

She tried to pull her hand away, but he tightened his hold, raising her hand and kissing the inside of her wrist. "Don't do that!" she cried.

"Would you rather I kissed you somewhere else? We aim to please." He grinned.

"I don't want you to kiss me at all!"

"Not even like this?" Mike turned her into his arms, his mouth descending so swiftly that she didn't have a chance to avoid it. And once their lips met, it was too late.

74

His mouth moved over hers in a slow seduction that sent shivers of excitement through her. It was a kiss that began gently with an unhurried exploration, a teasing hint of promises to be fulfilled. Samantha trembled against him, caught between fear of that powerful body and the necessity to feel it against her own. What the outcome would have been she never knew, because Mike released her.

Holding her flushed face in his palms, he inspected the drugged blue eyes and tremulous mouth with satisfaction. "I think I've proved my point."

"You're detestable!" she gasped.

"Because I'm determined to make you realize that you're a woman instead of a man?"

"I never tried to be a man."

"If you really believe that, then you're deluding yourself." His gray eyes swept over her slim jeans and checked cotton shirt. "Why else do you dress like that? And those delightful, but short curls." His fingers twined in the glossy strands. "Don't you know a man likes to bury his face in long, scented hair when he's making love?"

A blush stained Samantha's delicate skin. "I'm sorry if I don't please you," she said, stung by his criticism. "I guess you'll just have to forego making love to me."

"Let's go in the bedroom and discuss it." He grinned, pulling her in that direction.

"Are you crazy? I wouldn't go in there with you!"

"I thought you said you weren't afraid of me?" he taunted.

"I'm not. I'm just being prudent."

"You don't have to worry, Samantha. I'm not going to attack you." He turned her to face him, his voice husky as he said, "You're going to ask me to make love to you one day."

The burning light in his eyes made her heart beat

so fast that it was an effort to say, "Don't count on it."

"Oh, but I am counting on it, sweet Samantha," he said softly. "I'm counting on it very heavily."

There was such confidence in his voice that it unnerved her. When she caught her lower lip between small, white teeth, Mike laughed. Putting his arm around her waist, he urged her into a room that was spacious and unmistakably masculine.

The king-size bed was covered with a brown velvet spread, and the massive, handsome furniture was scaled to his own outsized proportions. There were no trinkets or feminine touches around, just large crystal ashtrays, piles of books, and a few souvenirs of purely male pursuits.

Mike watched her assessment of the room. "You don't like it?" he asked.

"Oh, yes, it's lovely."

He took off his tie, tossing it carelessly on top of a highboy as he unfastened the top buttons of his cream-colored silk shirt. Flinging himself on the bed, he patted the side next to him. "Lie down and tell me what you don't like about my bedroom."

"Certainly not! And I do like it, it's just—" She broke off to say sharply, "You shouldn't put your shoes on that beautiful bedspread."

"You sound remarkably like my mother." He laughed. "If you won't lie down, will you at least perch some place, so I don't feel like a cad. I'm really too tired to play the gentlemanly host. I've been up since six this morning."

Samantha made a tentative move toward the door. "Maybe I'd better leave then."

"Don't go. Come over here and rub my back. Don't you think you owe me that?" When she hesitated, Mike said impatiently, "You're quite safe, I'm too tired to attack you."

She approached the bed with trepidation, sitting gingerly on the edge as he turned on his side with his back to her. She stroked it, timidly at first, then with more assurance, running her hands over the hard muscles and tracing them down to the narrowing waist.

"Ahh, that feels good." He sighed.

But when he pulled his shirt out of the waistband of his slacks and guided her hands onto his bare skin, Samantha felt her pulse begin to skyrocket. His back was smooth and warm, without a trace of fat on its lean length, the sinews hinting at the lithe grace of a panther. Her hands roamed over him, glorying in the perfection of the most beautiful male body she had ever imagined.

She stroked his broad shoulders and arms slowly, wanting to touch all of him, wanting to put her lips on that warm brown skin. The realization made her gasp. She snatched her hands away as though they had been burned.

Mike rolled over on his back, looking up at her. "Mm, that was nice. You should have been a nurse."

"But not a doctor," she said acidly, to cover her ragged breathing.

"Do we have to fight the battle of the sexes tonight?" He sighed. "I'd rather hear why you don't like my bedroom."

Samantha started to get up, but his arm around her waist prevented it. "I do like it, honestly. I was just wondering how it would look with . . . with your wife's things in it."

"Are you proposing to me?" He smiled.

"Of course not!" She stiffened against his encircling arm. "Even if I wanted to marry you, which I don't—unlike your friends, I don't poach on other people's property."

"I wasn't aware that I belonged to anyone."

"Not even your fiancée?" she asked sweetly. "That should make for an interesting marriage."

"I have a feeling that we're talking at cross purposes. Who am I supposed to be engaged to?"

"I wouldn't know. I don't travel in your exalted circles," she said frostily.

"I hate to spoil your impression of me as a complete bounder"—he chuckled—"but I'm not engaged to anyone. Where did you get that idea?"

"Well, you said . . . I mean when I asked about the five bedrooms . . ."

"I said I was going to fill them up with children." He nodded. "I didn't say when."

"I just naturally assumed . . ."

"No wonder you were so wary of me. Does it set your mind at ease to know that you weren't kissed by an engaged man?" he teased.

Her eyes flashed angrily. "I'm not exactly a mid-Victorian!"

"You act remarkably like one—except that the Victorians led quietly licentious sex lives. They didn't talk about it, they enjoyed it."

"I'd rather not talk about it either," she said primly.

"Why not? Are you afraid of sex, Samantha?"

It was what Brooke had asked her, and shook her head impatiently. "You have no right to assume that, just because I don't hop into bed with every man I meet."

"I'm very happy to hear that," he remarked gravely.

Stung by the twinkle in his eyes that told Samantha he was mocking her, she commented acidly, "Even though it's a restraint you don't practice?"

"I'm a man." He shrugged.

"And a very physical one."

"I haven't had any complaints." He grinned. "I

haven't had to use coercion either, I might add. Although you obviously find this hard to believe, the women were just as eager as I."

Samantha could have told him she didn't find that at all hard to believe. She kept her voice scornful. "I suppose there have been a great number of them."

"Samantha, you shock me." He chuckled. "Surely you don't want all the graphic details?"

Her cheeks flamed painfully. "Certainly not! I can't think of anything less interesting than your sex life."

"Well, now, I wouldn't go that far."

"I don't know why we're even talking about it. The whole subject is distasteful."

"You don't think sex is here to stay?"

Although she knew he was baiting her, Samantha couldn't help rising angrily to it. "You, and men like you, make a mockery of something that should be tender and beautiful."

"I agree with the tender and beautiful part, but why does it distress you to think that it can also be wild and wonderful?"

"It doesn't distress me," she said hotly. "I . . . maybe it will be."

"You don't seem in any hurry to find out," he remarked wryly.

"That's what this is all about, isn't it? You're making fun of me because I believe in marriage."

"You think I don't?"

"Not as long as you can get what you want without it," she maintained.

"Sweet Samantha, I didn't think anyone could be as innocent as you. Do you honestly think the only reason a man gets married is because he couldn't get that particular woman into bed?"

"We weren't talking about all men, we were talking about you."

"And I suppose Donald, that paragon who is too bloodless to have taken you long ago, is different?" he asked contemptuously.

"You have no right to talk about Donald like that!" she flared. "How do you know what self-control he's practicing?"

"And you, Samantha? Do you find it difficult to remain virtuous?" When she flushed and looked away, Mike's mouth thinned grimly. "You don't even want to think about sleeping with him."

To her dismay, a shudder ran through her. "That's not true, I do!" she gasped.

He shook his head. "You don't love him, Samantha. How can you even consider marrying him?"

His hands were sliding slowly up her rib cage and she grabbed desperately for them before they reached her swelling breasts. "You and Brooke are two of a kind!" she cried. "You both think marriage is one long Mardi Gras filled with fun and excitement. Well, it isn't."

He looked at her with compassion. "You poor child. Your little sister knows more about life than you do. What kind of marriage are you going to have with no fun and excitement in it?"

"I didn't say that. You're twisting my words around. I just said there is more to it than sex. There are shared interests, and . . . and compatibility. Things you find out by really getting to know someone, not just going to bed with him."

He watched her intently. "You don't think you can meet someone for the first time and know that's the person you want to marry?"

"How could you possibly?"

"Cynics call it chemistry, romantics call it predestination," he smiled. "It doesn't matter, it just happens."

"I'd be afraid to trust it," she said skeptically.

"You're afraid of everything, in spite of that brave exterior," Mike said harshly. "You're a timid little girl hiding in a woman's body, terrified to come out and play with the big kids. Well, by God, I'm going to drag you out if it's the last thing I do."

He jerked her forward and Samantha sprawled across his firm body before she knew what he intended. His arms closed around her as she struggled frantically to get up, her body pulsingly aware of his hard length beneath her.

"Let me go," she cried.

"In a little while," he soothed. "As soon as I've shown you why you aren't going to marry Donald."

"Nothing you can say is going to change my mind," she panted.

He rolled her over on her side, wrapping one leg around hers so their bodies were closely joined. "I hadn't planned on doing a lot of talking." He smiled.

His hands moved deliberately to the buttons on her blouse. With a gasp, she caught at them. "What do you think you're doing?"

"Do you really want me to spell it out for you?" he asked mockingly.

Samantha started to struggle in earnest then, but Mike captured both wrists in one hand, pinioning them behind her back. His superior strength was too much for her. When her shirt was open to the waist, Mike's glowing eyes studied her satin skin. Bending his dark head, he kissed the hollow in her throat, his warm mouth sliding down to the valley between her aching breasts. A shiver of pleasure shot through her, shocking in its intensity.

Frightened by the sensations he was evoking, Samantha cried, "You said you weren't going to rape me."

"I'm not." The tip of his tongue delicately

touched one nipple, and her fingers clutched at his shoulders. "Do you remember what else I said?" he murmured huskily.

"I . . ." She was drowning in her own emotions, unable to think clearly.

"I said you were going to ask me to make love to you." His fingers trailed over the flat plane of her stomach and beyond. "You are, aren't you, sweet Samantha?"

"I . . . I don't know." A shower of burning embers followed his hands and mouth.

"Let me show you what it can be like." He rubbed his cheek against her breast, then realizing that its slight roughness was rasping the delicate skin, he smoothed it with gentle fingertips that were unbearably sensuous. "We'll be joined in our own private world, my darling, and I'll give you ecstasy like you've never dreamed of. You want me, don't you?"

His mouth covered hers in a long, drugging kiss that lifted her beyond the realms of passion into sheer bliss. Her fingers twined through his thick dark hair and she arched her body against his, wanting to be part of this wonderful man, not just tonight, but forever.

The realization that she was in love with Mike came as a shock. It acted like a brake, slowing the throbbing sensations that were cascading through her heated body. This *couldn't* be happening! Not love! Surely what she felt was only the base desire an experienced lover like Mike could awaken. But Samantha knew it wasn't so. She had been fighting against it for a long time, trying to blot it out of her consciousness, refusing to admit what her heart knew to be true.

Mike buried his face in her neck, sighing against the scented softness, "I want you, Samantha."

A quiver ran through her body. Yes, he wanted

her—for now. Just like he had wanted all the others. She was nothing to him except another conquest. Perhaps slightly more challenging because she was virgin territory. That meant he would tire of her sooner though, since she didn't have the expertise to keep him interested for long. Tears filled Samantha's eyes and overflowed, leaving a crystal trail down her pale cheek. She was being offered a small sample of something that would leave her hungry for the rest of her life.

Mike lifted his head when a betraying drop touched his face. "Are you crying, Samantha?" he demanded incredulously.

She turned her head on the pillow. "No," she said in a muffled voice.

He wrenched her chin around, seeing the evidence she couldn't hide. "Are you *that* afraid?" Levering himself off of her, he said contemptuously, "You can stop crying. I told you I wasn't going to attack you."

She wiped away the tears with trembling fingers. "That wasn't why . . . I'm not crying, Mike, honestly. I *want* you to make love to me," she pleaded.

"Forget it," he said coldly. "I don't play around with children."

His sudden rejection was devastating. "Do I look like a child?" she asked passionately.

Gray eyes, like chips of ice, swept over her body. "No, you look warm and desirable, but it's only an illusion. You're a beautiful empty shell. I thought I could show you the joys of being a woman, but your father did his work too well." His eyes rested on her bare breasts, something flickering for just a second in their depths. Turning his back, he said harshly, "Get your clothes on and get out of here. And don't bother me again, Samantha."

Her fingers were shaking as she tried to fasten her

blouse, a task made more difficult by the tears that misted her vision. How could Mike have turned into this cold, awful stranger? And yet, the rigid set of his shoulders as he stared out into the darkness indicated he wasn't as indifferent as he pretended. Did he really want her to go?

Approaching him diffidently, she said, "I . . . I'm leaving now."

He turned around, looking at her clinically. "Before you do, maybe you'll answer a question. Why were you willing to go through with it since you obviously regard the act of love as a fate worse than death? Was it curiosity? A desire to know what all the fuss is about?"

"No! I—"

"Well, I'm sorry to disappoint you," he cut in harshly, "but I don't give lessons. Go practice on Donald, that ought to be good for a barrel of laughs."

He wouldn't even listen! He didn't want to understand. All he cared about was that his toy had proved unsatisfactory. She faced him with blazing eyes. "I don't need your advice, and I don't need *you!* Don't worry about my ever bothering you again, I'd sooner be staked to an anthill!"

He sauntered over to stand very close to her, threatening her with the sheer size and power of his body. "Ah, that's better. That's the Samantha we all know—the real one. The one who wishes she were a man."

He was so close their bodies were almost touching, but she stood her ground. Clenching her fists, she cried, "If only I were! I'd batter you into a pulp!"

"Too bad nature gave you that luscious body instead," he said sardonically. "What a waste."

With an outraged cry, she turned and ran out the door, his mocking voice following her down the stairs. "Give my regards to Donald, and tell him to contact me if he wants any advice on what turns you on."

Samantha never remembered afterward how she had gotten home. Pacing up and down her small living room, all she could think of was the devastating scene she had just been through. How could any man be that cruel and unfeeling? And to think she had imagined for one small moment that she was in love with him. Love? She *hated* him—and always had. Her first instincts had been correct. Mike Sutherland was a manipulative, deceitful monster! He wasn't fit to breathe the same air as Donald.

Donald. Samantha paused in her frenzied pacing. He was the one comforting thought in this whole miserable mess. She still had Donald. *He* was the one she was really in love with. If she had ever given him a chance, his kisses and caresses could have aroused her the way Mike's did. Mike was right about one thing—and one thing only—she had been very unfair to Donald. Although he had never tried to urge her into bed, he was probably suffering as much as she was now. And there was no reason for it, no real reason at all. She would go to him right now and tell him so.

Before Samantha could allow a strange reluctance to change her mind, she caught up her car keys and ran out the door.

The impetus that had impelled her almost vanished when Donald greeted her in his pajamas and bathrobe. "Samantha, what brings you here at this hour?"

"Did I get you out of bed? I . . . I didn't realize it was so late," she stammered.

"Come in. I was only reading. Is anything wrong?"

"No, I . . . I just wanted to see you."

He smiled and kissed her cheek. "How nice. Can I get you anything? A cup of coffee?"

She shook her head. "I just want to talk to you. Can we sit down?"

"Of course." He looked down at his pajamas. "Would you like me to get dressed first?"

Samantha could almost hear Mike's mocking laughter in her ears. Blotting it out determinedly, she said, "You're fine like that."

"You seem different tonight, Samantha. Are you sure there is nothing the matter?"

Ignoring the question, she took a deep breath. "I came here to talk about us, Donald."

"What about us?" he asked warily.

"How long have we been going together, Donald?"

"I don't know—several years."

"Exactly. And in all that time, you've been a perfect gentleman."

"At least I try to be." He smiled.

"That's just the point. I realize how difficult your restraint must have been. I haven't been fair to you. A man's needs are more urgent than a woman's, but you've never complained."

He took both of her hands in his. "I would never ask you to do anything you would regret. I respect you, Sam."

The use of her nickname made a small vein begin to pound in Samantha's temple. "I know that, but perhaps we've been expecting too much from each other. When two people are in love, it's only natural that they . . . they want to be together," she finished lamely.

Donald got up from the couch next to her and went to sit in a chair. "Naturally, I agree with you wholeheartedly, but I thought we had agreed to wait."

Samantha looked down at her laced fingers. "We don't have to," she said in a low voice.

He cleared his throat. "We have discussed this thoroughly, Sam, and I thought we were in agreement. You're obligated for two and a half more years of Brooke's schooling, although I'll never understand why she has to go to such an expensive college." He frowned. "And then there's your mother. You've been complaining that business has been falling off. Well, mine isn't so hot either. Until I get that partnership they have been promising me for years, I don't see how I could take on the responsibilities of your whole family."

Samantha looked at him in stunned surprise. "I wasn't asking you to marry me."

"But you said that we—" A dull red stained his cheeks. "You can't possibly mean—"

"We're adult people, Donald. We're planning to be married someday."

"I can't believe that you're actually suggesting we cheapen ourselves by indulging in some sordid relationship."

"Don't you want to make love to me?"

"Of course I do, after we're married. You don't know what a compliment I'm paying you, Samantha. Sex is something a man gets from a certain kind of woman, not the one he asks to be his wife."

Her eyes narrowed. "Have you ever slept with a woman, Donald?"

"What kind of a question is that?" he asked indignantly. "You said yourself that I'm a gentleman. Would you expect me to tell you?"

"I don't want to know who, just if."

"I don't know what's gotten into you tonight, but I don't like it," he said distantly. "I would expect that kind of talk from Brooke, but you have always been a lady."

"Are you sure, Donald? Do you really know anything about me?"

"I'm beginning to wonder."

"Well, don't let it keep you up nights." She shrugged into her jacket.

"Samantha, wait!"

"What for?" she asked shortly, her hand on the doorknob.

He took her arm, trying unsuccessfully to lead her back. "We have to talk."

"I don't want another lesson in economics," she said bitterly.

"That's the real problem isn't it, darling?" he soothed. "You're upset because I said we'd have to wait a little longer to get married. The other was just your way of trying to shock me into it."

She looked at him as though seeing him for the first time. "Is that what you honestly think?"

"I know it's hard on you, sweetheart. It's hard on me too. Don't you think I want to make love to you?"

"I'm really not sure."

"How can you say that?" He put his arms around her. "Of course I do. I just want it to be right between us, you know—beautiful."

"Not wild and wonderful?" she asked achingly.

He took his arms away. "Who has been putting ideas in your head? That sister of yours? Your mother ought to keep a closer eye on her. That kid has entirely too much freedom."

Samantha looked at him with dawning wonder.

"Is that why you dislike Brooke? Because she has her arms out to life? Because she isn't afraid to express joy or sorrow or passion? She doesn't keep every emotion bottled up inside her like I do."

"Then it's time she did. You're worth a dozen spoiled little brats like that."

"Please, Donald, I don't want to talk about Brooke."

"Well, it just aggravates me the way you work your head off for that idle kid."

"I think I'd better go." She sighed.

"No, don't go." He was suddenly contrite. "Come sit down and we'll talk about the house we're going to build one day. That always cheers you up. A lovely, brand-new, modern house, won't that be nice?"

Unbidden, a picture arose of a beautiful English brick mansion, its interior filled with Persian rugs and exquisite antiques. The patina of age gave it a dignity and charm that could never be equaled by something raw and new. What would it be like to live there, to wake up each morning in a big bed with a brown velvet spread, to come home each night to someone's welcoming arms?

"Come on, darling," Donald coaxed. "Let's talk about our house."

Samantha's gaze was far away. "It's only a castle in the air."

"Don't be that way, Sam. We'll have our house. You just have to be a little bit patient."

"What?" Her eyes focused on him with difficulty, as though she had forgotten where she was.

"We'll laugh about this after we're married," he said, taking her in his arms and nuzzling her neck. "And don't think I won't remind you that you were the impatient one."

"Don't do that," she said sharply, moving her head away.

"I was only teasing, honey. We won't ever refer to this again."

"That's very forbearing of you," she said acidly. "It's time I went home, Donald."

"Not before you kiss me good-night," he said playfully.

She looked at him dispassionately. "Aren't you afraid I might lose my head and tear your clothes off?"

"You're still angry," he said sadly.

"No, I'm not angry"—she sighed—"just tired and very confused."

"I know, darling. You need a good night's sleep. Everything will look better in the morning."

Taking her in his arms, he kissed her gently. Samantha closed her eyes, waiting for something to happen. When it didn't, she put her arms around his neck, urging her body against his and forcing his head down fiercely.

"For once in your life, Donald, kiss me—*really* kiss me!"

He made a startled move away, but she clung to him, forcing his mouth open. After a moment, his arms tightened and he kissed her back, his tongue moving into her mouth. One hand cupped her breast tentatively, and Samantha pressed against it, wanting desperately to feel something besides revulsion. Her movements incited him. His mouth crushed hers until she could taste blood where her teeth were forced into her lip. His hand tightened painfully on her breast.

When she cried out, he released her immediately. "I'm sorry, Sam, did I hurt you?"

"No, it . . . it's all right."

His breathing was rapid, but there was a smug look on his face. "I told you we shouldn't fool around with things that can get out of control. You're too innocent to know how a man can act when his passion is aroused."

Through the pain Donald had inflicted, Samantha could feel Mike's gentle fingers on her breast, his warm mouth soft and seductive, arousing her unbearably. A shudder ran through her slender body.

Donald patted her shoulder. "Don't think about it, darling. But maybe now you understand what I was trying to tell you."

"Yes, Donald, I'm afraid I do understand," she whispered.

He leaned down and kissed her cheek. "Now I think it's best if you do go home. Drive carefully, and don't forget to lock your car doors. I'll call you tomorrow."

Samantha drove home in a daze, her life in shreds around her. She had gone to Donald hoping he would blot out all thoughts of Mike, but she had only succeeded in accomplishing the opposite result. Donald's prowess as a lover was laughable compared to Mike's. Surely that wasn't the major consideration though. Samantha stared blindly at the road, trying to prove Donald's superiority, and failing. When she needed help, it was Mike she turned to automatically. He might grumble a lot and they fought fiercely at times, yet she knew she could always count on him.

With a feeling of desolation, Samantha realized she could no longer count on Mike. "Don't bother me anymore," he had said. Her hands gripped the steering wheel. Well, he needn't worry, she never would! She didn't need either one of them. Tonight had been a disaster, yet it was her own fault for allowing herself to be vulnerable. Who needed men anyway? She could stand on her own two feet. Hadn't her father taught her to be self-reliant?

A high tide of indignation sustained her until she marched into her apartment, got undressed, and climbed into bed. Then despair crept into her bones and she hugged the pillow and wept.

Chapter Five

Samantha dragged herself through the next ten days somehow, the dark circles under her eyes mute testimony to the sleepless nights she was spending. Everyone was worried about her, but Pete Grogan was the only one brave enough to say anything.

"Are you okay, Sam?" he asked one morning.

"I'm fine," she answered shortly.

"I thought maybe something was bothering you," he persisted.

"What could be bothering me?" she asked in a thin, taut voice. "The Remingtons are due home in two weeks and it looks like their house won't be finished, the excavation for the Taylor swimming pool caved in, the bank refuses to extend our line of credit. What could be wrong?"

"I know we've had a run of bad luck lately, but all businesses have their rough periods."

"This isn't a period, it's an era—an epoch!" she expanded wildly.

"Calm down, Sam. What good is it going to do to make yourself sick over this?"

"No good at all," she said bitterly. "But if I thought it would help, I'd get double pneumonia."

"Things will get better," he soothed.

"Yes, I know. And it's always darkest before the dawn. Run that one past me."

He regarded her appraisingly. "Feeling sorry for yourself isn't going to solve anything."

"If I don't, who will?" she asked flippantly. Her shoulders sagged suddenly and she put her head in her hands. "Oh, Pete, what am I going to do?"

The sympathy in his eyes wasn't reflected in his casual tone of voice. "Why not dump the whole mess on Sutherland and walk away with a bundle?"

"Never!" Samantha sat up straight, her eyes flashing. "He will never get his sly hands on Morgan's! That's what he's counting on. I'll bet he's in back of half of the plagues that have been visited on us."

Pete sighed. "You're not making sense, Sam. Mike Sutherland has no personal interest in Morgan Construction."

The truth of that statement was like a dagger in her midsection. "Did you want something special, Pete, or did you just come in to chat?" she asked stiffly.

When he had gone, Samantha took herself firmly in hand. Pete was right, feeling sorry for herself wasn't very constructive. There had to be a solution to their problems somewhere. If only she didn't feel so drained of energy. Nothing seemed to matter that much anymore, one way or another, and that was a dangerous trap to fall into.

She went to bed early that night, tired enough for once to sleep soundly. The telephone must have been ringing for a long time before she surfaced sufficiently to answer it. Even then she was disoriented, not knowing what time it was, or even if it was night or morning.

"Wake up, Sam," Pete's urgent voice ordered.

"I am awake," she said thickly. "What time is it?"

"It's ten-fifteen," he said impatiently.

She looked vaguely at the darkened window. "Why are you calling me at this hour?"

"That's what I've been trying to tell you. There is a fire at the Remington house. You have to get down here right away."

"Oh, no!" The mists of sleep dissipated abruptly. "How bad is it?"

"Pretty bad. The firemen are here now. You'll have to come down and give them some information."

"Of course." Samantha hesitated. "How did it start?"

"Nobody is sure yet. It's bedlam right now—water all over the place, and three engine companies. They don't take any chances in a neighborhood like this."

"They aren't chopping holes in things are they?" she asked in horror.

Pete's shrug was conveyed through his voice. "You know how it is."

"How about all those fancy knickknacks? Were any of them destroyed?" she asked fearfully.

"You'll see for yourself. I can't talk anymore, Sam, someone wants to use the phone."

She flew into her clothes in record time, grabbing the first thing that came to hand. A very short time later, she pulled up in front of a scene that made her mouth go dry. The flames were out, but thick smoke was still billowing from the Remington house. The once white exterior was smudged and grimy, and there was a gaping hole where the front door used to be.

Firemen were pulling smoldering furniture onto

the lawn, calling instructions to each other, while a circulating red light on the fire chief's car cast a flickering disco-like pattern over everything. A radio on one of the fire engines crackled with static, interspersed with the dispatcher's voice, adding to the general confusion.

"What happened?" she gasped as Pete came toward her. "It looks like a disaster!"

"I guess it could be worse. The fire was contained in the front of the house. Only a few of the over-stuffed pieces were burned."

"Still, the damage will run into thousands of dollars."

Pete avoided her eyes. "I suppose so."

"Will we be held responsible?" she asked fearfully.

"I'm afraid we might."

"Even if it wasn't our fault?"

"Who's to say?" He shrugged. "Our workmen were here. Face it, Sam, it could have been negligence on their part."

It was what she was afraid of. After all, hadn't one of her men cut a cable not too long ago? And then there were those exposed wires Mike had pointed out at the same time. She sighed. "I don't know what I'm ever going to tell the Remingtons, but at least we're insured."

"That's what I wanted to talk to you about," Pete said hesitantly.

Samantha's blood turned to ice. "Don't tell me we're *not* insured!" she begged.

"It isn't that simple."

"Either we are or we aren't," she cried.

"Well, we are, but not completely. You see, Rufus had a blind spot about insurance. He thought it was a waste of money. He used to say that any boss who couldn't police his own jobs shouldn't be in the business. I used to argue with him, but you know how stubborn your dad was."

"How much coverage do we have?" she asked fatalistically.

"The bare minimum. We're liable for the first fifty thousand."

"Fifty thousand!" Samantha's legs threatened to buckle, and Pete reached out to brace her.

"You have to understand. Rufus figured he could cover anything except a total disaster."

"Which this is to me," she said numbly. "What do you think the damage will run?"

He looked away. "It's hard to say."

"Don't hand me that, Pete. You've probably got it figured up already."

"Well, I haven't been through the whole house yet, so it would just be a guess," he answered evasively.

"How much?" she asked inexorably.

Their eyes met and he sighed. "Anywhere between fifty and a hundred thousand."

Samantha felt like she had been hit with a sledgehammer. So this was the way it was going to end—in a puff of smoke. "I see," she said woodenly.

Pete looked anxiously at her white face. "Are you all right, Sam?"

She stared at him vaguely. "Yes, I'm fine."

"Look, don't go pushing the panic button. Maybe I'm wrong. It will take a thorough inspection before we know for sure. And if it is that bad—well, we'll figure something out."

"Sure, Pete, we'll manage." It was almost as if she were anesthetized, aware that she had sustained a mortal blow, but unable to feel anything yet.

"That's the girl, keep your chin up. I have to go see about getting that door boarded up, and I think the chief wants to talk to you."

The next hour had a nightmare quality about it. Samantha answered questions, standing on the lawn while the clean-up work proceeded around them. After that, she was allowed inside to view the damage, which made her stomach knot into a tight little ball. Two of the fire engines departed with a great clashing of gears and equipment, and after a suitable time the last one left also. The fire was over. Just another statistic for the records.

Pete inspected the boarded-up front door. "That will hold it for now. Go home and get some sleep," he advised. "There isn't anything more we can do around here tonight."

"You're right, Pete." Samantha wondered if she would ever be able to sleep again. "You go ahead."

He looked at her sharply. "You too. There isn't any sense in hanging around here, working yourself into a state."

"I'm not. I'll leave in a couple of minutes," she promised.

"Well . . . okay." Obviously reluctant, he started toward his car, fatigue carving deep lines in his weather-beaten face.

After he had driven away, Samantha drifted slowly around to the backyard. The fog was coming in. It was cold, with the damp penetrating chill that seeped through clothing effortlessly. Samantha shivered, scarcely conscious of her discomfort. She felt disembodied, cut off from a world wrapped in a silence that was eerie after all the recent noise made by the firemen and the neighbors who had come to gawk.

The neighbors. She turned to look in the direction of Mike's house to her left. Why hadn't he been among the little groups of people? Being right next door, he should have been worried about his own property. Perhaps he wasn't home. The softly diffused amber lights coming from that direction indicated otherwise.

Something sparked in Samantha's numbed brain as a remembered scene flashed through her mind. A picture of Mike pointing out a coil of exposed wires and asking, "Don't you know you could start a fire this way?" He would know which ones to touch together. Suppose the fire wasn't accidental? He had tried every other way to get control of Morgan's—pirating, seduction, insults. He was very aware of her financial picture. Mike would know that a disaster such as this would wipe her out. What if he decided to be the *deus ex machina?*

A small remnant of sanity warned Samantha that she was being absurd, but she was beyond reason. The magnitude of her personal disaster had robbed her of all perspective. The only thing she could think of was that *somebody* must be responsible. Something malevolent was ruining her life.

A slow anger started to burn in her veins, growing in intensity as she imagined Mike Sutherland's satisfaction. He was probably congratulating himself this very minute, rubbing his hands in glee over his victory. Well, he wouldn't get away with it! Somehow she would find the proof and expose him for the scheming devil that he was. And she would tell him so—right now!

When the door wasn't immediately opened to her urgent ring, Samantha pounded on it with small, clenched fists, taking out her rage and frustration on the innocuous panel. Suddenly the door was flung open and Mike towered over her, a scowl on his face.

"What do you think you're—Samantha! What are you doing here?"

"Surely you aren't surprised to see me?"

"Of course I'm surprised. It's after midnight."

"I notice you weren't asleep." She looked pointedly at the fawn doeskin slacks and brown turtleneck pullover that hugged his powerful chest. "I suppose the noise next door kept you awake."

His eyes narrowed on her white face. Taking her arm, he drew her inside and closed the door. "I spoke to the firemen. I guess it was before you arrived."

"Yes, it was out by the time I got here. They respond quickly in a neighborhood like this, don't they?" she remarked, almost conversationally.

"They do a good job everywhere."

"But more so in Pacific Heights. You couldn't have been too worried about your property."

"I wasn't. It wasn't much of a fire," he said negligently.

A shudder ran through her at his calm dismissal of an event that was cataclysmic for her. "You saw to that, didn't you?"

"What are you talking about?"

"Tell me, Mike, did you get the idea the night you fixed that severed cable?"

His fingers bit into her shoulders like steel spikes. "Do you know what you are saying?" he asked ominously.

Her voice was high and thin. "Crossing a couple of little wires is just child's play for a man who knows how to dynamite without blowing up the whole countryside, isn't it?"

His hands tightened like a vise, but Samantha didn't even feel the pressure that would leave bruises for days afterward. "Are you accusing me of setting that fire?" he demanded.

"Oh, I don't expect you to admit it—even though

there aren't any witnesses. That would be too straightforward for you," she taunted.

"By God, if you were a man, I'd wipe up the floor with you," he grated through clenched teeth.

She thrust her chin in the air. "Don't let that stop you, Mr. Sutherland. It's about the only thing you haven't done to me."

"You can't honestly believe I had anything to do with that fire next door," he said incredulously.

"I don't have the proof yet if that's what you mean, but I'm going to get it. Oh, yes, I'm going to get it if it's the last thing I do on earth!"

His eyes were penetrating. "I realize how aggravating this must be for you, but you're letting yourself get emotional."

"Just like a woman, is that it?" she asked furiously. "Going all to pieces over a minor annoyance."

"Oh, for God's sake, Samantha, will you pull yourself together?"

She stood very straight, her hands clenched at her sides. It was infuriating that she still had to tilt her head back to look up at him. "Don't worry, I don't intend to go all soft and feminine on you."

He looked her up and down insultingly, taking in the old windbreaker, the tousled hair, and the smudge on her cheek that she didn't know was there. "I wasn't really expecting you to. You wouldn't know how."

Anger scalded her. "Fortunately for me! You'd like it if I was one of those featherbrained females you're accustomed to. The kind that are taken in by that phony charm you hand out. Luckily I saw through you the first time we met."

"What do you want, a medal?" he asked brutally. "Why don't you go home and write a long list—all the things I hate most about Mike Sutherland." He turned away contemptuously, but she ran after him, grabbing his arm and tugging at it.

"Go ahead and laugh while you can. You're not going to get away with what you did tonight! I'm going to go to the police."

"If you want to make a fool of yourself, I don't suppose I can stop you," he said scornfully.

"You don't think they will listen to me, but you're wrong."

"Really?" He leaned against the wall of the spacious entry hall, regarding her sardonically. "I happen to be a prominent contractor. Do you seriously believe you're going to convince the police that I'm a part-time pyromaniac?"

She nodded positively. "When they have all the facts. When I tell them how you tried and failed to make me sell out to you."

"Is that what this is all about, Samantha?" he asked softly. "Morgan Construction? Or is it the fact that I tried to do something else?"

"I don't know what you mean." Her hand fell away from his arm.

"I think you do. I think this wild outpouring of invective is because I not only tried to do something else—but succeeded."

His eyes swept over her mockingly, and Samantha caught her breath. "I don't know what you're talking about," she said, turning toward the door.

He pulled her back. "Don't go now. Not when we're getting to the heart of the matter."

"I've said all I came to say," she muttered, struggling in his iron grip.

"But I haven't." His voice was silky. "I haven't even begun."

"Threats aren't going to change my mind," she said with a courage that was beginning to ebb.

"The only thing I'm going to threaten is your peace of mind. You have succeeded in convincing yourself that you hate me because I'm the big bad wolf who is going to swallow up your company, but that isn't the real reason, is it?"

Samantha bit her lower lip, finding it increasingly difficult to meet those comprehensive gray eyes. "If you had left me alone, I'd still be . . . none of this would have happened."

His hand moved to the back of her neck, his fingers combing sensuously through the soft curls. "None of what, Samantha?"

He was so close that her breathing felt constricted. "The . . . the fire."

"The fire would still have occurred. I didn't start it, you know that. What's really bothering you is that I broke through that facade of being 'one of the boys' that you present to the world." She tried to dislodge his disturbing hand which only tightened in her hair, pulling her head back. "Did you have even yourself fooled? Didn't you know there was a woman underneath?"

"Let go of me! You're not making any sense," she cried breathlessly.

He watched her struggles dispassionately. "You lash out at anyone who tries to make you face facts, but it doesn't change them."

"You're very clever at turning everything around," she said bitterly. "According to you, if I wore high heels and let my hair grow long, I'd be an instant success. At what—getting into your bed?"

Mike's stern face relaxed in a smile. "It would be a start."

His infuriating habit of making her feel unfeminine enraged Samantha, especially now when she had lost everything. Casting wildly about for a way to pay him back she said, "Thanks for the advice, but I don't find you any more attractive than you find me."

His eyes narrowed dangerously. "Are you asking for a demonstration of how wrong you can be?"

Before she could escape, his arm circled her waist, jerking her against his hard body. His hand held her head immobile so his mouth could ravage hers in a kiss that was punishing in intensity. There was no tenderness in the way he took what he wanted, only a desire to prove his male superiority. Forcing her lips open, he probed ruthlessly, demanding a subjugation she refused to give. There was savage determination in the way he ground her hips against his hard loins, an uneven display of power she couldn't match.

Samantha's strength failed in this pitiless onslaught, her body going limp against his.

With the collapse of her defenses, his brutality ceased. The bruising pressure lessened, his arms holding her more gently now. His mouth softened too, seeking to give pleasure as well as receive it. She trembled against him, lost in the seduction he wove so easily around her.

His arms were a haven that she wanted to rest in forever. All the misery of the past few hours was dissipated as she gloried in the joy of being close to him once more. It was useless to try to deny it—she loved this man with every fiber. But it was hopeless. All she could ever have were a few fleeting moments. Tears of resignation trailed down her cheeks at the bleak thought.

Mike lifted his head, his bemused expression hardening into cynicism. "More tears, Samantha? I thought those were reserved for something heavier than a kiss."

His return to mockery was the last straw. The

tragedy of her life overwhelmed Samantha, and she couldn't stop the tears. Putting her hands over her eyes so Mike couldn't see the devastation, she turned blindly toward the door.

"Samantha, wait!" He caught her by the shoulders, trying to pull her hands away. When that failed, he took her in his arms, cradling her head against his shoulder. "Something is really wrong, isn't it? Tell me what it is, darling."

When that only made her cry harder, he smoothed her hair gently, making crooning sounds as he kissed her temple. After her sobs had subsided into gulping breaths, he led her into the living room which was lit only with one shaded lamp. Easing her onto a couch, he held her close, stroking her back tenderly.

"Whatever it is, kitten, I'll fix it. Tell me about it," he murmured.

"Oh, Mike, I'm so sorry. Can you ever forgive me? I know you didn't have anything to do with the fire."

"Hush, darling. Just tell me what's wrong."

"I don't know what I'm going to do. I'm at the end of my rope. Tell me what to do, Mike," she begged.

"I will, sweetheart. As soon as you tell me about it."

For a long moment she allowed herself the luxury of inhaling his warmth and compassion, pretending that he really cared about her. But that was a dangerous fantasy. She had already had enough hard knocks tonight. Setting herself up for another might well be the death blow. Sitting reluctantly upright, Samantha knuckled away the tears like a weary child.

"You don't have to be kind after the terrible thing I accused you of," she said.

"I want to help," he said simply.

She shook her head, looking down at her tightly

clasped hands. "There is nothing you can do. And besides—you told me not to bother you again."

"That was said under great provocation." He smiled. "You knew I didn't mean it."

"No, you were right. I have been nothing but a nuisance to you. I don't blame you for getting angry."

"I'm going to get still angrier if you don't tell me pretty soon what is upsetting you," he said, his expression belying the words.

"It's the fire, Mike. I'm wiped out. If there is anything left after the settlement, which I doubt—any equipment or anything—you can have it at cost."

"Whoa! Wait a minute! What are you talking about? Your insurance will cover the damage."

"That's what I'm trying to tell you. We aren't covered."

"That isn't possible." He frowned. "How can you run a business without insurance?"

"Just another example of my incompetence." Samantha sighed. She explained about Rufus and his ideas on the matter. "We never discussed it, but that doesn't absolve me. I should have found out when I took over."

"Why didn't Pete tell you?"

"He knew how pressed we were for money. I guess he thought we could squeak by."

Mike swore briefly under his breath. "Of all the irresponsible—"

"Don't blame Pete. It was my responsibility and I goofed."

He scowled at her. "You mustn't be so hard on yourself. How could you be expected to operate a construction yard without help? You were thrown in on a more or less sink-or-swim basis."

She gave a little laugh that threatened to turn into

a sob. "Aren't you changing your tune? You are the one who told me it was no business for a woman."

"Forget all that. Right now you need some constructive advice."

She shook her head. "It's too late. If I hadn't been so knuckleheaded, I would have sold out to you long ago, then this would have been your headache. Although your men would never have made this mistake," she said bitterly.

"This is no time for self-pity," he said sharply.

Samantha hung her head. "You're right."

A long forefinger raised her chin. "The question is, what are we going to do about it?"

"It isn't your problem, Mike. I never should have come here tonight. You were right about my refusing to face facts. I had to blame somebody so I blamed you. It's good of you not to have tossed me out the door long ago."

"I find myself less inclined to do so all the time," he said softly.

Her long eyelashes fell before the light in his gray eyes. "I think I'd better go," she murmured.

"Not in your present state. I'm not going to let you go home to worry yourself into a decline over this. You look like you've lost your last friend."

"I've lost my father's business, that's worse," she said soberly.

He took her cold hands in his warm ones. "You haven't lost anything, Samantha. I'll give you a loan to cover any liability you have for the Remington house."

"I couldn't accept it. We are barely getting by now, there is no telling when I could pay you back."

"I'm in no hurry." He smiled.

"I don't want charity," she said stiffly. "If I can't cut it on my own, then I shouldn't be in business. You said that yourself."

"Will you stop quoting me? What are you, Boswell to my Johnson?"

"It's true, Mike. It's time I accepted my limitations."

"Why do you insist on punishing yourself? You've taken on a tough job. Men all over the country are scrambling to stay in business."

"That's the operative word isn't it—men?" she asked bitterly. "You agree with me, you're just trying to sugarcoat it."

"You have a terrible habit of putting words in my mouth, Samantha. What I really believe is that you are female Atlas, longing to lay down the burden, but unable to because of a misguided sense of conscience." He sighed. "However, if I can't make you see the light, I'll help you hold up the world."

His kindness almost brought back the tears so she affected an offhand manner. "You have never backed a loser in your life, why start now?"

His hand cupped her cheek. "Is that the way you see yourself?"

"Well, you couldn't exactly call me a howling success at anything could you?" she asked, trying to smile.

"No," he answered, dashing her hopes. "But that is only because you have spent your short life trying to be something you aren't, and don't want to be."

"Since you are so omnipotent, maybe I ought to turn the rest of my life over to you," she said bitterly.

He became very still. Cupping her face in his palms, he looked deeply into her eyes. "Maybe you should."

Something electric flashed between them as they stared at each other. Mike's head was poised over hers, close enough for her to see the dilated pupils that turned his eyes slate-gray. She trembled under the warmth of his hands, drowning in her need to be closer to him. Bruised and battered from the traumatic events of this night, she longed to find solace in his arms, to feel them close around her and have him carry her to the heights of passion that would make everything else unimportant.

Her lips parted as she invited his mouth to join them in the first step to rapture. Mike's sharply indrawn breath acknowledged the invitation. His slowly descending head blotted out everything except the anticipation of ecstasy.

A strident voice cut through the dream. "Mike, how long do you think I'm going to—" The words broke off abruptly as a beautiful blonde surveyed them from the doorway. Her seductive body was encased in a scarlet sheath that was a showcase for charms that couldn't be hidden in any case. "Well, excuse *me,*" she said sarcastically. "Am I interrupting something?"

Samantha looked at her blindly, unable to comprehend the other woman's presence. Mike's reaction was similar, but he recovered fast.

Standing up in one swift movement, he crossed the room with long strides. "I'm sorry, Regina. Something rather urgent came up."

"Yes, I can see that," she remarked acidly.

"A colleague of mine has a problem," he said smoothly.

"It looked like you were about to solve it for her when I came in," the woman said spitefully.

Ignoring that, Mike said, "If you will just go back in the den, I'll join you shortly."

"Maybe I'd better leave," the blonde said distantly, flipping back her long hair.

"If that is what you would prefer, I'll call a taxi," Mike said pleasantly.

Regina's coldness vanished. She ran her palm over

his shirtfront. "You don't really want me to go, do you, Mike?" she asked coaxingly.

His face was expressionless. "That is entirely up to you."

"Well you can't blame me for being teed off." Her voice was aggrieved. "You left me sitting all alone for twenty minutes. If it was anyone but you, I would have walked out long ago."

He took her elbow, leading her from the room. "I have explained the situation, this is—" His voice trailed off as they disappeared down the hall.

Samantha sat immobilized, her numbed mind refusing to credit what her eyes had seen. What kind of insatiable satyr was he? Righteous indignation ignited her. All the time Mike had been comforting her—no, a lot more than that!—he had another girl stashed away in the other room.

She thrust away the realization that she had come here uninvited. That didn't excuse him. He didn't have to be so tender, breaking down her already shaky defenses until she had practically offered herself to him—again. Tormenting her had gotten to be a pastime with Mike, something he couldn't resist. Well, he was going to have to get his kicks somewhere else, because she was tired of providing him with laughs.

Samantha sprang up from the couch, practically running into the hall. Before she could make her escape, however, Mike blocked the door.

"Samantha, don't go!"

"What did you have planned, an orgy?" she asked bitterly. "I'm sorry, but I don't go in for that sort of thing."

His hands went to her shoulders convulsively, and he shook her hard. "You know better than that."

"Do I?" Samantha brushed the hair out of her eyes. "The only thing I know is that I am the fool of the world. You've been able to twist me around your little finger like a rubber band, but no more. The first time we met I knew you were the enemy, and first impressions aren't wrong. You have destroyed me the way you set out to do, but your victory isn't going to be quite complete."

"You're being hysterical. I didn't know you were coming. I couldn't help it that I had a guest."

"I would have been surprised if you hadn't," she cried. "Heaven forbid that the great Mike Sutherland should sleep alone one night!"

"Aren't you rather jumping to conclusions?" he asked evenly.

"I don't think so. Given your well-known appetites, I can't see you and that blonde discussing Schopenhauer."

"You can't see anything beyond that ridiculous little nose of yours," he said grimly. "I had no idea virgins were that fascinated with sex."

"That's another of your misconceptions," she raged. "As if it matters to me who you sleep with."

"Are you sure it doesn't, Samantha?" he asked silkily.

"Don't flatter yourself. I know you're working your way through the female population of San Francisco. I'm just happy that I'm not part of the crowd."

"Happy—or frightened?" he asked, moving so close that she could smell his pungent after-shave lotion and sense the leashed anger in his powerful body.

Samantha panicked. Stepping back, she bumped into the wall, flattening herself against it desperately. "Don't use that stale line on me," she warned scornfully, although her voice had a slight quaver. "I'm too smart to fall for it."

He advanced relentlessly, penning her in with

spread arms, his palms resting against the wall. "Yes, you're very smart, Samantha, or should I say self-sufficient? So secure that you can go through life without leaning on anyone. You don't need love, or even affection. You think you can do it all yourself."

"Yes, I . . . I can." She faltered.

"Poor child." He touched her cheek with gentle fingers. "I feel sorry for you."

"I don't need your pity," she flared.

"You need something. What else makes you keep turning up on my doorstep?"

"This is the last time," she vowed. "You don't have to worry, I will never bother you again."

"Oh, you bother me, Samantha," he said, tracing the shape of her mouth with a gentle forefinger. "You bother me a lot."

"I'm sorry if I interrupted your date," she cried. "But I'm sure your powers of persuasion will prove equal to the occasion."

"Do you indeed?" He smiled. "My powers don't seem to have had any effect on you."

His teasing touch was destroying her. Samantha knew it was something he did automatically, yet she couldn't help responding. Drawing a quivering breath, she asked disdainfully, "How many women do you need in one night?"

"Only one," he said, kissing the corner of her mouth. "But if I can't have her, I'll have to settle for poor substitutes. I'm a man, with a male's appetites. You're responsible for my looking elsewhere." His closed lips moved over hers caressingly, taunting hers to open first.

She turned her head away with an effort. "I would have to be out of my mind to believe that."

"You want to believe it. Why not let yourself and see what happens?" he urged.

Her eager body was in complete accord. Samantha tried to resist, but her need was too great. She wanted this man so incredibly much. He sensed the weakening and gathered her in his arms. She clung to him, lifting her face and twining her fingers in his hair.

When his mouth closed over hers, she entered another world, an enchanted land where all her dreams were fulfilled. Mike was all she wanted out of life. As long as he held her like this, nothing else mattered. His hands slid over her body, sending her into a trembling ecstasy that was shattered by a querulous voice from the other room.

"Haven't you gotten rid of her yet, Mike? How long does it take?"

Samantha's eyes flew open, her stricken gaze meeting his. She tore herself out of his arms. How often could this man humiliate her? She could just imagine his promising the blonde that he would dust off this troublesome female in nothing flat. Unfortunately he was a very physical man. When he had a warm body in his arms, it didn't particularly matter which one it was! Samantha's cheeks burned with shame as she eluded his detaining hands.

"I can't let you go like this," Mike said tautly.

"I don't think you have your priorities straight," Samantha cried bitterly. "She has first claim on your bed."

She rushed out the door, slamming it behind her before Mike had a chance to reply. Gunning her car away from the curb, Samantha drove like one possessed, yet she couldn't go fast enough to outdistance her anguished thoughts.

This was positively the end! She never wanted to see Mike Sutherland again. When she was with him, he had the power to melt her resolve, but that was only because she was as blindly stupid as all the other poor souls who fell in love with and were used by him. At least now she knew her weakness and could guard against it. It was like having an illness for which there was no cure. But at least she could avoid the deadly danger of exposure.

Angrily wiping away the tears that wouldn't stop, she congratulated herself on being well rid of him.

Chapter Six

Samantha was so tired the next day that just putting one foot in front of the other seemed like too much of an effort. Even if she could have slept, which was impossible after all that occurred, Mike had phoned her innumerable times last night before finally giving up. At least she supposed it had been Mike. After hanging up on him the first time, she hadn't answered the phone.

But that didn't stop her from thinking about him and the curvy Regina. Her mind conjured up all kinds of pictures, one more hateful than the next. Mike's dark head bending slowly to that blond one, his hands caressing her back with lingering, seductive strokes. And worst of all—their two bodies intertwined in that big upstairs bedroom.

The last image had pulled her out of bed to pace the floor restlessly. She knew this nonsense had to stop. If it wasn't Regina, it would be some other woman. She couldn't continue to tear herself to pieces over a fickle man who wasn't worth a second thought. Her mind agreed with all the good advice; it was her body that was finding it difficult to accept. Toward morning, she finally fell into an exhausted sleep, with the result that she was late getting to work.

Pete was sitting at her desk when Samantha entered the office, the phone cradled on his shoulder while he wrote a message. He looked up when the door opened, breaking off his conversation. "Wait a minute, here she is now." Holding the receiver out to her, he said, "I'm glad you finally showed up, it's Mike. He's been calling every five minutes."

Something remarkably like fear entered her eyes. She shook her head violently. "I don't want to talk to him."

Pete put his hand over the phone. "You *have* to talk to him, Sam. I already told him you were here."

"Then tell him I went out again." She turned and fled out the door.

Samantha wandered aimlessly around the construction yard for a while, giving herself a pep talk. Hadn't she decided in the small hours of the night not to let Mike bother her? She had already started the process of getting over him, Samantha assured herself. It was just that she didn't want to talk to him because she was embarrassed at making a fool of herself last night. How could she have displayed such weakness in the face of her mortal enemy? After she left, did he make a funny story out of it for his girl friend's amusement? Samantha covered her ears as though she could actually hear their derisive laughter.

Back in her own office, she shuffled through some papers, looking at figures that might as well be

Greek for all the sense they made. She was adding up a column of numbers for the fourth time when the door burst open, crashing against the wall with an explosive sound.

Mike filled the doorway like an avenging angel, six feet four inches of taut fury. "Who the hell do you think you are to refuse my phone calls?" he stormed.

The unexpected sight of him, even furious as he was, did funny things to her heartbeat. Samantha took a deep breath to steady herself. "There is no law that says I have to talk to you."

His legs were slightly spread, tightly clenched fists resting on his narrow hips. "There is, however, something called common courtesy, which you wouldn't know about."

"I'm sure you know about the common part anyway," she spit at him.

"I ought to break your scrawny little neck, do you know that?"

She leaped out of her chair. "For your information, I am not scrawny! I'm sorry I don't measure up to your voluptuous girl friend, but on the other hand, I doubt if it will give me worry lines."

Suddenly, Mike began to laugh. "Here I am, threatening to beat the daylights out of you, and the only thing that bothers you is that I called you scrawny."

"It doesn't bother me a bit, actually. I just consider the source." She put her tilted nose in the air.

His anger seemed to have dissolved. "Perhaps I was a little hasty," he said, looking at her mockingly. "Scrawny isn't exactly the word for you—I think immature describes it better."

Unreasoning rage swept over Samantha, driving out caution. "You didn't seem to mind last night when you forced yourself on me!"

"Is that what I did, Sam?" He was laughing at her openly, the masculine version of her name underscoring his derision.

"Yes, you did," she insisted stubbornly, knowing as he did that it was a lie. "You took advantage of the fact that I was upset and didn't know what I was doing."

"I hope I'm around more often when you're upset. I like the way you lose control," he taunted.

"I thought you said I was scrawny," she challenged.

His gaze was insulting as it swept her slender body, lingering on the small, firm breasts. "Well, as you discovered for yourself, I have a very healthy male appetite. While you're not exactly full-blown, you do have the necessary . . . um . . . equipment."

Samantha gritted her teeth. "It's just as I suspected—*any* woman will do."

"Oh, I wouldn't say that," he drawled. "You present a challenge, so I'm willing to overlook your deficiencies."

"Don't you think I'd be a little inexperienced for your taste?" she asked scathingly.

"That can be rectified." He was clearly enjoying himself.

"I thought you didn't give lessons."

He shook his head. "We're going to have to do something about that memory of yours. Do you remember everything I say?"

Samantha looked down at the cluttered desk. To her eternal sorrow, everything about him was indelibly etched on her heart and brain. "I suppose I do," she answered his question. "Nobody ever talked to me like that before."

"No man, you mean."

"All right, no man," she conceded.

"Perhaps that was because you never tried them as sorely as you've tried me."

"Me?" she cried inelegantly. "You are the one who has made my life miserable."

"How did I do that, sweet Samantha?"

"You know perfectly well. It's the reason you're here now, to gloat over me." Even as she accused him of it, Samantha knew Mike would never do such a thing.

He denied it himself. "What you really mean is that I awakened that beautiful body, and now you're having trouble dealing with it." His firm mouth twitched with amusement. "If it will help, I take back what I said about not giving lessons."

"Oh!" Her breath came out in an explosive little gasp. "You are detestable! Wasn't that blonde last night enough for you?"

"Frankly, no. You pretty well destroyed my amorous mood. I took her home right after you left."

"I'll bet!" she scoffed.

"Whether you believe it or not, it's true. The lady didn't think too kindly of you, I might add."

Samantha suppressed a wild joy. "I don't suppose it was what she expected," she said distantly. "I'm quite amazed myself."

"Did you picture us frolicking in the nude through the house, stopping to make love in unlikely places?" He grinned. When her flaming cheeks betrayed her, Mike started to laugh. "That *is* what you thought, isn't it?"

"Certainly not!" She looked at a point somewhere beyond his shoulder. "It is of no interest to me where you make love."

He sauntered slowly over until he was standing very close to her. "Since you remember everything I say, you must know that my preference is for a bed. I told you that when I took you out to dinner."

"Did you? I . . . I must have forgotten."

"I haven't," he murmured, trailing a gentle fore-finger down her cheek to the corner of her mouth. "Will you have dinner with me tonight, Samantha?"

She took a step back, away from his disquieting hand. "What's the matter, is your girl friend busy tonight?"

"I don't know. I didn't ask her."

"You really should. You owe her a return engagement after last night's incompleted pass," she said nastily.

He raised a sardonic eyebrow. "Are you giving us your blessing? Well, so be it. Just remember that you are responsible for driving me into the arms of another woman."

"You mean you *are* going to take her out?" Samantha asked, outraged.

"Unless you've changed your mind."

Samantha was almost speechless with rage. Of all the insulting men she had ever met, Mike Sutherland clearly won first place! Without any pretense at all, he was telling her that it didn't matter which woman he slept with as long as it was someone. Did he think he was conferring a favor by giving her first chance at him? It took a great effort not to fling herself at him like a wildcat. Only the sure knowledge that he could subdue her with one hand stopped her.

He was watching the play of emotions over her mobile face with unconcealed amusement that added to her fury. Quickly lowering her long lashes to veil the expression in her eyes, Samantha said, "Why would you want to be with me?"

"I can think of a few reasons," he said dryly.

She fluttered her lashes coyly. "What if I proved . . . unsatisfactory? Maybe I ought to take you up on the offer of those lessons."

His eyes narrowed appraisingly. "If that's what you want."

"Would you teach me anything I asked?" she murmured in a seductive voice.

He was regarding her warily now, but when she turned the full power of limpid violet eyes on him, Mike caught his breath. "Anything, anytime," he said huskily.

Samantha bent her head, picking at a piece of invisible lint on her blouse. "There *is* something I have been wanting to do, Mike," she breathed. "And I've never felt like this with any other man."

A light flamed in his eyes as he reached out to touch her cheek. "What is it, honey?"

"This!" With all her might, Samantha kicked him in the shins.

He gave a mingled howl of pain and rage, hopping around on one foot and clutching his leg. After one triumphant look, Samantha ran for the door, but the slight pause had been her undoing. Mike recovered in time to reach out a long arm and slam it shut before she could escape.

"No, you don't! This time you're going to get what's coming to you," he grated.

"Let go of me, you big brute!"

"In due time," he said grimly, dragging her across the room by a firm grip on her arm.

"I'll scream," she warned.

"Go ahead, it won't do you any good. Even the Marines couldn't get you out of this one. For once in your short, spoiled life, you are going to get what you deserve."

Her eyes widened. "What are you going to do?"

"What someone should have done a long time ago." Sitting down on a straight-backed chair, Mike pulled her facedown across his knees.

When she realized what he intended, Samantha fought like a tiger, but he held her as easily as if she had been a kitten instead. "Don't you dare lay a finger on me, Mike Sutherland!"

"I intend to use all five, plus my palm," he assured her.

"You're nothing but a great big bully!" she gasped. "Only a coward would attack a defenseless woman."

Samantha continued to struggle even though she knew it was useless in the face of his relentless determination. She was almost resigned to her fate when miraculously, Mike's grip loosened and he swore softly under his breath. "You're right, I can't do it," he groaned.

He jerked her face up, still holding her across his knees and she immediately tried to lash out at him with her fingernails. Pinning her hands underneath her body, he said, "Lady, if you're defenseless, I would hate to see you when you're trying to protect yourself."

Samantha's head was resting on his hard thigh, the silky curls in wild disarray. Her cheeks were flushed with anger as she stared defiantly up at him. "It's all your fault. You didn't have to overreact just because I hurt your macho pride."

"You did a lot more than that. My shin hurts like the devil."

"I hope it does! If you'll let me up, I'll fix the other one for you."

Mike's eyes narrowed dangerously. "You still haven't learned your lesson, hm? Maybe I'd better teach it to you after all."

She arched her body in a vain attempt to break his steel grip. "Go ahead, hit me then. That ought to make you feel like a big man."

"I don't seem to be able to administer the corporal

punishment you deserve, so I think I'll try something else." There was a grim smile on his firm mouth as his hand moved to the collar of her blouse.

"Wha . . . what are you going to do?"

"There is more than one way to tame a wildcat." His long fingers undid the first button.

"Stop it! You can't do this," she gasped.

"Watch me."

"No, don't!" The second button came loose and Samantha's creamy throat was exposed. His fingers stroked its length before moving inexorably on. A streak of fire seemed to flame everywhere he touched. "Mike, please!" she begged.

"Oh, it's please now, is it?" He paused, a long forefinger tracing the widened V of her blouse, barely touching the heated skin that longed traitorously for closer contact.

"Yes, I give up. I apologize. I'm sorry!" she cried wildly.

"Words, Samantha. You're only sorry that I caught you before you got away."

"No, honestly! I won't ever do anything like that again if you'll just let me up." She tried desperately to free her hands.

"I wonder why you're so frightened now?" he mused. "You were spitting like an angry cat when you thought I was going to wallop you." Another button gave way.

"Mike, this is an office. Anyone could come in and see us."

"Didn't you notice that I locked the door?"

"That's even worse! If anyone tried to get in they would think—oh, why did you do that?"

"I didn't want to be interrupted while I administered your well-deserved punishment. Although I'm glad now that I couldn't go through with it." His smile was taunting. "This method is going to be much more pleasurable." Her blouse was completely unbuttoned now and he pulled it out of the waistband of her jeans.

Samantha twisted and bucked while he watched her efforts calmly. When she was exhausted, he unhooked her bra, freeing her firm, round breasts to his appreciative eyes. His palm smoothed the satin skin, sliding down to make a slow circle on her flat stomach. A long shudder ran through her and she closed her eyes, savoring the almost unbearably pleasurable sensation.

His warm mouth touched one taut breast, taking the hardened tip delicately between his lips. A flame of desire enveloped her, so demanding that she arched her body upward, turning her head from side to side, blindly searching for release from the tension that gripped her.

His mouth covered hers and she parted her lips with a sigh, welcoming him into the private recess. His exploration was seductive, making every secret part of her body long for his attention. At her soft moan of delight, Mike released her arms. They circled his neck immediately, her fingers threading convulsively through his thick dark hair.

After a long time, he raised his head and looked at her with blazing eyes. She was completely acquiescent in his arms, her face radiant with pleasure.

"No fight left, Samantha?" he asked softly. "Your spirit seems to depart in direct relation to your clothes. If I can ever get you completely nude in my arms, I might have you tamed yet."

He turned his head in a listening position as she stared at him with drugged eyes. Setting her swiftly on her feet, he held her between his knees, rapidly buttoning her shirt and tucking it into her jeans as though he were dressing a child. She braced herself with her hands on his broad shoulders, glad of the support of his thighs because her own legs were trembling.

Giving her a brief kiss on the mouth, he chuckled. "If you don't want anyone to know what's just gone on in here, I suggest you get that dazed look off your face." He moved with catlike grace to the door, unlocking it only moments before Pete entered.

"Mike, how are you?" Pete gave him a hearty handshake, his face wreathed in smiles.

While the two men were greeting each other, Samantha retreated behind her desk, taking a surreptitious look in a small mirror she kept in a drawer. Her reflection was in no way reassuring. Surely anyone could tell by looking at her! Those overly bright eyes and flushed cheeks were a dead giveaway, not to mention her mouth, swollen by Mike's kisses.

"I see you finally caught up with Sam," Pete said.

"Yes, it took a while, but I finally got to her," Mike said mockingly.

She couldn't look at him. "Perhaps you will leave now that you have accomplished what you came for," she said, shuffling some papers around the desk.

"Oh, but I haven't," he said softly.

Her eyes flashed with dislike.

"That's what you think! If you ever step foot in here again, I'm going to call some of the boys and have you thrown out."

"Sam!" Pete's voice was distressed.

"That's all right, Pete." Mike was struggling to contain his merriment. "I think Samantha is still in shock over recent events."

"That's no reason for her to talk to you like that after what—"

"Does he have you buffaloed too?" she interrupted hotly. "Maybe he's a big man around his own yard, but he is just an intruder here. Will you kindly get out of my office, Mr. Sutherland?"

"If that is what you would like, Miss Morgan."

"You know it is." His derisive look snapped her self-control. *"Get out!"* she shouted, clenching her fists.

"Now just a darn minute, Sam." She had never seen Pete even ruffled, but he was clearly angry now. "What you need is to be taken over somebody's knee." At Mike's explosive snort of laughter, Pete looked briefly in his direction before continuing sternly, "I don't know what has gotten into you. How can you talk to Mike like that after all he has done for you?"

After all he has done *to* me, she thought bitterly. "This is something that doesn't concern you, Pete," she said distantly.

"Listen to me, little girl," he snapped, "this business is just as important to me as it is to you. I should think you'd be throwing roses at Mike not brickbats."

Mike had been lounging against the door, watching the proceedings with contained amusement. Now, he moved forward. "It isn't her fault, Pete. I hadn't gotten around to telling her."

"You mean she doesn't know?"

Samantha looked at the two men. "Know what?" she exploded. "Will one of you please tell me what is going on?"

"Why don't you do the honors, Pete?" Mike said easily.

"It's about the fire last night. This morning real early, Mike went over and made an inspection. He had a hunch about how it started—the location, and the way it was contained in the front of the house mostly. And by George, he was right." Pete regarded Mike with shining eyes. "I don't see how you did it."

Samantha looked at him blankly. "Am I supposed to be elated because he found some faulty wiring?"

"It was wiring all right, but the fault wasn't yours," Mike explained gently. "The fire was started by a defect in the main panel of the electric alarm system located by the front door. I did some checking and discovered that it hadn't had the periodic inspection it should have. The security company is responsible for the damages, you aren't."

Samantha's legs gave way and she sat down with a thump, unable to credit what she had just heard. This would make all the difference in the world. They weren't wiped out. She hadn't failed Rufus after all.

"So you can see why you owe Mike a debt of gratitude," Pete said. "I think an apology is in order."

"It isn't necessary. I don't think Samantha's nervous system could take any more jolts." Mike grinned.

She took a deep breath. "Pete is right, I do owe you an apology. What you did was . . . unbelievably kind."

"Even though it wasn't in my best interests, isn't that what comes next?" he taunted softly.

"Please, Mike, I'm trying to make amends," she pleaded.

"As well you should," Pete told her severely, not quite ready to let her off the hook. Turning to Mike, his expression changed to respect. "I never would have thought of the alarm system. It was sure decent of you to check it out."

Mike shrugged that off. "We couldn't let the Dragon Lady lose her security blanket, could we?" he asked with a wry smile.

"I'm going over to the Remington house now, Sam," Pete said. "I've beefed up the crew there and with any luck at all, we'll have it cleaned up and finished by the time they get back from Europe." After pumping Mike's hand vigorously, he scurried out.

It seemed very quiet in the office after he left. Samantha gazed intently at her fingernails, tracing the shape of one with the ball of her thumb. She was quiveringly aware of Mike watching her, yet she couldn't force herself to meet his gaze.

He finally broke the silence. "Speechless, Samantha?" he teased. "I'll have to circle this date on my calendar."

"You can say anything you like to me, Mike. I deserve it."

He tipped her chin up, but she still wouldn't look at him. "What's this? No rebuttal?" When she shook her head mutely, he frowned. "I can't say I like this new, meek little Samantha. What happened to the hellcat I've grown used to?"

Her eyelashes fluttered on her flushed cheeks. "Gone forever. I'm through hurling unfounded accusations."

"Oh, really? Then maybe this is the time to renew my offer to buy Morgan Construction."

Her eyes flew open and she jerked her chin away. "What!"

"You heard me. I want to buy you out."

"Aren't you expecting rather excessive gratitude?" She scowled.

His mouth curled with amusement. "Ah, that's better. The fire is coming back in your eyes. All that's lacking now is the suggestion that I bailed you out so you would feel obligated."

She stared at him with dawning comprehension. "That *was* the reason, wasn't it?" she asked slowly.

"I should have known you would never give up. Well, this time you've outsmarted yourself." Her eyes flashed deep blue fire. "I'm back in business and I'm going to stay. Your devious plan didn't work!"

He threw his head back and laughed. "Samantha, you are a delight. I can lead you in any direction I choose. Don't you know, silly child, that if I wanted to get your company by trickery, the easiest way would be to let you go bankrupt? I could pick up the pieces for small change."

The truth of his statement made her feel like a fool. He had only been teasing her, and as usual, she had leaped to judgment. "I don't know what makes me say things like that," she said helplessly. "Why do you put up with me, Mike?"

"Why, indeed?" he murmured, gazing at her soft mouth.

"I would do anything to take back the rotten things I've said to you—but I can't sell you my father's company. It was his life, and now it's mine. Can't you see that?" she pleaded.

"Is this what you really want to do for the rest of your life, Samantha? Don't you know there are challenges out there if you will only come out of your cocoon and meet them with all that verve you have bottled up inside?"

She bit the corner of her lip. "You just refuse to understand."

He sighed. "All right, we won't talk about it anymore." He turned a straight chair around and straddled it, resting his arms on the back. "Would you like to hear about my new project?"

"Oh, yes, I'd love to," she breathed, grateful to him for not pursuing the subject.

"It's a development of medium-priced homes."

"You're going to build single houses?" she asked,

vaguely disappointed. This didn't jibe with the Mike Sutherland she knew, the grandiose builder of dams and bridges. If he did deign to build a house, she would expect it to be a palace.

He nodded his head. "Hundreds of them. I've acquired a large tract of land down the Peninsula. I intend to build houses that people can afford—young ones, old ones, anyone who has been dreaming of a place of his own."

"Isn't that easier said than done? Money is so tight nowadays."

"My houses will be within reach," he said firmly. "That's the whole purpose of this development. It will be a self-contained city, actually, with a market and a drugstore and a laundromat, among other things."

"Not a laundromat," she objected. "Having her own washer and dryer is the dream of every woman who has had to wrestle a heavy basket of clothes in and out of the car. I should think that would be the very first thing they would buy."

Mike raised his eyebrows. "I hadn't thought of that."

"You might even include it with the house," Samantha said, warming to the subject. "On hundreds of machines, you could get them a little above cost. It would probably add just pennies to the mortgage, and what a blessing to the buyers not to have to lay out the cash."

His eyes narrowed on her thoughtfully. "What about a community center? If I built a large clubhouse-type affair, do you think it would be used?"

"Oh, yes, Mike, that's a super idea! With a kitchen in it. Be sure and include that. If it had kitchen facilities, it could be used for birthday parties and anniversary celebrations and, oh—a million different things. It would be a wonderful place for teenagers to get together for dances too, someplace where their parents wouldn't be in the next room telling them to turn down the hi-fi." Her face was lit with animation.

Mike lowered his chin to rest on his folded hands, looking up at her with secret satisfaction. "How about the homes themselves? What does a woman look for in a house?"

"I suppose it varies with the individual."

"What would you want?"

A picture of Mike's beautiful mansion flicked at her consciousness for a moment, only to be suppressed firmly. "I like lots of storage space. There is nothing worse than having to move a whole stack of towels before you can get to the sheets and pillow cases underneath. Oh, and I would like those wonderful pull-out bottom shelves in the kitchen so you don't have to stand on your head to get at the pot in back. If it wouldn't add too much to the cost, that is."

He looked at her consideringly. "How about decorating? If you were buying one of my houses, would you want to walk into the finished product, or would you prefer an allowance so you could pick your own paint and paper?"

"Oh, my. I would have to think about that."

"That's what I want you to do, Samantha, think about it." His big hand reached out and covered hers on the desk. "I'd like you to come and work for me, help me plan my city."

She caught her breath. "All those questions—was this what it was leading up to?"

He nodded. "First I had to see if you were interested."

"Well, of course I'm interested. Who wouldn't be? But I can't just—"

"Think of the satisfaction, Samantha. The knowledge that you've contributed something to hundreds of people."

"What? The choice between paint or wallpaper?" she cried. Everything was happening too fast. Mike was putting the pressure on, and she knew her inability to withstand him. "It sounds like you want some kind of glorified decorator. That's not my field."

"I'm asking you to join my staff as an architect, to be in on the planning. Wouldn't you like to see a city grow out of your drafting board?"

Suddenly she *could* see it. Rows of houses on curving streets, each with a garden and trees. The community center should be something special. Not consciously quaint or anything like that, but not coldly impersonal either, not plastic. Of course Mike might have very different ideas. They would be bound to clash a lot. That was rather funny, really. When didn't they?

"Well, Samantha?" His voice was seductive.

She looked at him in confusion. "I haven't . . . I'm afraid I don't have enough experience."

"You wouldn't be expected to handle it all alone, no one person could. There is a whole staff that will work with you."

"When does all this begin?"

"The financing is being arranged now. We expect to begin grading within a month."

"So soon!"

He shrugged. "That will give you plenty of time to get cleaned up here. If my offer is satisfactory, we can have the papers drawn up and signed in the next few days."

Samantha came down to earth with a thud. "You mean it's a condition of the job that I sell to you?"

He looked at her with exasperation. "My dear

girl, how do you expect to run this business and also work for me?"

"I hadn't . . . I mean . . . couldn't Pete take over temporarily?" she asked hopefully.

"There used to be three of you. Do you honestly think Pete could do it all alone?"

"Maybe I could help out after work," she said slowly. "He could hold down the fort until your job was finished."

Mike ran his fingers through his thick dark hair, restraining himself with an effort. "I don't think you understand. I'm not offering you part-time sketching to do in your spare time. Sutherland City will take at least three years to complete, maybe more. The hours will be long and irregular. Sometimes you'll have to work night and day, but the rewards will be great, and I'm not talking only monetarily, although you'll have those too. I'm offering you a chance to be part of a vision—to do something really worthwhile."

Mike was leaning over her, his hands spread wide on the desk. He was big and male and intensely alive. He had never backed down from a challenge in his life, and he obviously couldn't understand how she could.

Unable to meet his eyes, she shook her head. "I'm sorry, but I can't. Not if it means selling Morgan's."

In the short silence, Mike straightened to his towering height. She could feel his contemptuous eyes burning into her bowed head. "You would pass up an opportunity like I'm offering to run a tacky little business like this?"

"Don't you dare talk like that! My father—"

"Your father is dead, Samantha," he grated. "You did your sacrificing while he was alive. You don't have to immolate yourself on the altar of his memory like some pagan virgin."

"That's not what I'm doing!" she cried. "You don't even try to understand."

"Oh, I understand all right," he said grimly. "Better than you think. I teased you about this place being a security blanket, but that's what it is, isn't it?"

"No!"

"As long as you can hide out here, you're still Daddy's little girl, aren't you?" he asked relentlessly. "You don't have to make any decisions, you can just keep on doing what Daddy told you to do."

"That's not true!"

"You can't even let yourself be a woman, although deep down, that's what you really want. You do want to be a woman don't you, Samantha?"

"No! . . . I mean, yes . . . oh, you're mixing me all up."

He came swiftly around to where she was penned in behind the desk. Samantha tried to retreat, finding no place to go. "Poor frightened little kitten," he said, touching her cheek gently. "So afraid to follow your normal instincts. You want me to take you in my arms and make love to you right now."

"No, I—" Her denial ended in a gasp as his arms circled her waist, pulling her against his demanding body. Thunderous excitement raged through her at the contact, shattering her with its intensity. "Please, Mike," she whispered.

His dark head bent inexorably toward her. "Please what, my darling? Is this what you want?"

His mouth covered hers, gently parting her lips, his fingers tangling in her back curls and holding her head when she would have moved away. She gave a low moan of protest, which he ignored, trailing his hand sensuously down her back and urging her stiff body against his long length.

She was locked in an embrace that sent fire racing

through her veins, her anguished movements against him only feeding the flames. His warm mouth wandered over her face, kissing her closed eyelids and sliding to her ear, which he traced delicately with the tip of his tongue.

Samantha might have been able to withstand a savage assault. She was powerless against this slow, seductive ravishment of her senses. With a deep sigh, her arms crept around his neck, her hands wandering restlessly over the breadth of his wide shoulders and muscular back. She was completely lost in his magnetism, murmuring his name over and over.

Mike lifted his head, looking down at her passion-flushed face. "I could get you to do anything I wanted right now, couldn't I, Samantha? You would sell me your soul if I asked." With a suddenness that was shocking, he set her on her feet. "But that isn't what I want," he said harshly. "I want you to come to me of your own free will."

She looked at him blindly, not understanding what had happened. "I don't know what you mean." Hadn't she surrendered, given in completely?

"I want more than your body," he said grimly. "When you are ready to give me that, call me. Until then, I don't want to see you."

The door closed behind him on a note of finality. Samantha sank slowly into a chair, staring blankly at the empty room that had been so charged with electricity when Mike had occupied it. What did he want from her? Her unfulfilled body ached for an explanation.

Knowing the answer, she put her head in her hands. Morgan Construction stood between them like an insurmountable wall. Mike wanted it and he would never give up until he got it. He was like a great black wolf outside her door, always waiting, scheming, enticing. If one thing didn't work, he tried another. She was tied up in knots, not knowing where the next attack was coming from.

Had he really meant it when he said he didn't intend to see her again unless she called him? Even though the thought tore her into pieces as small as confetti, Samantha knew it would be for the best. She couldn't go on yearning for a man who was so ruthless he would destroy anyone to achieve his objective. Mike knew how vulnerable she was and never hesitated to exploit it. If only she weren't so alone. If only her father were still alive.

Thoughts of family reminded Samantha of how long it had been since she had seen hers. A wave of homesickness swept over her suddenly, as though Brooke and Cecily lived twenty-five-hundred miles away instead of only twenty-five.

On an impulse, she pulled the phone forward and dialed a number. "Mother," she said, with a catch in her throat, "I want to come home."

Chapter Seven

$\mathscr{B}$irds were twittering in the trees outside, heedless of the fact that it was Saturday morning and people were trying to sleep. Samantha didn't really mind, though, she was so used to getting up early that she probably wouldn't have slept much longer anyway.

Looking around the lovely bedroom with its crisp organdy curtains and blue shag rug, she was reminded of all the happy times spent here when she was growing up. The bulletin board on the wall over the little white student's desk still had a few snapshots tacked to its cork surface. Samantha smiled, remembering what treasured possessions they had been. Now it was difficult to recall the names of half of the boys in the photos.

After showering, she reached automatically for a pair of jeans, then rejected them in favor of a white linen skirt and a lemon-yellow blouse that tied in a soft bow at the neck. Jeans were for work. This weekend she planned to forget that there was such a place as Morgan Construction.

Samantha went down to the large, cheerful kitchen that glistened with every modern appliance. She started the coffee, then turned her attention to the refrigerator. It was well stocked as usual. She put enough bacon for all of them in a pan and cracked eggs in a bowl, thinking how pleasant it was to do all the domestic things she never had time for. It would be nice to have a home and someone to cook for. Her hands stilled momentarily, then resumed their work determinedly. This weekend she had come back to the nest. She refused to allow any painful thoughts to intrude.

"Good morning, darling. Did you sleep well?" Cecily Morgan entered the kitchen.

"Like a log." Samantha kissed her mother's cheek, marveling as always at her youthful appearance.

She looked like a woman half her age, her figure still trim and her face relatively unlined. Cecily's short blond hair was always done in the height of fashion, her face fully made up, and her clothes chic. It had been a little daunting for two young girls who were prone to sprout pimples before a big date or rip a hem at just the wrong moment. But as they grew older Brooke was able to emulate their mother's confidence and high style. Not so Samantha. She always felt gangling and awkward around her petite mother.

"You've started breakfast, dear, how lovely," Cecily said. "But you really shouldn't have. We see you so seldom that I was planning to wait on you hand and foot."

"I'm not a guest, Mother," Samantha said sharply.

"Of course you aren't, darling, but a little pampering never hurt any woman," Cecily said complacently.

She would certainly know. Her husband had treated her like a tiny princess, shielding her from all the harsher things in life. Cecily, in return, had been the perfect wife, deferring to Rufus in all things. Samantha sighed. It would be wonderful to be treated like a delicate piece of china, yet she knew she could never endure the submission that went with it. She and Mike were always—her hands gripped the bowl. Why did everything lead back to him?

"We won't wait for Brooke," her mother said. "Heaven knows when she will be down. It was so late when I heard her tiptoeing in that I didn't dare look at the clock." She gave her daughter an impish grin. "Otherwise I would have been forced to take a stand."

Samantha raised her eyebrows. She knew that her mother disliked unpleasantness, avoiding it at all costs, but wasn't that carrying permissiveness too far? After all, Brooke was only nineteen. Donald's words rang unpleasantly in her ears. "That kid has too much freedom." Still, he could be right.

"Do you know where she was last night?" Samantha asked casually.

"She went to a party with Stuart Rayburn and they probably went to the Moon Watch afterward."

"The Moon Watch!" Samantha said sharply. "That isn't a very reputable place."

"That is undoubtedly why the young people all congregate there right now," Cecily said calmly. "Next month I expect it will be someplace else."

"I don't like the idea of Brooke going to a dive like that." Samantha frowned. "I shouldn't think you would either."

Cecily's laughter had the tinkle of musical bells.

"Oh, Samantha, how funny that sounds. Don't you remember when you and Victor Poole used to go to that terrible place with the silly name? What was it again—oh, yes, the Kit Kat Klub, of all things."

Samantha gave her a startled look. "I didn't know you knew about that. Who told you; Dad?"

"Oh, no, your father never knew. He would have been furious."

It took a while to digest this. "I thought you told Dad everything," Samantha said slowly.

Her mother's smooth brow was serene. "My dear child, no marriage could survive a burden like that. Besides, he would have worried dreadfully."

"And you didn't?"

The amusement on Cecily's face was replaced by tenderness. "Sit down, Samantha." She pulled out a chair at the breakfast table. "As you will find out, a mother always worries about her child, no matter how old she gets. But one worries about important things, like will she choose the right man, will she be happy? The other is trivial. Your father and I taught you and Brooke to have high standards, to think for yourselves without bowing to peer pressure, and to use good judgment. If I were going to worry about unimportant things like the places you went at night, I would have to worry every time you stepped out of the house." Her eyes twinkled with merriment. "Things happen during the day also, you know."

Samantha looked at her mother in dawning wonder. She had never realized that so much common sense lay under that tranquil face. "I'm afraid I have underestimated you," she said humbly.

"Don't let it bother you, darling. Most people do."

Brooke made her entry, stretching and yawning. "Oh, good, I haven't missed breakfast." Giving

Samantha a hug, she said, "It's super special having you here, Sammy. I think this calls for champagne. How about it, Mother?"

"If you like, dear. I believe there is a bottle in the refrigerator."

"If you two are trying to make me ashamed because I haven't been home in so long, you've succeeded." Samantha laughed.

"Was it that handsome hunk that's been keeping you in town?" Brooke asked eagerly.

Cecily raised her perfect eyebrows. "A new boyfriend, Samantha?"

"This isn't a boy, it's a man—and what a man!" Brooke sighed.

Cecily looked interested. "I'd like to meet him."

"Wouldn't we all? But Sammy got there first, the lucky thing."

"What is his name?" her mother asked.

"I don't . . . he isn't . . . Brooke is making up the whole thing." Samantha leaped to her feet and went over to the sink, beginning to beat the eggs furiously.

"Nobody could make up a man like that. He's six foot two—"

"Six four," Samantha murmured before she could stop herself.

"Even better." Brooke's eyes glowed. "Gorgeous thick dark hair that you want to run your fingers through, a physique like a linebacker—the kind with big, wide shoulders tapering down to slim hips and long muscular legs that you'd love to feel wrapped around you."

"Brooke!" Samantha gasped.

Cecily merely laughed. "My goodness, he does sound too good to be true."

"How far have you gotten with him, Sammy?"

What would her sister say if she told her she had struck out—repeatedly. "Brooke is romanticizing again," Samantha told her mother. Turning back to the sink, she proceeded to whip up the eggs she had already beaten. "He's just a business competitor. We don't even like each other."

"I see." Cecily's eyes rested thoughtfully on her daughter's rigid back.

"That wasn't the way it looked when I—"

"Why don't you set the table, Brooke?" her mother interrupted. "I will pour the coffee."

. Brooke took the hint. Unfortunately she switched to a topic almost equally unpalatable. "Are you still seeing Donald Dullsville?"

"Honestly, Brooke! Don't you ever run out of those childish names?" Samantha asked angrily.

"Not so far." Brooke grinned. "Donald inspires me."

Samantha forked bacon out of the pan. "It might interest you to know that he feels the same way about you."

"Who cares about the opinion of a wimp?" Brooke asked airily.

"I wish you would stop picking on Donald," Samantha cried hotly, her nerves fraying. "Some of those little twits *you* run around with are candidates for a kennel commercial!"

"I suppose you are referring to Danny Wilton— just because he failed a few subjects. Donny Dimwit probably flunked recess!"

Cecily began to laugh. "I could almost believe you were ten and fifteen again."

The sisters looked at each other and started to laugh too, all tension dissolved. Brooke hugged Samantha impulsively. "It's only because I love you, Sammy. I just worry so that you might marry the—marry him," she finished.

Samantha ruffled her sister's hair. "Don't worry. I'm probably going to be an old maid."

It was said lightly, yet Samantha knew it to be true. There would never be another man like Mike. Her defense of Donald had been purely reflexive—habit, blended with nerves.

After breakfast, Cecily gave Brooke a list of errands to run. As they watched her drive away, her bright hair streaming out of the convertible Rufus had given her on her eighteenth birthday, Cecily said to Samantha, "Would you like to come out to the garden with me? It's been so long since we have had a nice, quiet chat, just the two of us."

With a sigh of contentment, Samantha stretched out on a padded lounge, one of several that decorated the wide flagstone patio. "You don't know how heavenly it is to have absolutely nothing to do."

Her mother carefully donned a pair of garden gloves to protect her long, polished nails. Picking up a basket and some garden shears, she began to clip the dead blooms off a rosebush.

"Have you been busy at the yard?" she asked casually.

"Pretty much so," Samantha said noncommittally.

"That's nice isn't it? It must mean business is good."

"I can't complain." Samantha shrugged.

Cecily eyed her soberly. "No, you never did."

Samantha changed the subject. "How is the Tuesday-Wednesday Club these days?" It was an ongoing joke in the family, Cecily's bridge club that was supposed to meet on Tuesday, but sometimes met on Wednesday—except when it didn't meet at all.

"Is something wrong, Samantha?" her mother asked gently, refusing to be diverted.

"What could be wrong on a heavenly day like

143

this?" she said lightly, lifting her chin to look up at the clear blue sky decorated with little white cotton clouds.

"I try not to pry, as I believe you know, darling, but if there is anything you would like to discuss, I would be happy to listen."

For one fleeting moment, Samantha longed to lay her burdens in someone else's lap. To pour out her troubles at the construction yard, her disillusionment with Donald, but most of all, her misery over Mike. If only there were someone she could talk to. Her mother certainly wasn't the one, however.

Samantha dismissed the subject as though it wasn't worth talking about. "Everyone has a problem here and there. It's nothing for you to worry about."

Cecily began clipping dead roses again, dropping them meticulously in the basket. "You sounded exactly like your father just then. Is it the business, or that new man Brooke spoke about?"

"Neither. Why do you persist in thinking there is something wrong?"

"Perhaps it's because you are getting so thin, or maybe it's those shadows under your eyes. A woman generally spends sleepless nights over two things— men or money."

"There is also black coffee. That keeps a lot of people up nights," Samantha said in a feeble attempt at a joke.

Cecily stripped off her garden gloves and sat down, looking at her daughter penetratingly. "I have always taught you to make your own decisions, my dear, and I am not trying to interfere now. But ever since your father died, I have been waiting for you to make up your mind."

Samantha looked at her blankly. "About what?"

"About what to do with your life."

"I thought that was pretty well mapped out."

Cecily sighed. "When Rufus convinced you to go into the business, I wasn't very happy about it. There were so many other places you could have utilized your talents, but he was determined and you were amenable. If you had ever shown signs of doubt, I would have fought him on the matter." At Samantha's startled look, her mother smiled. "Oh, yes, my dear, I fought with your father sometimes, but only for what I truly believed in. And I usually won."

"I hadn't realized," Samantha said slowly. This weekend was showing her a side of her mother she had never even guessed at.

"You seemed happy enough in your work so I didn't interfere, but it is a different matter now. What is it, Samantha? Are you having trouble carrying on alone?"

Samantha smoothed her skirt carefully. "We're having a few little problems; it isn't anything I can't handle. I don't want you to worry. Nothing is going to change."

"My dear child, *everything* changes," her mother said gently. "You can't live in a vacuum. If you are concerned about Brooke and myself leading the kind of life we always have, you shouldn't be. This house is much too large for us, especially now that I don't entertain on the same scale. I have been thinking for some time that I would like less responsibility, less upkeep. A smaller house would be nice, or even one of those lovely apartments."

"Brooke would hate it," Samantha said uncertainly.

"She is rarely home anyway." Cecily laughed, then became serious again. "And if you are worrying about Brooke's tuition, that is not an insurmountable problem either. She could always get a part-time job. Under that flighty manner of hers lies a very keen mind and a lot of determination. Don't ever worry about Brooke," she said dryly. "She will get by."

"I didn't have to work when I went to college, and I would hate to think that she had to. Especially since it would be my fault," Samantha said somberly.

"We are a *family,* Samantha," her mother said sternly. "And you are a member of it, not the patriarch. You don't owe us your whole life. You should be thinking about getting married and having babies. When I was your age, I was already started on a family."

"That's because you were little and gorgeous. I'm afraid nobody wants me, Mother." Her smile was forced.

"I can scarcely believe that."

"Spoken like a real, doting parent," Samantha teased. "It's true though, whether you want to believe it or not. Even Donald is only interested in a long-term lease."

"And you, Samantha? You want more than that?"

"I used to think so." She sighed.

Cecily hesitated for a moment. "It sounds as though you should give it more thought," she said lightly.

"What do you think of Donald, Mother?" Samantha asked unexpectedly.

"Heavens, child, what kind of question is that?"

"A very pertinent one since he was almost your son-in-law."

"Almost?" Cecily's eyebrows were question marks. "Have you broken up with him?"

"I . . . I think so."

"Don't you know?"

Samantha shrugged. "Yes, I guess I really do. It's

just that we went together for four years. Old habits are hard to break."

"If that is all he was, a habit, then you made the right decision."

"I suppose so, but I'm going to miss him in a way. Donald isn't at his best with other people, but we did have fun together a lot of the time. And he was always a gentleman. I got so tired of wrestling in the backseats of cars, and later, in men's apartments. Why do men always have to get so physical?" she cried.

Cecily looked at her beautiful daughter with hidden amusement. "I can see that Donald was the wrong choice for you. When the right man comes along, you won't mind his getting . . . um . . . physical." Samantha's cheeks suddenly bloomed to match the roses in the garden. Cecily looked at her piercingly for a moment before saying casually, "You haven't mentioned why you dislike this new man that your sister mentioned."

Fortunately, Brooke herself arrived home at that moment, creating a diversion.

"Look who I met in the shopping center," she announced. Followed by two young men in tennis shorts, Brooke came through the sliding glass doors and onto the patio.

"Hello, Mrs. Morgan," the older of the men greeted her mother before turning eagerly to Samantha. "I couldn't believe it when I heard you were here, Sam. I haven't seen you in a dog's age."

Stan Rasmussen was a man she had gone out with years ago. Brooke had had a wild crush on him, which had amused Samantha because she couldn't get that excited about him herself, although he was very good-looking. If she remembered correctly, he was in the real estate business, and doing very well at it.

"Hi, Stan. You're looking well." Samantha smiled.

He sat down on the lounger next to her. "Not half as well as you do. You're still the most beautiful girl in Hillsborough."

"Except that I live in San Francisco now, and there is more competition there." She laughed.

His eyes went over her in warm appraisal. "You can stand it."

"If I'd known I was going to get all this flattery, I would have come home long ago," Samantha said lightly. "What have you been doing with yourself, Stan? I gather you aren't married or I would have heard about it."

He shook his head. "When you turned me down, I became a confirmed bachelor. I'm still looking for a girl like you."

Before she could answer, Brooke's boyfriend, Skip Baylor, came over. He was the current favorite, a blond, suntanned youth with an engaging grin.

"Hi, Sam. How's the lady construction worker?" He grinned.

Samantha had always liked him. Returning his smile, she said, "Fine, Skip, how's the mighty tennis player?"

"You'll have a chance to find out for yourself. Brooke suggested we all go over to the club for a few sets."

"It sounds nice, but I came home to spend some time with Mother this weekend."

"Run along and enjoy yourself, dear, I have some telephoning to do," Cecily said. "We can continue our little chat later."

"Yes, do come, Sammy," Brooke coaxed. "It will be like old times."

Samantha allowed herself to be persuaded, although she warned, "Wait until you see my game. I'm terribly out of practice."

"All the more reason," Brooke said. "Don't worry though, we'll get you back in shape."

"I'd say she's already that," Stan said, his eyes going over her curved body lingeringly.

The day proved to be great fun. By the time they returned in the late afternoon, Samantha's eyes were sparkling and her face was animated. They all went into the den where Cecily had drinks and snacks waiting. It was like stepping back into her carefree girlhood. Not a single problem had crossed Samantha's mind all day.

While they were bantering back and forth, the phone rang. Brooke bounded out to answer it, calling, "It's for you, Sammy."

Nobody knew she was here. Who could it be? Samantha looked up with a question on her lips, but the strange look on Brooke's face stopped her from asking. Samantha's heart started to pound so hard she could almost hear it. Could it be Mike? He could have tracked her down. Nothing stood in his way when he wanted something.

Almost running into the hall, she picked up the receiver. "Hello?" she breathed.

"Don't tell me I've finally gotten hold of you!" Donald exclaimed.

"Oh . . ." There was a short pause while her heart plunged back to its accustomed place. The odd expression on Brooke's face was caused by the restraint she was using in not calling him one of her derogatory names. "Hello, Donald," Samantha said flatly.

"I have been calling you for days. I left messages all over the place. Didn't you get them?"

She had received, and ignored, them. "What do you want?" she asked rudely.

"Don't be angry with me, Sam," he pleaded.

"I'm not angry, just busy. I came here to be with my family. What was it you wanted?"

"I want to talk to you, Sam." When she waited pointedly, he said, "Not like this. Not over the phone."

"Yes, it is a toll call isn't it?" she said nastily.

Donald's quiet voice reproached her. "That isn't like you."

He was right. It had been a rotten thing to say. "I'm sorry, Donald. I've been kind of edgy this weekend."

"And I'm responsible for it," he said with remorse.

All of her newfound tranquility had vanished with his telephone call. Why couldn't she have just one weekend to herself? "No, you're not," she said impatiently.

"You were very upset the last time we were together, and looking back, I don't blame you. I wasn't very understanding."

"It doesn't matter."

"Anytime I hurt you, it matters very much. I love you, Sam."

She was curiously unmoved by the declaration. After going with this man for four years, drifting into a comfortable understanding that someday they would marry, Samantha realized that she had no feeling for him at all. "I'm sorry, Donald, because I don't love you."

"Don't say that, sweetheart! I know I disappointed you, wounded your pride. I must have been out of my mind!"

"What you are saying is that you apologize for not sleeping with me," she said wryly.

"No! I'm not sorry about that. I want to marry

you, darling. Right now—tomorrow if you like. You were right, there is no reason for us to wait."

"Have you forgotten Mother and Brooke?" she asked dryly.

It cost him something, but he mastered his distaste. "We'll work something out. Maybe I can go over your books and find a way of cutting down your overhead. The main thing is that we'll be together. These last days without you have been hell, sweetheart. Do you realize it's been almost two weeks since I have seen you?"

Was that all it had been? How could so much have happened in such a short span of time? Samantha looked up to see Stan Rasmussen hovering in the doorway, making motions at her.

"Just a moment, Donald," she said, putting her hand over the mouthpiece.

"I didn't want to disturb you, but I have to be shoving off," Stan said. "We were talking about dinner at the Fogcutter tonight. Will you come with me?"

Before she could answer, Brooke appeared at his side. "Mother is going to a concert and she says you should go with us. We'll have fun, Sammy."

Hysterical laughter bubbled inside Samantha. She had one man on the phone asking to marry her and another casually asking her out to dinner. Well, why not? Given a choice, she preferred Stan's invitation.

"I'd love to go," she told him.

"Great! Pick you up at seven-thirty." With a wave of his hand, he went out the door.

"I can't talk anymore, Donald," she said into the phone.

"Don't hang up, Sam! Didn't what I said mean anything to you?"

"Not very much," she admitted.

"I won't let it end like this. We have too much invested in this relationship. At least say that you'll think about it."

"All right." She sighed, more to get rid of him than because she intended doing it.

Fortunately Samantha had left some of her dressier clothes at home since her closet space in the apartment was limited. For this evening, she chose a coral-colored knit with a scooped neckline and long sleeves. Only someone with a perfect figure could do it justice. It emphasized the slenderness of her curved body, the color setting off her dark, glossy hair.

During the short time they were alone together, Stan was lyrical with praise. He drove a two-seater Mercedes, and Skip's sports car had a minimal backseat, so it had been necessary to take both cars.

Dinner was a slightly frantic affair. The Fogcutter was a local favorite and they saw many people they knew. Old friends kept coming over to the table. There was much talk and laughter, reminiscences with old acquaintances and introductions to new friends.

Samantha enjoyed it, yet there were a few bad moments. Like when she noticed a tall, dark man across the room. His broad shoulders and the tilt of his head set her pulses racing. It wasn't until he turned around and she saw it wasn't Mike that she could start to breathe again. Suddenly all the hilarity seemed juvenile, like whistling in the dark to convince yourself you weren't lonely and miserable. It took a determined effort to recapture the gaiety.

After dinner they went to one of the local hotels to dance.

"Ah, this is better," Stan murmured, holding her very close as they moved slowly around the crowded dance floor. "I haven't had a chance to be alone with you all day."

"We aren't exactly alone now," she pointed out.

"No, but it's better than nothing. Not much, though. What say we shake this place and find a spot where we can really be alone?"

"Your apartment or mine?" she asked dryly.

He lifted his head to look at her searchingly. "Do you mean it?"

"Of course not. I was just anticipating you." She sighed. "Look, Stan, I didn't want to have an affair with you when we dated before, and I still don't. I'm sorry if this has been a wasted evening."

"Don't say that, Sam. Being with you is always a joy. I won't deny that I want to make love to you, but if the answer is no"—he shrugged—"well, it's no. I would like to go on seeing you, though. Who knows?" He grinned impishly. "I might wear you down yet."

"I can't promise that, but I've enjoyed being with you too, Stan," Samantha said, finding that she really meant it.

It was late when they left the hotel. Brooke and Skip declared that they were hungry, but Samantha and Stan declined to join them in their quest for pizza.

After the younger couple left, Stan said, "How about going up to the reservoir for a spot of heavy breathing?"

"Well, at least you're honest." Samantha laughed.

"With you, always. So how about it, if I promise not to come on strong?"

"It's getting late, Stan. I really should be getting home."

"Please, Samantha, I only want to talk. We've been surrounded by people all night. Just for half an hour?" he asked hopefully.

"Okay, but no longer," she warned.

Crystal Springs Lake glittered in the moonlight, a long meandering body of water bordered by thick trees. It was hard to realize that those dense woods were filled with deer. It was so close to the city. The shy, lovely creatures kept to the forest most of the time, yet occasionally at night, the headlights of a car would pick out a graceful shape bounding across the road to get to tenderer shoots.

"I had forgotten how lovely it is up here," Samantha said. "It's been so long."

"Why don't you come home oftener, Sam? Your mother and Brooke really miss you, not to mention your old friends."

"I don't know." She sighed. "I always seem to be so busy. There are always problems." She smiled at him. "I shouldn't complain. All businesses have them, I suppose."

"Yours must be especially tough in times like these," he answered sympathetically. Unless you're a big outfit like Sutherland Construction, you're bound to feel the crunch. Those guys are recession-proof. I heard they just bought a huge tract of land down by Mountain View. There is a lot of talk in the industry about it. They're planning to build a mini-city. Man!" Stan's eyes gleamed. "Wouldn't you like to be in on that?"

"I . . . I suppose so."

"The whole thing is run by one man, a fellow named Mike Sutherland. Now *there* is a guy I'd like to meet," Stan said admiringly. "He's a real original. Some of the stories I've heard about him are unreal. Do you happen to know him?"

"Not really." Samantha turned her head to look out the window. "I think it's time we went home, Stan."

154

"I'm boring you," he said with remorse. You came home for some R and R, and here I am bending your ear about business. That must be the last thing you want to talk about. How dumb can I get?"

"It isn't that. I'm just rather tired all of a sudden."

"I'm some kind of a jerk! Here I have a gorgeous girl alone in the moonlight, and what do I talk about?"

She gave him a small smile. "It isn't the subject matter. I guess I just don't feel like talking anymore."

"Neither do I." He moved closer, sliding his arms around her.

"Stan, you promised."

"Just a kiss, Sam. For old time's sake?"

His head came down, blotting out the moonlight, his mouth covering hers gently. At first, Samantha stiffened automatically, then she relaxed in his embrace. After all, why not? She wasn't a child, what was a kiss between friends?

His kiss progressed beyond friendship, however, the initial gentleness giving way to increasing ardor. He crushed her tightly, his lips parting hers in a demand she tried to respond to. Maybe this was the answer. Sliding her arms around his neck, she allowed him to probe the warmth of her mouth, tried to share some of the desire he obviously felt for her.

Her response elated him. Burying his face in her neck, he murmured tender words against the smooth skin, straining her ever closer. Samantha endured it, trying to feel *something*. But when his hand moved to cup her breast, she shivered with revulsion.

"Let me, darling," he whispered. "Don't fight it." His mouth covered hers again, holding it for a long time while he sought to arouse her passion. Samantha didn't try to resist.

Finally he raised his head. Their eyes met in the moonlight. "It's no good, is it?" Stan asked.

She moved away, wrapping her arms around herself. "I'm sorry," she whispered.

"There is someone else, isn't there?"

"Yes." A fringe of dark eyelashes swept down to veil the misery in her eyes.

Stan surveyed her bent head for a long moment, then he sighed. "Well, all I can say is, he's a lucky guy." He turned the key, and the roar of the motor tore the velvet silence. "I'll take you home."

Samantha was starting up the stairs when her mother called from the kitchen, "Is that you, Samantha?"

Groaning inwardly, she arranged a smile on her face. At the moment she didn't feel up to facing Cecily, whose sharp eyes missed very little. "Yes, Mother. I was just going up to bed," she added hopefully.

Cecily appeared in the doorway. "Have a cup of hot chocolate with me first."

Samantha hesitated. "I'm rather tired."

"A nice cup of hot chocolate will make you sleep like a baby," Cecily urged, rather uncharacteristically.

"All right, Mother." She sighed.

"Did you have a nice time tonight?"

"It was . . . very pleasant."

"Your enthusiasm is underwhelming." Cecily laughed. "Poor Stan, I think he had high hopes for this evening."

"It wasn't Stan. I really had a good time. It's just—oh, I don't know. I guess you can't go back again."

Cecily raised her eyebrows. "Why would you want to?"

"Why not?" Samantha asked somberly. "It's so easy being a little girl."

"But not as much fun as being a woman." Her mother smiled.

"That's easy for you to say. You were married right out of college. You don't know what it's like out there."

"As a matter of fact, that is the one thing I regret. The fact that I didn't experience more of the world first. Not that I would have changed a thing about my marriage."

"Did you love Dad very much?" Samantha asked curiously.

Cecily's expression was tender. "Yes, dear, very much."

Samantha concentrated her attention on the steaming cup in front of her. "What would you have done if Dad hadn't loved you?" she asked casually. "I mean if he hadn't wanted to marry you?"

Cecily considered this. "I suppose I would have kept after him until he did."

"You can't *make* someone marry you," Samantha said sharply.

Cecily laughed. "Drink your chocolate, dear, while I tell you about my sorority sister, Corinne Blake—it was Corinne Masterson in those days. She was a lovely girl, but by no stretch of the imagination could you call her beautiful." Her bemused eyes were looking into the past. "Corinne fell madly in love with Jonathan Blake and we all felt sorry for her because he was what you would call a Big Man on Campus. He was handsome and clever—the girls simply flocked around him. He could have had his pick."

"I know the type," Samantha murmured.

Cecily eyed her daughter compassionately. "Yes, well, when Corinne told us she intended getting

Jonathan to marry her, we all thought the poor girl was out of her mind. Imagine our surprise when she actually did it."

"Are you making this up, Mother?" Samantha demanded disgustedly.

"No, it's the truth, I swear to you. They live in Arizona now and have three lovely children. Everyone says they are divinely happy."

"It sounds like one of those fairy tales you used to put us to sleep with. Men like that just don't marry women like your friend Corinne," Samantha said bitterly.

"Isn't it fortunate that she didn't know that, dear?" Cecily asked dryly.

"Okay, then tell me how she accomplished this miracle?"

"I wouldn't exactly call it a miracle. She was a woman and he was a man. I always told you a clever woman could accomplish anything she set her mind to. All it takes is faith—plus a little initiative."

Samantha sighed. "Lord knows I wish I could believe that."

"He helps those who help themselves," Cecily commented crisply. "And now if you have finished your cocoa, I think I will be off to sleep too."

Alone in her bed sometime later, Samantha stared at the ceiling. Her mother made everything sound so simple, but it wasn't that easy. Mike might as well have been the man in the moon for as much chance as she had of snaring him. Especially since he had made it abundantly clear that marriage wasn't what he had in mind. There was no question about what *he* wanted.

Maybe she ought to settle for that since tonight had proved with chilling finality that Mike was the only man who could awaken her. At least she could take the job he offered. That way she would get to see him once in a while.

Cecily had removed the biggest obstacle today when she said she and Brooke wouldn't mind giving up this big house. Her mother had even indicated that she wanted Samantha out of Morgan's. But that wasn't what her father would have wanted. Could she give up his company, even to Mike, the man she loved?

The job he was dangling in front of her nose was one she longed to accept. It was the condition he had imposed that stopped her. Why was everything tied to the sale of Morgan's? How could she help but be suspicious. He didn't really need another architect, and if he did, they were lined up waiting to work for Sutherland's. There couldn't be anything personal in the offer either. She couldn't begin to compete with the kind of women who were his for the asking.

No, the facts were clear whether she wanted to face them or not. All Mike really wanted from her was Morgan Construction, and if he made love to her one more time, she would probably give it to him.

In spite of her mother's thinly disguised pep talk, Samantha knew what she had to do. Tears ran down her face as she said good-bye to Mike in her heart. It was the only way.

Chapter Eight

Samantha returned to the office on Monday morning in a resigned state. It had been good to get away, to put things in a proper perspective. She had forced herself to make a decision. It had caused great pain and many tears, but at least she was through tormenting herself. Once she faced the fact that she would never see Mike again, a kind of numbed calm descended on her.

Pete commented on it. "I'm glad to see you're taking it so well about not getting that addition job we bid on."

"You can't win 'em all," she said brightly.

"That's the spirit, Sam. We have plenty of work to keep us going."

They both knew that wasn't true, so Samantha was glad when the phone rang. She wondered if Pete found it as difficult as she to keep up this cheerful act. Maybe so, because he took the opportunity to leave the office, giving her a wave of his hand.

"Morgan Construction," she said crisply into the phone.

"Where were you all weekend?" Mike asked without preamble.

The unexpected sound of his voice made the blood rush to her head. Her ears rang with little bells that might have been caused by the telephone wires, or might have been the sound of her heart singing.

"Samantha? What happened to you?" he demanded.

"I . . . I'm here."

"I asked you a question. Where were you?"

"I went to the country."

"With whom?" he asked sharply.

She was recovering a little. "If you must know, I went home to see my mother and sister."

"Oh, well, that's all right then."

"I'm glad I have your permission," she said acidly. "Where did you think I was?"

He chuckled. "For a minute I was afraid you went away with Donald. But I don't know what I was worried about. Knowing both of you, you would have had separate rooms."

"You . . . you . . ." she sputtered.

"Don't tell me you've run out of adjectives?" he asked mockingly. "Would you like me to supply a few? How about evil-minded? Depraved? Or lecherous, that's a good one."

"Yes, you're all of those and more!" she stormed.

"My, my, that weekend in the country didn't do anything for your disposition. Did you miss me?"

"As a matter of fact, I didn't," she said coldly. "I was too busy taking up where I left off with an old boyfriend."

"Warmed-over lovers are like stale beer," he said cynically.

"Not Stan. He improved with age. He even kisses better," she lied.

His voice was choked with merriment. "I didn't know you were a connoisseur of kisses. Tell me, how do I rate in your little survey?"

The mere thought made her bones feel like liquid. "So far down the scale that it's laughable," she forced herself to say scornfully.

"Perhaps I ought to come over and find out what it is you like," he said softly.

"I don't give lessons," she said.

"I guess I deserved that, didn't I?" he asked quietly.

She hadn't realized the connotation when she said it. Samantha's cheeks flushed bright pink and she said quickly, "Why did you call, Mike?"

"I wanted to know if you had made up your mind about that job I offered."

"Yes." That was all she could get past the lump in her throat.

"Do you plan on telling me?" he asked pleasantly.

"I can't take it," she said in a low voice.

"I see."

"I . . . it . . . it just wouldn't work. There are all kinds of reasons I can't—"

"Don't sweat it, Samantha. I'm not entirely surprised," he said casually.

"Or disappointed," she said bitterly.

"Oh, I wouldn't say that." His voice was cool. "You know me, I always like to get what I go after."

"I'm aware of that." Her tone matched his.

"What are you going to do now?"

"The same thing I've been doing."

"Until you get it right, is that it?" he asked sardonically.

"Although it might surprise you, Mr. Sutherland,

I have work to do. So if you are through being insulting, I would like to get back to it."

"Wait, Samantha, I have something else I want to talk to you about. As I said, your decision didn't surprise me. I can see that you are determined to push that peanut all the way up the mountain no matter how many times it rolls back down again."

"Morgan Construction is not a peanut," she cried in outrage. "Even though it might seem like it to an elephant like Sutherland's!"

"Let's don't go into that again. What I wanted to say is that since you insist on being harebrained, I have a remodel job for you."

"I wouldn't work for you!"

"It isn't for me," he said crisply. "It's for my parents. My mother wants to throw two small bedrooms into one to make a large den for my father."

"Why don't you do it?" she asked suspiciously.

"Be reasonable, Samantha. I don't do little jobs like that."

"Not even for your parents?"

"*Especially* not for my parents! Well, how about it, do you want the job?"

For a moment she was tempted. It would be interesting to work on a penthouse. Perhaps even more pertinent, she had a burning desire to meet Mike's parents. But there must be a hook behind the tempting bait. Samantha refused to bite again. "Thanks, but I'm afraid we're too busy to take it on right now," she lied.

There was a strangled sound of annoyance. "Don't hand me that! Don't you think I know you are barely keeping your head above water, you little nitwit? Your suppliers have put you on C.O.D. *Take this job!*" he roared.

Her anger rose to meet his as she realized his

intent. "I don't need your charity," she raged. "Morgan's was in business before you were born and it will be here long after you're gone. Leave me alone, Mike Sutherland! Just leave me alone!"

He controlled himself with an effort. "All right. But I'm afraid I'm due for an early demise if your prediction is to come true. Do whatever you want, Samantha, just don't come crying to me when you fall down again. It will be a cold day in hell before I pick you up."

"And it will be a colder one before I ask you to," she shouted.

They hung up simultaneously, both with a crash.

Samantha didn't tell Pete about the remodel job Mike had put her on to—or the fact that she had turned it down. He would think she was crazy, especially since she couldn't explain. But I'm *not* crazy! she told herself fiercely. Rufus would spin like a top if he knew she had accepted charity—and from that man of all people! She could get along without him quite nicely.

For the next couple of days it didn't look like it. Life followed its, by now, predictably disastrous course. Machinery broke down, bills came in marked "please remit"—the whole spectrum. Then suddenly, everything turned around.

It began with a phone call, like so many momentous events in Samantha's life. A Mrs. Robert Tremayne had bought a charming old Victorian in Presidio Terrace and wanted it completely renovated.

Pete returned from an inspection with a glowing report. "It's a real beauty, Sam. Handwork like you don't see anymore. Those carved moldings alone are irreplaceable. It would be a joy to work on that place."

"Did you see Mrs. Tremayne? Did she seem receptive?" Samantha asked eagerly.

"She's a very nice lady. She took me all through the house and explained what they wanted. I made a few suggestions too that she seemed to like. If we get the job, I think she will be very easy to work with."

"*If* we get the job. Oh, Pete, let's figure up this estimate really carefully. Let's bring it in as low as we possibly can."

Almost a week went by before they received an answer. A week of bated breath and crossed fingers. Then Mrs. Tremayne phoned to say the price was satisfactory, and could they start as soon as possible?

From the beginning everything went smoothly. It was the very antithesis of the Remington house. Mrs. Tremayne was delighted with their progress, material was delivered on time, even the weather cooperated.

To add to Samantha's euphoria, other work started to come in, all of it from fashionable parts of town. In no time at all they had crews working on Russian Hill, in St. Francis's Woods, and on Marina Boulevard, that lovely street facing the yacht harbor and the bay. They even had to put on more men.

"I'm almost afraid to believe it, Pete," Samantha said. "Do you think we have a fairy godmother somewhere?"

"I don't know and I don't care," he replied. "As long as this keeps up, why ask questions?"

He was kept so busy that Samantha had to check on some of the crews herself. It was a hard-and-fast rule of Pete's that each job must be inspected once a day. That was what ensured the quality of Morgan's work.

"You'll have to go by that Taylor Street job

today," he told her one morning. "I won't have time."

The apartment on Taylor was in one of the most beautiful residential buildings in San Francisco. Situated on top of Nob Hill, the prestigious high rise commanded a magnificent view of the city. Samantha had found it hard to keep her mind on her work the first time she visited the apartment they were remodeling. The vistas through the wide glass windows were compelling.

That day the weather was particularly sparkling. Driving up the steep hill, Samantha inhaled the clean, tangy air with pleasure. As she gave her car to the uniformed doorman in the courtyard she was glad that she had chosen to wear a dress this morning instead of the usual jeans. It was only a tailored lavender shirtdress but it made her feel more in tune with these posh surroundings.

A few things had delayed her, so it was shortly before noon when she arrived. The work was going along fine, however. She was in and out in a very short time. When she pressed the button for the down elevator, Samantha's mind was already busy with the next order of business. She stepped in without noticing that the light said this elevator was going up.

She was riffling through some estimate sheets when a mocking voice said, "Do my eyes deceive me, or is this Samantha Morgan? I didn't recognize you without your jeans."

There could be no mistaking that deep voice. Samantha's heart did a fast somersault as she looked up into Mike's teasing gray eyes. "What are you doing here?" she asked rudely.

"Is that any way to treat an old friend?"

"Since when are we friends—old or otherwise? We can't even say a civil word to each other."

"No, *you* find that difficult. I am always a perfect gentleman. Well, almost always," he amended, laughing at her raised eyebrow.

The elevator stopped. "Your nonexistent manners no longer concern me," she said haughtily.

Stalking out ahead of him, Samantha was dismayed to find that this wasn't the lobby. In fact, it was someone's penthouse apartment. The elevator opened directly into a magnificent marble-floored foyer the size of a small room. A lovely console graced one wall, with a baroque gilt mirror over it that reflected a beautiful oil painting on the opposite one.

"This isn't the lobby," Samantha exclaimed, dismayed to find that the elevator doors had closed.

"No, but it looks interesting. Let's take a look around," Mike said.

"Are you out of your mind? We have to get out of here."

"What's the hurry?" With his hands in his pockets, he sauntered into the living room. "Quite a view. Come here and look at it."

"Mike, please! Even *you* can't get away with this. Come with me before the owners call the police." Her concern led her to tug his arm, trying to drag him away.

A tall, stately woman suddenly appeared at the head of the free-standing spiral staircase that rose from a corner of the two-story living room. "I'll be right down, Mike," she called. "Fix yourself a drink."

Samantha turned to him with glittering eyes as comprehension dawned. "You *know* these people," she said accusingly.

"Slightly. This is my parents' home."

"Here I was worrying that you would land in jail,

and all the time you were making a fool of me," she raged.

"No, I wasn't, kitten." He reached out to her, but she angrily batted his hand down. "I was enjoying your concern. It's so seldom that I'm the recipient of it."

"Well, you won't be again! You *ought* to be in jail!"

He caught her arm as she whirled toward the entry. "Don't go, I want you to meet my mother."

"And I'm looking forward to meeting your friend." The beautiful older woman who had appeared extended her hand. "Hello, I'm Felice Sutherland."

Samantha's eyes were still sparkling with anger, but she remembered her manners. "How do you do? I'm Samantha Morgan."

"It's delightful to have you here, my dear," Mrs. Sutherland said. "What can I get you to drink?"

"Oh, but I can't stay. I only—"

"Of course you can," Mike said easily. "You haven't even seen the apartment yet. Mother loves to conduct tours."

They smiled affectionately at each other. "He teases me because I love this place so. It's really funny. You would expect Mike to want an ultramodern apartment like this instead of rattling around in our big old home. I'm happy about it though. I would hate to see it go out of the family."

"I can understand that," Samantha told her. "It is such a beautiful house."

"You've seen it?" Mrs. Sutherland asked.

"Oh, yes, Samantha pops in at odd hours," Mike said, murmuring for Samantha's ears alone, "Very odd hours." She clenched her fists as he walked toward a glass tea cart that held an assortment of bottles. "The usual for you, Mother? And what would you like, Samantha?"

Somehow, Samantha found herself with a drink in her hand, sitting on a down-filled couch facing two-story windows that displayed a breathtaking view of the bay and beyond. In the near distance small white sailboats dipped and bobbed on the choppy water like little paper triangles, while farther out, a line of freighters made their measured way toward port.

"I don't think I would ever get anything done if I lived here," she commented. "I would probably stare out of the window all day."

"Yes, one never quite gets used to the view." Felice smiled. "My only regret is that the terrace isn't more useful. It runs all the way around the apartment, but we are up so high that the wind makes it quite uncomfortable at times."

"I should think some kind of a windbreak could be devised," Samantha said thoughtfully.

"You've started the wheels turning, Mother, I can tell." Mike grinned. "Too bad you didn't take their job, Samantha. You could have figured out something for the terrace as well."

Felice raised her eyebrows. "Is this the young woman you told me about?" she asked her son.

"The one and only," he said, regarding Samantha with an unreadable expression.

His mother looked at her more closely. "What interesting work you are in, my dear."

"It is fascinating to see all different kinds of places," Samantha agreed. "That's why I'm here today, as a matter of fact. We are remodeling the Sandhills' apartment on the nineteenth floor. Do you happen to know them?"

Felice expressed surprise. "Yes, of course. A delightful couple. Didn't Mike tell—"

"What are you giving us for lunch, Mother?" he cut in smoothly. "Not any of that creamed stuff in a patty shell that you serve the Opera Guild ladies, I hope."

An indefinable look passed between them. "Nothing more exotic than vichyssoise," she said, after an imperceptible pause. "Followed by cracked crab, French bread, and salad. Does that meet your approval?"

"Sounds good to me. How about you, Samantha?"

She wasn't expected. How could Mike put his mother in a position like that? Shooting him a look of outrage, she said, "I couldn't possibly stay for lunch."

"Of course you can," he replied. "You have to eat somewhere."

"I wish you would stay," Felice urged graciously. "I would like to get to know you better."

"Mother has the greatest cook in town," Mike threw in as an inducement. "Although it doesn't take much talent to crack a crab."

"I could have had Marcel prepare it in those tiny crepes he does so well with the Mornay sauce," Felice said wickedly. "Delicate I grant you, but so delicious."

"You wouldn't dare," Mike growled.

"No, I suppose not." She smiled at Samantha. "There is so much of him to fill up."

Samantha's eyes went to his long-limbed, broad-shouldered frame, remembering the feel of it all too well. She hastily averted her gaze.

Their banter was casual and affectionate, carrying Samantha along with it. Without quite knowing how it happened, she found herself seated at the dining-room table sometime later. It was set beautifully with pale blue organdy place mats appliquéd with white flowers. The silver was sterling and the cut-crystal goblets that held ice water were Waterford.

As the soup was being served, Felice said to Samantha, "You must tell me about your work."

"I'm sure Mike could tell you more. He's the giant in the field," Samantha said.

"He does rather stand out." Felice smiled at her tall son. "I'm interested in the construction industry from your viewpoint, though. It is an unusual business for a woman."

"That's what Mike says," Samantha remarked dryly. "He doesn't think I should be in it."

"I'm not surprised," Felice said. "My son is a charming young man in most respects, but while it pains me to admit it, he is a terrible male chauvinist."

"You've found an ally, Samantha." Mike grinned. "Mother is the original women's libber. Her only trouble is that she was born in the wrong time slot. A little earlier and she would have been marching with the suffragettes, a little later and she would have pursued a career."

"It's true." Felice sighed. "It makes me simply wild to think that my generation was relegated to giving parties and doing good works."

"I'm lucky that she had to settle for being a housewife, or I never would have been born," Mike teased.

"That is nonsense," Felice said crisply. "Young women today combine a career and a family quite effortlessly. Isn't that right, Samantha?"

"You're asking the wrong one, Mother. Samantha doesn't even intend to get married."

"That isn't so. I do expect to marry someday," she cried hotly. What Mike said was true, but she wouldn't give him the satisfaction of admitting it.

"Anyone I know?" he murmured.

They were both looking at her expectantly, and Samantha felt her cheeks grow warm. Felice took pity on her.

"You mustn't mind Mike. He takes it as a personal affront that some of us can get along quite well without men."

"Or maybe some of you just think you can," he said mockingly.

"You see what I have had to put up with?" Felice sighed. Turning to her son, she said, "If you don't behave yourself, Samantha might think twice before having anything further to do with you."

There was a derisive gleam in his eyes. "It's too late for that."

Samantha's heart skipped a beat. What did he mean by that? Too late for her to help herself? Did Mike guess that she was in love with him?

Once more, Felice came to the rescue. Sending her son a quelling look, she said, "Pass Samantha the salad dressing and stop badgering the child."

The rest of lunch passed more pleasantly. Felice was a masterful hostess and she kept the conversation flowing easily from one interesting topic to another. Not until much later did Samantha realize that Mike's mother had found out a great deal about her without asking any pointed questions.

"I hope you will come back again," Felice said warmly, when they were leaving. "I'm sure my husband would enjoy meeting you. Perhaps Mike will bring you to dinner one night."

The slightly seeking look in her eyes was replaced by satisfaction as Mike kissed her cheek. "That's what I was planning to do," he said.

"I liked your mother very much," Samantha said shyly when they were downstairs waiting for their cars.

"I thought you would," Mike answered. "You'll like Dad too." The white Ferrari was brought around. "Take a ride with me," he said impulsively.

"I couldn't possibly. I have to go back to work."

"The world won't stop spinning if you take a little time off." He walked her around to the passenger side, cutting her off her halfhearted protests.

Samantha knew she should have stood firm, yet this was such an unexpected treat that she couldn't resist the opportunity of being with him a little longer. It was self-destructive and foolish. How could she go about the task of forgetting him if she kept indulging herself like this? But when he turned his head, giving her a slow smile, Samantha knew it was hopeless anyhow. She would never get Mike out of her heart.

He surprised her by maneuvering the car onto the freeway. "Where are we going?" she asked.

"For a ride."

"But where?" she persisted.

"There is something I want to show you."

As the miles slipped by, Samantha guessed their destination. "You're taking me out to the development site, aren't you?"

He nodded. "I thought you might like to see it."

She looked down at her clasped hands. "It won't change my mind, Mike."

He covered her twisting fingers with his big hand. "Relax, kitten. I have no ulterior motive. It's a long, boring ride alone, that's all."

The site of Mike's proposed city was now just acre upon acre of rolling meadowland, emerald-green grass polka-dotted with white daisies. Majestic trees that had taken years to achieve their impressive height cast pools of welcome shade.

Not far from the road, men were peering through transits, surveying the ground. In the distance ponderous grading machines were at work, making growling sounds as they bit into the rich soil.

Mike left Samantha standing on a knoll while he went to confer with the men. When he returned, he eyed her questioningly. "Well, what do you think of it?"

"Do you want the truth?" she asked.

"Of course."

"I think it's beautiful just as it is. It seems a shame to disturb all this tranquility."

He looked at her impassively. "You don't ever want anything to change, do you, Samantha? Left to your own devices, you wouldn't even have wanted to grow up. How old would you have chosen to remain? Ten? Fifteen? No older than that, I'm sure. Not old enough to be forced out of the nest."

It was essentially what her mother had said, yet it was more palatable coming from her. "You didn't have to bring me all this distance to give me a lecture," she said stiffly.

Mike sighed. "No, I didn't. Especially since nothing penetrates that stubborn little mind of yours." Putting his arm around her shoulders, he said, "I don't want to argue with you today. Come and see where we're going to put your clubhouse."

"You really thought it was a good idea?" she asked, diverted from her resentment.

"Positively inspired."

Walking through the ankle-deep grass, Samantha's tension eased. Mike's arm stole around her waist and she was rewarded with a warm smile. Happiness shot golden sparks through her entire body. If only it could always be like this!

Samantha gave a delighted exclamation as they came across a small pond that had been hidden by a dense stand of trees. "You didn't tell me about this!"

"Didn't I?" Mike gazed indulgently at her rapt face, lingering on the soft, parted lips.

"Oh, Mike, you could do wonderful things with this. Make it a communal swimming area, for instance. Or maybe it could be stocked with fish and ducks and things. Think how educational it would be for the children to see them in their natural setting."

"Very educational," he agreed, smothering a grin. "Especially if the ducks ate the fish. It would teach them about survival of the fittest."

"You're laughing at me, but I don't care." A look of alarm crossed her face. "You're not planning on filling this in, are you, Mike?"

"How could I?" he teased. "You would probably throw yourself in front of the bulldozer."

"I might," she agreed. "Tell me some more. How far from here is the shopping center going to be? I don't think it should be too close. We want to keep the clubhouse a quiet place where people can hold meetings and such during the day without a lot of outside noise," she explained, unaware that she had used "we" instead of "you."

Something kindled behind Mike's eyes, but his voice was casual. "You see that grove of trees in the distance? The ones growing almost in a circle. That was the spot I had in mind. What do you think?"

"Yes, that seems far enough away." She looked around wistfully. "I know it's unavoidable, but it seems a shame to destroy all these beautiful trees."

"We're not going to. The days of a developer coming in and bulldozing down everything in sight are over, thank the Lord. We are going to preserve as many as we can."

"I'm glad." She put her hand on the trunk of a particularly lovely silver birch. "Could we save this one?" The words echoed in the clear air. Samantha's cheeks flushed as she realized her use of the plural. "I . . . I meant . . ."

Mike's firm hands on her shoulders brought her close, confusing her even further. "It gets in your blood, doesn't it, Samantha? Standing here where it's all going to happen, you can see it growing before your eyes, can't you?"

"Yes, I . . . I guess so."

"You want to be part of it. Admit it."

Her mouth felt dry as she said, "I suppose anybody would."

"Then go for it." He drew her so close she could feel the warmth of his body and smell the tangy masculine scent of him. "Take the first step. That one is always the hardest, but after that you'll be free. Trust me, Samantha."

His palms framed her face, his eyes burning into hers with an intensity that demanded the response he wanted. She was under siege by a dominant male force intent on her complete subjugation. Samantha felt her willpower slipping. His advantage was reinforced by the fact that she wanted so badly to give in. If only he would satisfy the nagging doubts in her mind, she would surrender willingly. If he would agree to a compromise, then she would know he wanted her, and not merely what he could get from her.

"I want to work with you, Mike," she whispered. "You said this city would take three years or more. Let me keep Morgan's for the first year and then I'll sell out to you."

Sudden anger flared in his eyes, like a jungle animal deprived of a prey he had been stalking. He dropped his hands, looking at her with contempt. "I should have known you didn't have the guts."

"And I should have known you wouldn't agree," she said bitterly.

"Let you keep Morgan's for an escape hatch? So you can bolt back into the safety of your little refuge every time you feel threatened by a real emotion? You're damn right I won't agree! I want you, Samantha. God alone knows how much I want you, but not like that. If you come to me, it's going to be for keeps—on my terms."

"Well, don't count on it. I don't need your job. In spite of everything you have tried to do, I'm making a success of Morgan Construction. We have more business than we can handle."

"Bravo! You've lived up to your father's expectations. That should make you very happy," he said sardonically.

"It does," she maintained, wondering why she didn't feel more so.

"I have to speak to one of the men for a minute," he said coldly. "Then I'll take you back."

Samantha retraced her steps, feeling utterly bereft. How different it had been with Mike's arm around her. Every daisy had been a small delight to step over carefully; now she crushed them disinterestedly underfoot.

He joined her shortly, starting up the powerful car with a roar. They drove for about five miles in silence. Mike was sitting so close she could touch him, yet he might have been alone. His face was preoccupied. It was as though he had erased her from his mind.

Unconsciously Samantha sighed, capturing his attention. "Sorry," he said. "One of the men presented me with a little problem." Samantha longed to ask questions, knowing she had forfeited the right. "Your family's home is around here, isn't it?" he asked, making a conscious effort at conversation.

"Down the road a little way," she said dully.

"It's no wonder you took an apartment in town. That must have been quite a commute."

"Yes, it got to be too much," she agreed.

The polite exchange was devastating. She wanted to shout, "Yell at me, shake me, do anything except treat me with this terrible disinterest!"

"I've never lived in the country. I suppose it makes for a different kind of childhood," he commented, continuing the empty conversation.

She shrugged. "I never lived in the city until I grew up. I wouldn't know."

"What were you like as a child, Samantha?"

"Average," she said tersely.

He took his eyes off the road to inspect her lovely face briefly. "I doubt if you were ever that," he said with a slow smile. "I wish I'd known you then."

"You wouldn't have looked at me twice. I was all arms and legs and long hair in a ponytail. Brooke was the beauty. She was little and cuddly like Mother. They both made me feel gigantic."

Mike's face was suddenly austere. "I would like to meet your mother."

"She's beautiful. Everybody adores her."

Mike glanced at her enigmatically. "Since we're so close, why don't we stop by?" he asked casually.

"You mean now? Oh, I don't—"

"Do we take the Burlingame or San Mateo cutoff?"

Without really wanting to, Samantha found herself giving him instructions. In a very short time they drove up in front of the pleasant house in the suburbs. She led him up the brick path with a strange feeling of trepidation.

"Mother might not even be home," she warned, hoping she was right.

Samantha wasn't quite sure why she didn't want

the two to meet. It wasn't as though Cecily was the matchmaking type, although a lot of good it would do her if she were. And she certainly didn't try to urge her opinions on anyone. But that last weekend she *had* expressed an uncharacteristic interest in Samantha's getting married. She didn't want this visit to get her mother's hopes up. One disappointed person in the family was enough.

"Darling, what a delightful surprise!" Cecily exclaimed a few moments later. Her eyes widened at the sight of the man looming over her daughter. "And you've brought a friend. How lovely."

Samantha was puzzled at Mike's reaction when she introduced them. He usually exuded effortless charm toward any woman from sixteen to sixty, but his manner now was coolly correct. It couldn't have been anything her mother said, because she was reacting as all the others did to his rather overwhelming good looks and masculinity.

When they were seated in the den and refreshments had been offered and refused, Cecily turned to her daughter with a twinkle in her eyes. "I see what Brooke meant," she murmured.

Samantha blushed painfully. "We're on our way back from Mountain View. Mike is starting a development out there. A small city actually."

"How exciting," Cecily said. "My husband was in construction and Samantha is running the business now. But how foolish of me!" she cried. "Of course you know that."

"Oh, yes, I'm certainly aware of the fact," Mike said grimly.

"It sounds like your paths have crossed," Cecily murmured.

Mike gave Samantha a grin. "Like swords you might say."

"I have never experienced it myself, but I suppose the world of business must be very competitive," Cecily said.

He regarded her levelly. "Your daughter holds her own."

"I'm so happy to hear that."

Mike's look of contempt was scarcely veiled. "Yes, I thought you would be." He looked pointedly around the gracious room filled with expensive furnishings.

"Would you like to look at mother's roses?" Samantha asked in a strangled voice. "She's famous for them."

"I'm sure Mr. Sutherland isn't interested in roses," Cecily said, a slight frown on her clear brow.

"I'm afraid my only experience with them is ordering them by the dozen," he agreed.

"That's the way it is with most men." Cecily smiled. "I suppose it's a woman's hobby."

"Was it Samantha's?" he asked coolly. "When she had time for feminine pursuits. Before she took over the full-time running of a business I mean."

"Mike!" Samantha had never seen him like this. His words were polite enough on the surface, but there was a biting edge to them that was shocking. She jumped to her feet. "I'm sorry, Mother. I think we'd better go."

"Sit down, dear." Cecily gave Mike a thoughtful look. "I believe Mr. Sutherland is asking what you were like as a girl."

"Mr. Sutherland is being downright, intentionally insulting!" Samantha cried hotly.

"That *is* what I was asking," Mike said to Mrs. Morgan, ignoring Samantha. "What was she like before Morgan Construction became her whole life?"

Cecily's eyes softened as they flicked over her

daughter's disturbed face. Turning back to Mike she said, "I think you are wrong about that."

"Am I?" he demanded harshly. "Then you are as deluded as your daughter."

"I won't let you talk to my mother like this," Samantha cried.

"Go in the kitchen and make us some coffee, dear," Mrs. Morgan said calmly. "This conversation is becoming very enlightening."

Samantha positioned herself in front of her mother's chair. "I wouldn't leave you alone with him for a second!"

Mike's grim face relaxed in a natural smile for the first time. "I have no intention of doing your mother bodily harm. She is turning out to be quite an exceptional lady. Do as you're told and go make some coffee." He turned her toward the door, giving her a little swat on the bottom.

In the face of her mother's firm nod and Mike's determination, Samantha reluctantly left the room.

"And don't listen at the keyhole," he called, making her furious because it had crossed her mind.

When they were alone, Cecily said quietly, "You seem to be a very angry young man, Mr. Sutherland. Would you like to tell me about it?"

"Call me Mike, please. And first let me tender my apologies. Samantha was right, I *was* rude and I'm sorry."

"Your apology is accepted, but I'm more interested in why it was necessary. I have a feeling that you are usually quite charming."

Mike smiled briefly. "That's kind of you after my inexcusable behavior. I can only offer the excuse that I came here with a preconceived notion."

"Which was?" Cecily asked curiously.

"That you and your other daughter were vampires," he said bluntly. "Draining Samantha of her youth, her future, everything a young, beautiful woman has a right to."

"And now you have changed your mind?"

"I don't know." He seemed at a loss. "You're not what I expected. However, the facts remain. She is sacrificing her life for you and Brooke."

"I hope you will believe that is not what we want," Cecily said, looking directly at him. "It never even entered our minds. You have to understand, Mike, Samantha was tremendously under the influence of her father. She always went to him with her problems, so I never realized until recently that she had any." Cecily shook her head. "What that young woman needs is a strong man."

"To be a father figure?" he asked harshly. "I don't think a really strong man would care for the job."

A flicker of annoyance crossed Cecily's face. "Men are so obtuse sometimes," she murmured, almost too low to hear. "What I had in mind was a man dominant enough to force her to accept and enjoy the fact that she is a woman. My daughter needs masterful handling, Mike, because I am sure she is frightened to death of the idea." She gave him an innocent look. "Oh, well, I am sure she will find that man someday."

Their eyes met and he gave her a slow smile. "Perhaps the job I offered her would provide the impetus. Who knows what might happen if she got out in the world."

"Job?" Cecily showed her surprise.

"I want to buy Morgan Construction, and I want Samantha to come to work for me."

She looked thoughtful. "What was her reaction?"

"Panic."

"I'm not surprised."

"Maybe you could give her a nudge in the right direction."

Cecily shook her head. "Oh, no, I never interfere. Of course if she should ask me, I would gladly give my opinion."

"Which would be?"

She gave him an oblique look. "I want my daughter to be happy, Mike." Her mouth curved in a smile of pure sweetness. "I am also a very selfish woman. I have a great yearning to be a grandmother."

When Samantha came back into the room carrying the coffee service, she was astounded to catch Mike in the act of kissing her mother's cheek.

"I don't suppose I will ever understand you," she said heatedly on the way home. "Your behavior was absolutely atrocious when we arrived. You were scowling and making nasty remarks, and all of a sudden you're grinning like a Cheshire cat."

He captured her hand and brought it to his mouth, kissing the palm. It sent shivers through her in spite of her anger.

"Your mother is a very remarkable woman, Samantha."

Yes, that was the answer. Cecily could tame a fire-breathing dragon. Mike had come prepared to dislike her, and she had captivated him with ease. If only she had inherited some of her mother's charm, Samantha thought sadly.

Chapter Nine

Business continued to be brisk at Morgan Construction. So good, in fact, that Samantha had to decline her mother's invitation to come for the weekend.

"I'm sorry, Mother, but I'm working on Saturday. We have a couple of jobs that simply have to be finished. I have crews on overtime. Besides, I was just there," she pointed out.

"I know, I'm being greedy, darling," Cecily said. "It was so delightful seeing you that I was rather getting used to it."

"I enjoyed it too," Samantha assured her. "Maybe next weekend."

By the end of the week, she was exhausted. It was gratifying to be so busy, but the body could only take so much. Samantha promised herself that she was going to sleep all day Sunday.

The doorbell put an end to that plan. She resisted

its noisy intrusion as long as she could, frowning in her sleep and burrowing under the pillow. Finally the insistent clamor brought her awake. Her outraged look at the clock showed it was only ten after nine.

Hopping out of bed, she looked for her robe without finding it. This made her angrier still. Stalking to the door, she threw it open. "Do you know what time—" The cross words died on her lips as she confronted a smiling Mike, looking impossibly handsome in a black turtleneck sweater and cream-colored cords.

"Don't tell me I woke you up?" he asked in mock surprise.

"Of course you woke me up! It's only nine o'clock, and it's Sunday morning. I had planned to sleep until noon."

He shook his head disapprovingly. "On a beautiful day like this? Don't you know sleeping is a waste of time? You can do that when you get old."

"I feel old already," she groaned.

"Cheer up, you don't look it." A flame turned his gray eyes luminous as he looked her over thoroughly.

Samantha was suddenly aware of the abbreviated baby-doll nightie she had on. Her legs were bare almost to the brief bikini panties underneath, and she knew her rosy nipples were very apparent through the sheer fabric. Mike seemed oblivious to her embarrassment. Sauntering in uninvited, he closed the door in back of him.

"What do you think you're doing?" she stormed.

"I knew you were going to ask me in. You just hadn't gotten around to it," he said smugly.

"You are the most—" Samantha stopped in the middle of the tirade she was about to deliver, aware

185

of her near-naked state. Anger waged a brief battle with modesty before she whirled and ran for the bedroom. "You stay right where you are," she warned over her shoulder.

"I wasn't going anywhere. I planned to devote the whole day to you."

Her mouth made a rounded O of amazement. But when his appreciative eyes continued to devour her body, Samantha slammed the door and rushed around getting into her clothes. She grabbed a deep blue cashmere sweater, the color of her eyes, and slipped into a white wool skirt. A pair of navy and white high-heeled spectators completed her casual outfit.

All the time Samantha was racing around getting dressed, her annoyance was building. Why couldn't Mike ever make a proper date? He was always popping in and out of her life, sure of his welcome. And the worst of it was, she couldn't deny the excitement his appearance always caused.

Her eyes were sparkling with resentment when she joined him in the tiny living room. Mike was leafing through a magazine, his long legs stretched out, ankles crossed. He greeted her with a slow, savoring smile that made her pulses start to flutter.

To cover it, she scowled at him. "Don't you have anything better to do than go around getting people up in the morning?"

"How else could I have breakfast with you? Unless you'd like to get back in bed and have me bring it to you there?" he suggested with a wicked grin.

"Don't be ridiculous!"

"I didn't think so." He laughed. "Okay, get your coat and we'll go out."

"I don't eat breakfast."

"You will when you taste what I have in mind. How do pecan waffles with pure maple syrup and link sausages sound?"

"Fattening," she said shortly.

"That's something you don't have to worry about." His eyes confirmed the fact by a comprehensive inspection that had Samantha squirming. Turning to the coat closet, he pulled out a black and tan houndstooth coat. "Here, put this on."

"Good heavens, no! The navy reefer is the one that goes with this outfit."

He obligingly took the jacket she had pointed to, holding it open for her to slip into.

"I didn't mean—I haven't any intention—" she began.

"I've been up since seven o'clock and I'm starving, Samantha," he said impatiently. "If you insist on arguing, we will do it after breakfast, not now. I warn you, I'm a bear until I've eaten."

Hustling her into her coat, he led her out the door with a firm grip on her arm, tucking her into the passenger seat of the white Ferrari. Angry words bubbled inside Samantha as she watched Mike walk around to the driver's side. They subsided when he got in next to her, his long, lean body so close they were almost touching. Why fight it? This was what she wanted more than anything.

Samantha hadn't asked where they were going. She never dreamed it was to his house. "What are we doing here? I thought we were going to a restaurant."

"Afraid I'm going to make you do the dishes?" he teased.

"That wasn't what I meant and you know it."

"All right. I brought you here because I thought it was time you saw the other important room in the house. You've already seen the bedroom." He grinned. "Although I would be happy to show it to you again."

Samantha stopped in her tracks. "If that is what you have in mind, I'd better leave now."

He laughed, ruffling her short glossy curls. "Relax, kitten. Your virtue is safe. I'm too weak from hunger to chase you around the house."

The kitchen he led her to was a large cheerful room, spacious enough to accommodate a round table and four chairs. Big windows looked out on a lovely back garden filled with flowers.

"Oh, Mike, what a beautiful kitchen!"

"Glad you like it." He was busily engaged in pulling out pots and pans.

"What can I do to help?"

"Just sit there and admire me while I work," he said, putting a pan of sausages on the stove.

"Aren't you going to wear an apron?" she asked critically.

"Aprons are for sissies," he scoffed.

He had pushed up his sleeves so his muscular forearms were much in evidence. Samantha looked at the lean, athletic length of him and started to laugh. "I don't think anyone would ever mistake you for one."

"It has never been a problem," he admitted.

She watched his deft movements with admiration. In the kitchen or on the construction site, Mike was completely in command, no indecision ever slowing him down. How wonderful to be that competent and sure of yourself. But why not? He was a very rare person.

Glancing absently in her direction, Mike suddenly stopped what he was doing, his eyes narrowing on her wistful face and parted lips. Crossing the room, he put his knuckles under her chin. "This is nice," he said softly. "It could get to be very habit-forming."

His dark head bent toward her, starting a thunder in her veins. If he kissed her, Samantha knew she would be lost. "I . . . I think your sausages are burning," she murmured.

With a muttered exclamation, Mike snatched the sputtering pan off the burner. He turned swiftly back to Samantha, but she had risen, putting the table between them.

"If you will tell me where you keep things, I'll set the table," she said, trying to keep the tremor out of her voice.

Mike was as good a cook as he had promised. The waffles were golden and light, the sausages browned perfectly, and the coffee delicious. Samantha's empty plate was a tribute to his prowess.

"I haven't eaten this much for breakfast in years. I'm absolutely stuffed." She sighed happily.

"What you need now is a brisk walk around the block," Mike declared. "Leave all of that," he instructed as she started to carry the dishes to the sink. "Tatsuo will be in later and he'll take care of it."

Samantha insisted on putting the plates in the dishwasher, but that was all Mike would let her do. Taking her by the arm, he led her out of the kitchen.

It was a brisk, sunny spring day, and as they wandered hand in hand through the neighborhood of beautiful homes, Samantha felt her heart soaring. Mike pointed out how some of the facades had been modernized without impairing their charm. They talked about different styles of architecture and discussed which ones they liked best. By the time they returned to the house, Samantha's face was sparkling with animation.

Mike lit the fire that was already laid in the fireplace in the den. From his kneeling position on the hearth, he looked up at her. "Aren't you glad it's nippy enough for a fire? There is nothing quite as romantic, I always say." Samantha tensed warily, feeling foolish when she realized he was teasing again. He switched on the television set before coming to sit beside her on the couch. "Would you mind watching the golf match for a little while?"

"I didn't know you were interested in golf," she said, making room for him.

He put his arm around her, smiling into her wide eyes. "There is a lot about me you don't know, but I think we're beginning to make progress." Samantha's long lashes dropped in confusion and Mike laughed. "Put your feet up and relax with me, honey."

His casual affection was completely unthreatening, making her feel warm all over, like a puppy wriggling with joy at her owner's caresses. Refusing to examine the analogy, she slipped off her shoes and curled up next to him, resting her head on his shoulder.

Judging by Mike's exclamations, the golf match was an exciting one. The long week Samantha had put in, however, started to take its toll. She was warm and comfortable, and her eyes gradually closed. At first she resisted, forcing them open again until the effort became too difficult.

Dimly she was aware that it had become quiet in the room. She frowned in her sleep when the support was removed from her head, smiling a moment later as she was gently stretched out on the couch and cushioned against something infinitely comfortable. Snuggling into Mike's arms, she gave a sigh of happiness.

Samantha slept for several hours, awakening to find her head pillowed on Mike's chest. She was cuddled in his arms, their bodies molded together for their entire length as they lay together on the couch. Her startled eyes flew to his face, finding that he was sleeping. He looked vulnerable somehow, with those all-seeing eyes veiled by spiky lashes, and the firm mouth that could be so taunting, relaxed now in a little smile. A lock of dark hair had fallen across his forehead and Samantha longed to brush it away. Did she dare?

When she made the first tentative move, his eyes opened, looking directly into her upturned face. His arms tightened. "Good morning," he said softly.

"It . . . it isn't morning," she managed to say, the pressure of his body against hers making speech difficult.

"I'm pretending that it is. I've always wondered what it would be like to wake up with you in my arms. Now I know. It feels wonderful." His hand slid down her back, urging her closer to his hard thighs.

Hot color rushed into Samantha's cheeks. "Mike! Let me up!"

"What for? Face it, kitten, you're already a compromised woman." He chuckled. "I can truthfully say that we've slept together."

"It wasn't . . . you didn't . . . Mike, stop it!" She was struggling to get out of his embrace.

A long leg wound around both of hers, immobilizing them while he pinned her down with his body. His mouth found the hollow in her throat, trailing a line of burning kisses up to her earlobe, which he bit delicately. "Didn't you ever play make-believe when you were a little girl?" he teased.

"Not like this," she gasped.

He raised his head, looking at her with eyes that suddenly darkened with passion. All the laughter was gone as he murmured huskily, "You're right. We aren't children anymore."

His mouth covered hers in a kiss that was wholly

adult. When she parted her lips to protest, he gained the entry he was seeking, probing the warm interior with a male expertise that had her senses spinning. Samantha uttered tiny cries, which he ignored, deepening the kiss and stroking her shoulder seductively, moving over to barely graze the place where her breast swelled gently.

In spite of her attempts to resist, he was lighting a fire in her blood that she couldn't stem. A tremor ran through her as Mike's hand roamed down her body, pausing while one forefinger touched the hard peak evident through her sweater.

"You don't know how much I've wanted to do this all day," he groaned. "Did you wear that sweater just to drive me out of my mind?" His hand slid under the ribbing to caress her bare midriff.

"No!" Samantha cried, as much in answer to his actions as his question. Her fingers clutched at his hand, stopping its inexorable progress upward.

Mike's head bent to her breast, taking the soft wool in his mouth as he sought the prize underneath. His lips accomplished their purpose, and when he pushed the sweater up, exposing her creamy skin, Samantha had lost the will to resist. With a small moan of surrender she clasped his head, holding it to her heated body.

"You're mine, my darling! Let me hear you say it," he exulted. Before she could answer, the telephone shrilled like a fingernail on a blackboard. Samantha's body tautened in his arms. "Let it ring," Mike growled, capturing her mouth once more.

Samantha grasped at the straw, losing her grip as he carried her higher and higher in a spiral that promised ultimate ecstasy. The phone that had stopped ringing started again as Mike was murmuring incoherent words into her neck.

Their eyes met and Samantha whispered, "You'd better answer it. It might be important."

Uttering a savage oath under his breath, Mike levered himself off of her. "Hello!" he barked harshly into the phone.

Samantha couldn't help the little smile that curled the corner of her mouth. It had better be important or Mike would devastate the caller.

The smile faded as some of the edge left his voice. "No, nothing is the matter. I'm just a little busy right now." There was a pause before he said, "You're mistaken. We didn't have a . . . an appointment." Another pause. "I can't help what you thought, I didn't say I would see you today." And then, "I'm very busy at the moment. You'll have to excuse me."

Samantha's blood chilled as she realized the import of the conversation. Mike had a date with another woman today, but when Samantha seemed like a better prospect, he decided to take the bird in the hand. How *could* he? The fact that he had almost succeeded was all the more galling! By the time he replaced the phone in its cradle and turned back to her, she was on her feet, straightening her disarranged clothing.

Putting his hand gently on her tousled hair, he said, "I'm sorry, darling."

She flinched away from him. "What you need is a social secretary to keep your dates straight."

"It wasn't like that, Samantha. I didn't—"

"The only thing that hurts a tiny bit, I'll admit, was hearing you say you were a *little* busy. Every woman likes to feel she is worth a man's full efforts."

"Be reasonable, darling. Did you want me to give her a play-by-play account?"

"No, of course not. She already knows how you go about it, doesn't she?"

Samantha turned away to hide the angry tears. He pulled her back against him, burying his face in her scented hair. "I won't try to lie to you. There have been a lot of women in my life. I'm thirty-eight years old, Samantha, I'm not a boy."

"If you don't mind, I'd rather not hear about your love life," she said coldly.

He turned her in his arms. "I only wanted to say that I've always played fair. I never told any of them I loved them. They wanted it as much as I did."

Samantha's heart was a cold little stone that had dropped somewhere in the pit of her stomach. Mike had never told her he loved her either—and she, too, wanted it as much as he did. But it wasn't enough. Even during the small time he allotted her he was plagued by his other girl friends. What self-respecting woman could put up with that, no matter how much she loved him?

"I'm going home now. If you hurry, you can still keep your other date."

He gave her a small shake, refusing to release her. "Will you stop acting like a child? So I got a call from another woman, so what? You're the one I want to be with."

"That's unfortunate, because I don't want to be with you," she said childishly. "Will you take me home or shall I call a taxi?"

He held her away, looking at her searchingly. "I can't believe you would overreact like this. Can't you tell that I—"

Samantha's misery threatened to overwhelm her, but she refused to break down in front of him. The only thing that sustained her was that Mike thought only her pride was hurt. He didn't know her heart was broken.

Setting her chin to stop its quivering, she broke in

bitterly, "The only thing I can tell about you is that you have women stacked up like . . . like airplanes waiting to land at a busy airport!"

In spite of himself, the corners of Mike's mouth turned up. "That sounds very formidable. Don't you think I deserve a round of applause for having the strength to get up and go to work?"

"On top of everything else, you're a braggart!" she cried in outrage.

"You were the one attributing super powers to me. I wonder where you get your information?"

"Everybody knows about you," she said vaguely.

"Including you," he said flatly.

"Not firsthand perhaps, but I'm not interested in finding out for myself."

"That wasn't the way you felt a short time ago," he said softly.

It was something she couldn't very well deny. Samantha's cheeks flamed as she said scathingly, "Well, I've changed my mind. You're probably greatly overrated anyhow."

His eyes glittered dangerously. "You won't know until you have judged for yourself. Would you like a sample?"

"I've had one and I wasn't impressed."

He jerked her to him suddenly, grinding his body against hers. His kiss was a masterpiece of seduction. It started teasingly, his tongue sliding sensuously across her closed mouth. When she turned her head, he feathered her cheek with light kisses, his warm mouth gliding across to linger on the sensitive spot behind her ear. At the involuntary tremor that passed through Samantha, he transferred his attention to her lips. The deep invasion was wholly male, promising delights that set her body on fire. Samantha forced herself not to respond, although it was torture when every part of her cried out its need to belong to this man. To experience just once his total possession.

When he finally released her, she gazed up at him unflinchingly. "If that was supposed to make me compare you with other men I've known, let me say it again—I'm not impressed."

Contempt etched deep lines in Mike's face. "What would you know about a real man? Run back to good old safe Donald. He doesn't frighten you, does he, Samantha? He doesn't arouse *any* emotion."

"That's not true! You can't understand a relationship like ours that isn't purely physical. Donald loves me!"

"I notice you don't say you love him," he remarked cynically.

"Of course I do!"

Mike's expression was coldly curious. "I wonder if you're capable of love. God knows you have the body for it. Too bad you don't know how to get any pleasure out of it."

"Is that what's bothering you? Or is it the fact that I won't let *you* get any pleasure out of it?"

"I haven't lost any sleep over it," he said cuttingly. "Virgins aren't that good in bed. The chase is interesting, but the payoff can be a bore."

Samantha's face paled. She turned and ran without any destination in mind, just the desperate need to get away from this cruel man. He caught up with her outside, his fingers bruising her soft skin as he whirled her around roughly. Shoving her unceremoniously into the car, he slammed the door so hard the windows rattled.

Not a word passed between them on the ride to her apartment. Mike's thoughts were centered on something extremely unpleasant and Samantha huddled in a corner, too miserable to be frightened at the manic way he drove. When they arrived at her building, he reached across her and flung open the door, his face set in a hard mask.

Samantha walked to the entry with her head held high, but she flinched as she heard the car roar away—and out of her life.

Work was her salvation in the week that followed. She didn't hear from Mike, nor did she expect to. Under her goading, he had revealed his true feelings. Fortunately she hadn't revealed hers.

Pete came into Samantha's office while she was trying to answer two phones and sign a stack of letters at the same time. He perched on the edge of her desk until she finished on the telephone, a wide grin splitting his lined face.

"Quite a difference from a month ago isn't it?" he asked.

She nodded. "Sometimes I find myself longing for a little of that peace and quiet, though," she said ruefully.

"You know you don't mean that, Sam."

"I suppose not. But this hectic pace is getting me down." She sighed.

He eyed her critically. "You do look a little peaked. Maybe you should take some vitamins."

Samantha couldn't tell him that vitamins wouldn't help what ailed her. It was easier just to agree. "Maybe you're right, Pete. Did you want something special?"

"Yeah, I have to talk to you about that prospective client, Mrs. Forsythe. We might be headed for trouble with her."

"Oh, Lord! Not another Mrs. Remington?" she groaned.

"Could be, although she goes about it differently. This one is all fluttery and scatterbrained. She makes up her mind one minute and changes it the next."

Samantha shrugged. "Just so you get it in writing. Changes can be costly."

"Sure, I know that, but it isn't the only problem. I have to reassure her every step of the way that our men can do the job, and she's still afraid to take my word for it. This one is used to doing business with the top dog. She insists on talking to you."

"No problem. Set up an appointment. I'll be happy to talk to her."

"You won't be happy, Sam," Pete said sardonically. "But it's unavoidable."

Upon meeting Mrs. Forsythe, Samantha began to understand Pete's problems. She was a small woman whose slight plumpness was camouflaged by exquisite clothes that were a bit too youthful for her. Mrs. Forsythe had evidently been a great beauty, if not a great brain, in her day, and she was still used to being catered to. Her confiding, little-girl manner gave way to petulance when she was thwarted.

The meeting with Samantha and Pete didn't start out auspiciously. She had greeted them courteously enough, her manner sharpening when she discovered that Samantha was the head of Morgan Construction.

"But you simply can't be! You don't look old enough."

This was such a common complaint that Samantha was used to it by now. Why did age alone merit trust? Avoiding Pete's twinkling eyes, she stated her qualifications.

"Well, that's very nice," the woman said. "But I can't get over the fact that you are only a few years older than my daughter."

"I understand your concern, Mrs. Forsythe. I'm

sure we could do a good job for you, but perhaps you would like to talk it over with your husband first." Samantha was happy that their present prosperity made it unnecessary to pursue this job, which promised to be a headache.

"Yes, that might be best. I always leave all the decisions up to Mr. Forsythe. He says a woman shouldn't be burdened with them, and I agree."

"Do take all the time you like," Samantha urged. "We wouldn't be able to start your job immediately anyway. We're quite busy at the moment."

"Yes, I imagine. Felice told me she was sending all her friends to you."

The name rang a bell, causing a chill of apprehension to travel up Samantha's spine. "I beg your pardon?"

"Felice Sutherland. Her son Michael owns that big construction company, but for some reason he has prevailed on his mother to send everyone to you. Isn't that odd?"

Samantha's chest felt like it was constricted by an iron band. "I think you must be mistaken," she said evenly.

"Not at all. Felice has done everything short of blackmail. I heard you did the Sandhills' apartment in their building, and the Morrisseys' on Russian Hill." Mrs. Forsythe sighed. "I suppose I will have to hire you after all. It wouldn't do to get taken off Felice's party list. She does give the most divine affairs, and if you aren't invited—" Mrs. Forsythe clearly couldn't bear to contemplate such social ostracism.

Samantha stared at her in numb disbelief, unable to credit what she was hearing. It couldn't be true that Mike was in back of their sudden prosperity. Why should she believe this woman who didn't have brains enough to open a package of chewing gum?

Standing up abruptly, she said, "I have to be going, Mrs. Forsythe."

The woman eyed her white face. "You look upset, Miss Morgan. I didn't realize this job meant so much to you."

"It isn't that, I assure you."

"Was it something I said then?" Mrs. Forsythe persisted. A bejeweled finger touched her cheek. "Now what was it Felice told me? Oh, I know." She laughed. "She told me not to mention that I knew her. But it doesn't make any difference, does it?"

"Not any longer," Samantha said, almost running for the front door.

She couldn't bear to go back to the office, so Samantha drove around aimlessly, her thoughts traveling faster than the car. It couldn't be true, she told herself over and over. Why would Mike help her when he had been trying to get control of Morgan's from the very beginning? Every time she had credited him with a kind act, there had always been an ulterior motive behind it. The same must be true now. But what could it be? *What?*

It couldn't be any personal involvement. Remembering the last time she had seen him, Samantha started to tremble. His cruel words came back to haunt her. Under great provocation, Mike became unguarded enough to reveal exactly how he felt about her. She was an amusing little toy that he had enjoyed playing with until he tired of the game. Surely he wouldn't go out of his way for someone he cared so little about.

A horn blared loudly as she veered into another lane and Samantha swerved sharply back into her own. Her wanderings had taken her down to the Embarcadero, the broad street heavily traveled by trucks and lined with piers. Docked freighters and luxury ships were visible through the few vacant lots between the wharves. Pulling up in front of one, she cut the motor and sat staring out at the water, following the progress of a tugboat without really seeing it. Her thoughts were all turned inward.

Had Mike guessed that she was in love with him? Was that the reason he had come to her rescue? Pity? The thought was agonizing! But even as it tore her apart, she rejected it. During that hideous scene at his house, he had accused her of being incapable of love. If he only knew!

Samantha realized that she was gradually accepting the fact that Mike was her benefactor. No matter how bitter a pill it was, the evidence was too overwhelming. All the people Mrs. Forsythe had mentioned, including the woman herself, were friends of Mike's parents. Little things started to come back too. Mrs. Sutherland's surprise when she asked her if she knew the Sandhills. Mike hadn't told her yet that their charity was to remain anonymous.

Something curled up and died inside Samantha as she was reminded of all the confident words she had flung at Mike. I don't need you! I can stand on my own two feet! I don't accept charity! She covered her face momentarily with shaking fingers. How he must have been laughing at her! He knew, probably to a penny, what her bank balance was, knew when she reached the edge of bankruptcy.

The Remington job was his first life preserver, and they had almost bungled that. No wonder he was so exasperated when he had to bail her out repeatedly. Why hadn't he just thrown up his hands in disgust?

What difference did it make why? It didn't even matter that she had made a fool of herself in front of Mike and probably his mother too. The pain of that would come later. What she had to face now was the fact that she was a failure. Everything Mike had said about her was true. She couldn't run a pony ride for children! How amused he must have been when she smugly bragged about all the new work they had. Without his help, the business would have gone under months ago and her blind pigheadedness would have left her mother and Brooke penniless.

Samantha raised her head. Maybe that's why he had done it. Well, no matter, it was still charity whatever the reason.

Was he right too about her using Morgan's as a security blanket? Recalling her panic at the thought of losing it, Samantha was forced to face the fact that he was correct there also. It was the only job she had ever held. It was frightening to think of working for someone else—even Mike. At least she had turned that down, thank heavens!

Samantha heaved a deep sigh. There was no point in torturing herself any longer. It was time to make amends—to the best of her ability, that is. The bitter accusations she had flung at Mike would haunt her forever.

There was a phone booth on the corner. Before she lost her nerve, Samantha made her way to it. Her request to talk to Mike met with endless delays, but at least he appeared to be in the office. While she waited, Samantha watched a heavy cement truck lumbering up the street. Her mouth became increasingly dry as it occurred to her for the first time that he might refuse to speak to her. At last he came on the line, his cold voice not promising to make this easy.

"What is it, Samantha?" he asked abruptly.

"I'd like to talk to you," she said hesitantly.

"Go ahead. But make it snappy, I'm busy."

"Not . . . not like this. Could we meet someplace?"

There was a small pause. "What did you have in mind?" he asked, his tone still inflexible.

"Any . . . any place you like."

"I didn't mean that. I meant why this sudden urge to see me? As I remember it, I don't impress you."

Samantha closed her eyes briefly. He had every right to be angry. She could almost feel his enmity over the phone. "I'm sorry, Mike," she whispered.

"Okay, you've apologized," he said curtly.

"Wait! Don't hang up! That wasn't what I called for."

"I should have known," he commented mockingly.

"I mean it wasn't the only thing. I want to talk to you about . . . about Morgan Construction."

"Don't tell me you're in a jam again," he exclaimed disgustedly. "Can't you ever—"

"No, it isn't that," she cut in swiftly, unable to bear hearing a list of her inadequacies at the moment. She took a deep breath. "I wanted to talk about selling it to you."

"What!" When she was silent, Mike said, "Is this some kind of joke?"

"If it is, I'm not laughing," she said bitterly.

"What's going on, Samantha?" The coldness had gone out of his voice.

"It's quite simple. You said you wanted to buy, and I'm ready to sell."

"What changed your mind all of a sudden?" he asked warily.

She passed a weary hand over her forehead. "Does it matter?" A police car went by with its siren blaring, drowning out his reply.

When she could hear again, Mike was demanding, "Where are you?"

"Somewhere," she said vaguely, glancing around.

"I want to see you, Samantha—right now!"

"No!" She was glad now that he had refused to meet her. Panic struck at the thought of having to face Mike. It would be necessary to see him when they signed the papers she supposed, but that wouldn't be for several days at least. It would give her time to gather her shattered defenses together.

"Something has happened and I want to know what it is," Mike said forcefully. "We can't discuss it over the phone."

"There is nothing to discuss."

"Can't you at least tell me what's bothering you?"

She made a futile little gesture that he couldn't see. "It isn't important."

"Anything that has you this upset is damned important." His voice was husky. "Tell me about it, honey, and I'll fix it."

Tears sprang to her eyes as she realized that this man she loved was holding out a helping hand once more, offering his strength even though she had thrown the offer back in his face countless times. Unfortunately there was nothing he could fix this time. She had to grow up and begin standing on her own without Mike to prop her up. That was what he had been trying to force her to do all along. Well, she wouldn't be a burden on him any longer.

"Let me come and get you," Mike was pleading.

Samantha squared her shoulders. "There isn't any need."

"Be reasonable. You can't close a deal like this over the phone."

"Why not? Either you want to buy or you don't."

"Suppose I tell you I don't want to take Morgan's away from you?" he asked.

"You aren't taking it, I'm selling it to you. If you've changed your mind about the price, that's no problem. I'll take whatever you want to give me."

"The money I offered was fair," he said absently.

"Good, then that's settled. I . . . I guess the next step is for our lawyers to get together."

"I said I hadn't changed my mind about the price, Samantha. But what if I told you I've changed my mind about the whole deal?"

"You mean you don't want to buy?" Her voice trembled slightly.

"I didn't say that. I said what if?"

"Then I would look around for another buyer," she said firmly.

"I believe you're actually serious," he said slowly.

"I am."

"Well, in that case, I guess you've made yourself a deal." Mike was suddenly preoccupied. "I'll be in touch. Good-bye, Samantha."

"Good-bye" . . . my love, she added after hanging up the phone.

Chapter Ten

Samantha dressed carefully for her appointment in the attorney's office, smoothing the skirt of her beige dressmaker suit and adjusting the collar of the cornflower-blue blouse that matched her eyes. This was the last time she would see Mike and she wanted him to remember her like this instead of in her usual jeans.

Not that he would ever give her a second thought. He hadn't contacted her in any way since they had made the deal a week ago.

The three men—the two lawyers and Mike himself —had already assembled by the time Samantha was shown into the quietly luxurious office. Her breath was drawn in involuntarily as he rose to greet her. Mike had dressed for the occasion also, his dark gray banker's suit emphasizing his height and the width of his shoulders. His snowy linen set off the perpetual tan he had acquired by working out of doors so much. The unaccustomed attire made him seem remote and austere, a disinterested, godlike figure who was unconcerned over the fact that his intervention had shattered her life.

Introductions were made and the meeting proceeded after a few pleasantries.

"I think you will find everything in order, Miss Morgan," Josh Whitley, Mike's attorney said.

"Yes, I've looked it over and it's all quite straightforward," Henry Creighton told her.

The distinguished silver-haired man had been her father's attorney for many years. Samantha trusted him, but no matter what the terms of the contract were, she was prepared to sign. Anything to get this agony over with so she could start rebuilding her life—if possible. Over her protestations, they insisted she read through the endless pages.

"It isn't necessary. I trust all of you," she insisted.

"Since when?" Mike murmured derisively, too low for the men to hear.

"That's very flattering," Henry Creighton soothed, "but it's only good business to read anything you affix your signature to."

Samantha flushed as the two lawyers exchanged a meaningful glance. It was clear that they considered her a helpless little woman with no business sense. Well, wasn't she? Grimly she reached for the thick contract.

Samantha forced herself to appear attentive as they persisted in explaining endless clauses to her. In truth, her attention was riveted on the silent man sitting next to her. Strangely enough, Mike was taking no part in the conversation. He seemed rather bored by it all, his interest captured instead by her delicate profile, which he was examining minutely. It made Samantha so uncomfortable that she couldn't have concentrated on what the lawyers were saying if she had wanted to.

Eventually the torture was over. Everyone stood and shook hands on the deal. When the platitudes and good wishes began, Samantha felt as though she had endured enough. Heedless of how abrupt her good-byes might seem, she fled out of the office and down the hall.

Mike caught up with her as she waited for the elevator. "I thought we might have a drink to celebrate," he said casually.

She turned her head away so he wouldn't see the shimmer of tears in her eyes that were darkened by pain to a deep violet. "I'm afraid I don't have time."

"Why not, Samantha?" he asked softly. "You're retired now, aren't you?"

She turned a blank face to him. "Yes, I . . . I suppose I am."

"What are you going to do now?"

"I don't know."

He watched her carefully. "My offer is still open. You can start to work for me tomorrow."

The elevator arrived and they joined the people already inside. They were both silent during the swift descent, but when the doors opened on the lobby, he fell into step beside her, reopening the conversation.

"At least have a cup of coffee with me," he said, taking her arm and steering her down the street.

She pulled away, facing him angrily. "Why can't you leave me alone? You've gotten everything you want!"

"Is that what you think, Samantha?" Mike's gray eyes bored into hers as they stood like an oasis amid the people swirling around them on the sidewalk.

Her eyes dropped before the intense, yet unreadable, expression in his. "I'm sorry," she murmured.

She had gotten so used to casting Mike as the villain that she was acting irrational again.

He used her moment of remorse to lead her into a café. After the waitress had taken their order and gone, Mike said, "Okay, Samantha, what is this all about?"

"I don't know what you mean."

"I intend to get to the bottom of it so you might as well tell me. What made you suddenly decide to sell out?"

"Oh, that."

"Yes, that," he repeated flatly.

She concentrated on tracing intricate circles on the tablecloth. "I just got tired of the whole thing."

"Do you expect me to believe that? After guarding that business more fiercely than you guarded your virtue, it isn't likely."

Her pale cheeks flushed at his analogy. "It's true, though. The pressure finally got to me. I just didn't want to work that hard anymore."

Mike looked at her impassively. "After you called last week and I couldn't talk you out of selling, I knew you were overwrought. That's why I left you alone—to get over whatever was disturbing you. But you went through with it, and now I want some answers."

"You did *want* to buy Morgan's, didn't you?" she cried, a horrible suspicion forming in her mind. Samantha didn't feel she could stand being the recipient of any more of Mike's largesse.

"I bought it, didn't I" he asked impatiently.

"That doesn't answer my question. If you are telling me that I pressured you into this deal, I'm going to tear up your check," she cried passionately.

"Will you stop jumping to conclusions? I offered to buy the company from your father, remember? And don't try to change the subject."

Samantha's taut body relaxed. She had forgotten that negotiations were under way before she ever met Mike. It was difficult to think straight with him sitting so close, enveloping her in his potent male aura. He was tapping impatiently on the table and she looked away, remembering those long fingers seeking out the pleasure spots of her body.

"I'm waiting, Samantha." Mike's implacable voice dispelled the erotic picture.

There was concern on his face as he watched her intently. Taking care of her had gotten to be a habit that he couldn't break. He needed reassurance that she had really wanted to get out. Somehow she would have to give it to him.

"All right, it wasn't the reason I gave you. I didn't want to tell you the real reason because I'm not very proud of it." She stole a look at Mike's face which told her nothing. "I suppose my mother actually put the idea in my head, although she wasn't aware of it." Mike made a sudden movement, but when she looked up, he motioned her to go on. "As you know, I've always been worried about her and Brooke having enough money. Mother must have guessed, because we got on the subject somehow, and she told me they could get along fine if I decided I wanted to do something else."

"I told you that a long time ago," Mike said tersely.

"I had to hear it from her," Samantha explained. "Suddenly I realized how much I was missing out of life—dates, parties, pretty clothes. That's the part I feel guilty about. Maybe I shouldn't have abdicated my responsibility for such trivial things, but the temptation to lay down the burden, as you called it, became too great." She avoided his narrowed eyes. "I want to get married, have children."

Mike became very still. "Do you have a prospective father in mind?" he asked casually.

Samantha felt her heart give an erratic beat. If only her dream weren't such an impossibility. Her nails made crescent marks in her damp palms as she answered, "Not exactly."

Mike relaxed against the back of his chair. "Then since wedding bells aren't imminent, suppose you come to work for me?"

Refusing only made him more tenacious, so Samantha tried a new tack. "Maybe I will at that. Just give me a few days to get over my recent bereavement." The smile she tried to give was more a quivering of her soft mouth.

His narrowed eyes surveyed her miserable face. "Isn't that a strange way to describe something you supposedly wanted so much?"

Samantha paled. Had she undone all her good work? "Just a poor choice of words," she said hastily. She stood up swiftly. "I really do have to run. I have a million things to do."

To her relief, he didn't try to stop her. Samantha hurried from the restaurant, conscious of his thoughtful eyes watching her escape.

She went directly back to the office to see Pete. It was imperative that she tell him about the new status of Morgan's before he found out from anyone else. Since she had never discussed it with him, had indeed been violently opposed to the idea, it was bound to come as a shock. Samantha had kept her own counsel because she couldn't explain the reason for her turnaround. But Pete was bound to be hurt that she hadn't confided in him. She was right about his emotions.

"How could you do a thing like this without even talking it over?" he demanded.

"It all happened so fast, Pete."

"That's no excuse. I see you every day. You could at least have mentioned that you were considering it."

"I seem to remember saying the same thing about you and Dad when you were negotiating with Sutherland's," she said dryly.

Pete had the grace to look embarrassed. "It wasn't the same thing at all. You couldn't have changed your dad's mind."

"And you couldn't have changed mine. I'm a failure, Pete. I just refused to admit it until now."

"How can you say that? We have more work than we can handle."

"Thanks to Mike Sutherland," she answered bitterly. "You heard that Forsythe woman. Mike has been twisting arms to get people to throw their business our way. Without him we would have been bankrupt long ago."

"Okay, so he steered some jobs in our direction. The important thing is that we did them well, doesn't that prove you're competent?"

She shook her head. "It proves *you* are. Every time I was left in charge I goofed it up and Mike had to ride to the rescue. How do you think that makes me feel? He told me I couldn't handle it and he was right."

"I don't think he meant it that way, Sam. You're too sensitive. You're learning more every day," he said encouragingly.

"And when I'm a hundred and eight, maybe I'll know half as much as you and Mike do. Look, Pete, you're going to be a lot better off," she explained patiently. That was the first thing she had discussed with Mike, and he had assured her that Pete's future was secure.

"I'm not worried for myself. It's you I'm concerned about, Sam. This place has been your whole life."

"Maybe that's the trouble," she said shortly.

"But you can't just walk away. What are you going to do?"

"Don't you think I can get a job with someone else?" she demanded. "Is that what you're trying to say?"

"Of course not. Don't get your feathers up. You're a fine architect."

"Well, then, just accept it, Pete. I have. It wasn't a decision lightly made, I assure you."

"I just can't get used to the idea of Morgan's without a Morgan, I guess," he said slowly.

She let him talk, listening to all his reminiscences, and adding some of her own, until the pain got too great. Then she called a halt. "We're a fine pair. Here we are getting sentimental about a lot of trucks and bulldozers."

"I guess you're right." He made a game attempt at returning her smile. "You'll keep in touch though, won't you?"

"Of course, Pete." She flung her arms around him impulsively.

He patted her back awkwardly. "What are your immediate plans?"

"I'm going to take a few days off and go up to Silverado."

It was a plan she had formulated in the long week before the signing. Silverado was a quiet resort in the wine country of the Napa Valley, about an hour-and-a-half drive from San Francisco. She had phoned ahead to reserve a cottage on one of the two golf courses, knowing she was going to need some time alone. Time to sort out her life and try to patch together the broken pieces.

The road wound through beautiful country that

was wasted on Samantha. She didn't spare a look at the grapes ripening to plump sweetness on the leafy vines or the black and white cows grazing in the green fields. Woolly sheep on the rounded hills didn't rate a glance either. Nor did the roadside stands offering mounds of ripe tomatoes, flowerlike artichokes, and juicy oranges. Samantha's attention was riveted on the road.

She picked up her key at the main hotel and drove to the small house reserved for her. It was clean and nicely furnished, but it had the anonymity of rooms that changed hands regularly. Until she unpacked and put her own articles around, it would remain coldly impersonal. That suited Samantha fine. Her surroundings might as well be as austere as her spirits.

Leaving her suitcase in the living room, she went out the door without bothering to lock it. The clientele here were all respectable.

She had no destination planned, wandering aimlessly through the lovely countryside, keeping her mind carefully blank. Tomorrow would be time enough to face harsh reality and make plans. Surely she could be allowed one day of forgetfulness. At one point a particularly lovely meadow stabbed her consciousness. It reminded her of Mike's acreage many miles away. She forced it from her thoughts. That too was an impossible dream. A charitable offer extended to a loser.

It was getting dark when she finally turned back, shivering slightly now that the sun had disappeared. Her legs were tired too. She had walked much farther than she realized.

Samantha arrived back at the cottage, so preoccupied that she didn't notice the white Ferrari parked at the curb. It was a terrible shock when she entered the house and Mike loomed up in front of her. She

214

began to tremble so badly that he caught her in his arms.

"I'm sorry, sweetheart." He stroked her back gently, holding her slender body against the hard, reassuring length of his own. "I didn't mean to frighten you. Didn't you see my car parked outside?"

She shook her head wordlessly, burrowing into his shoulder and inhaling the wonderful masculine aroma of him. Mike's fingers massaged the tense neck muscles under the tumbled curls, soothing her until she was trembling for a different reason.

Knowing she couldn't allow that to happen again, Samantha moved out of his arms. "How did you know where to find me?" she asked.

"I stopped by your office."

"It isn't mine anymore," she said carefully. "It's yours."

Mike waved an impatient hand. "All right, I stopped by *the* office. I had a long talk with Pete."

"Oh, I'm glad," Samantha exclaimed, forgetting her own problems for the moment. "I told him he had nothing to worry about, but it must have been more reassuring coming from you."

"A man like Pete is an asset to any company. I'm fortunate to get him."

"Then everything is settled," she said brightly.

"Not quite. As I said, I had a long talk with Pete—about you, Samantha."

She forced a smile. "That must have been dull."

"On the contrary, it was extremely enlightening. Pete is very worried about you."

"Pete still thinks I'm fifteen years old." She shrugged.

"He's a good friend, and he is concerned about your future."

"I know." She clenched her fists. "He's like all the

215

rest of you, he thinks I can't get a job anywhere else."

"That's not true, you're just being emotional. And if I'm lumped in with 'all the rest,' let me say that I don't believe that for a moment."

"Yes, you do! You told me I couldn't cut it in the big outside world."

He shook his head. "I said you were *afraid* to, that's an entirely different thing."

Her shoulders slumped dejectedly. "Well, it's only a matter of semantics now. We'll all find out soon enough if I can get a job."

"Where do you intend to look?"

"I don't know, I haven't decided yet."

"You never gave any thought to accepting my offer, did you?" he asked quietly.

Samantha walked to the window and drew aside the curtain to look out at the golf course. "I considered it, but then I decided against it."

"It isn't charity, Samantha."

Her body went rigid. Mike must never know that she had found out about his machinations. The remnants of her pride depended on his believing that she had sold out for the reasons she gave him.

"I never thought it was," she said lightly.

He came over to stand in back of her. Every nerve ending was aware of him and she clutched desperately at the curtain, suppressing the urge to lean back against that broad chest and let his arms close around her.

"Then why did you reject the idea?"

She could feel his warm breath on her temple, stirring the fine hair. A wave of longing to feel his lips there swept over her, but she fought against the weakness. "Because we don't . . . I . . . you and I . . ." She stopped helplessly.

He turned her around, linking both hands behind

her waist. "Were you afraid I would chase you around the office all day?"

She braced her palms against his chest, feeling the steady beat of his heart beneath the fine linen. "Such a ridiculous notion never crossed my mind," she said breathlessly.

"Is it ridiculous?" he murmured, tilting his head to one side and giving her a mischievous grin. "You might be right about not chancing it. I would probably spend all my time trying to entice you onto the couch in my office."

Samantha's cheeks flamed. She was suddenly aware that her palms were moving over his shirt-front, her fingers slipping inside to touch the crisp hair that covered his chest. Snatching her hands away, she moved out of his arms. "Well, now you know why I turned down the job."

Mike crossed his arms, leaning against the windowsill and allowing her to walk away. "If that was the reason, I could understand it. But it isn't is it, Samantha?" He gave her a searching look that sought to reach into the recesses of her mind. "You're a fine architect. Have I undermined your confidence so badly that you are beginning to doubt it?"

"I don't know," she whispered.

"If I had known this was going to be the result, I would have let you go bankrupt," he said fiercely. He watched the startled consternation spring to her eyes. "Yes, I found out the real reason you decided to sell. Pete told me."

She might have expected this to happen. If only she had told Pete not to say anything to Mike. Her pride was in tatters.

"Well, now you know." Her legs refused to support her anymore and she sank into a chair. "I really admire your restraint," she said bitterly. "It must have been hard to keep a straight face while I was spouting all that nonsense about not needing any help from you."

"That's the part that bothers you, isn't it? Why do you find it so hard to accept? Everyone needs help at some time or other."

"Stop it, Mike! You never needed help in your life. You don't need anyone!"

He crossed the room to stand over her, his face an unreadable mask. "Don't be too sure of that."

"You did it all on your own even when you could have had help from your father, so you don't know what it's like to be a failure."

He hunched down in front of her and took her cold hands in his. "You're not. I don't ever want to hear you say that again."

"It's true. Even when you threw business my way, half the time I didn't know what to do with it. I can't imagine why you put up with me!"

"Can't you?" He smiled.

"Yes, I suppose I can," she said wearily. "You felt sorry for me, just the way you do now."

"You're wrong there. I don't feel sorry for you. You're doing much too good a job of it yourself."

"Oh!" she gasped, stung by his heartlessness.

"Now you're going to listen to some hard facts," he told her calmly. "At our first stormy meeting I told you that you weren't qualified to run a construction company. That doesn't have anything to do with your talent as an architect. I did some investigating and found out you are a damn good one."

"Thank you. I'm glad to hear I have one attribute."

"You have a lot more than one, but I'll get to that later." He smiled. "First I'm going to get rid of some of your misconceptions. Given time and proper guidance, I have no doubt that you could have made a great success of Morgan's."

"Oh, sure. As long as you were there to take care of all my mistakes."

The corners of his mouth tilted. "I can think of worse things than taking care of you."

"Like what? Having a root canal?" she asked bitterly.

"If it's the last thing I do, I'm going to instill some confidence in you," he said grimly. "I'm going to *prove* to you that you can be a success."

"Are you offering to sell Morgan's back to me?" she asked wide-eyed.

"Oh, no, my dear! Getting out was the first step in your growing-up process. I'm not going to let you drop back into your little safety net."

"How could I, now that I see it for what it was?" she asked sadly. "I'm like the man without a country, except that I'm worse off. I am a woman without an identity."

His hard hands gripped her shoulders, lifting her to her feet. "Being a woman is an identity in itself."

She shook her head. "I know the kind of woman you mean, but that isn't me. All my life I've longed to be little and cuddly like Brooke, but I'm not. I'm big and capable—at least I always thought I was until now—and there is nothing I can do about it. Don't you think I would have preferred it to be the other way?"

Mike uttered a smothered oath. Grabbing her wrist in one big hand, he dragged her after him. "Come with me," he ordered.

"Where are you taking me?"

Positioning her in front of a full-length mirror mounted on a closet door, he stood in back of her, looking at their reflections. "Shall I tell you what I see? I see an exquisite girl with eyes like violets sprinkled with morning dew. Her tilted nose is rather funny, but her mouth is generous and sweet. I see skin like a gardenia petal, so flawless and delicate that I'm almost afraid to touch it for fear of bruising its lovely texture. Her body is made for love. Those tantalizing breasts alone could drive a man to distraction." His hands cupped their fullness before trailing down her body.

"Mike, please—"

"Quiet, I'm not through yet. I see rounded hips, perfect thighs, and long slender legs. The girl I'm looking at is so beautiful that no man in his right mind would want anyone else. Now tell me what you see?" Her cheeks stained a bright pink as Samantha tried unsuccessfully to twist out of his grasp. "Tell me," he demanded.

"I see a woman everyone calls Sam," she said hopelessly. "Even Brooke's name is prettier."

He turned her in his arms then, raising her drooping head with his knuckles under her chin. "If Brooke is so irresistible, perhaps you can tell me why it's you I want instead of her."

"You only met her once."

"What does that have to do with it? I wanted *you* the first time I saw you."

Her startled eyes met his. "That's not so! We had a terrible row."

"When you threw the hard hat across the yard." He nodded. "But when we were alone together and I got a good look at that delectable body of yours in those tight jeans, it was a different story. I wanted to make love to you right there on the floor of the construction shack."

"Mike!" Samantha felt herself growing warm all over.

"It can't come as any great shock to you," he

teased. "That's what I've been trying to do ever since."

Her long eyelashes descended to her flushed cheeks. "You told me . . . you said you were only interested in the chase."

"As I remember, you said some rather unpleasant things yourself that day."

"I know, and I'm sorry," she murmured.

He cupped her cheek gently. "Don't tell me my fierce little tiger cat has turned into a purring kitten?"

An unwilling smile curved her mouth. "Was I very terrible?"

He raised one eyebrow. "Let's just say there were times when it took great effort to restrain myself."

She made a face at him. "Stop congratulating yourself. I remember once when you didn't."

"If you are referring to the time I threatened to spank you, it was well deserved. But I liked what came after a lot better. In the future I'll use that method of punishing you whenever necessary."

Tiny flames licked at her insides as Samantha remembered being held across his lap, reliving the way his seductive hands and mouth had brought her to full pulsating life. She tried to put it out of her mind. "There won't be any need," she said carefully. "Our business dealings are over." Hope flamed suddenly in her heart. "Unless of course, you would like me to stay on for a little while to help with the transition period?"

"That won't be necessary," he answered coolly. "I plan to put Pete in complete charge and bring some of my own men in under him."

The vain hope went up in smoke. It had been just a pipe dream anyway. "It's nice to know that Morgan's will be in good hands," she said, trying to smile.

"The best," he agreed callously.

Bitterness rose in her throat. "Too bad I didn't contribute to its success."

"Oh, but you did, Samantha. You provided the direction. Your idea of concentrating on remodel work was an excellent one. Sutherland's never bothered with it before, but there is a growing market out there. As a subsidiary, Morgan Construction will handle it."

"Except that it won't be called that," she said sadly.

"I hadn't planned on changing the name."

Samantha's startled eyes searched his face, finding that he seemed perfectly serious. She found it difficult to swallow the lump in her throat. "It . . . that's awfully kind of you."

"Kindness has nothing to do with it—I'm a businessman. Morgan's has always stood for quality and we aren't going to change that either."

"It's more than I could have hoped," she said simply. "In spite of what you say, Mike, I'll always remember you as a very kind man."

"You sound like you're going somewhere."

"Maybe I will at that." She turned away so that he couldn't see the emotions that were tearing her apart. "There is nothing to keep me here anymore except Mother and Brooke, and they don't really need me."

"How about me, Samantha?" His strong hands kneaded her tense neck muscles, stopping briefly so he could kiss the vulnerable spot at her nape. "I need you."

He turned her into his arms, but she put her palms against his chest, holding him off. "Don't make pretty, insincere speeches, Mike. I'm feeling too defenseless right now."

He drew her hips against his hard thighs, molding

her body so closely against him that she felt imprinted with every firm muscle and bone. Lowering his head, he murmured into the soft hollow of her throat, "Does this convince you?"

She twisted her head, trying to dislodge his tantalizing lips. "You don't even need me for that. You have dozens of women who will give you what you want."

"You're wrong, my darling. You are the only one who can give me what I want." His lips trailed a feathery path across her jawbone to her mouth where he nibbled lightly on her lower lip. "You want me too, Samantha, admit it."

"Why are you doing this to me, Mike? Why are you tormenting me?"

"Because you're like a fire in my blood," he murmured deeply. "I have to have you."

"No!" she cried. "It's all wrong!"

He anchored his hands in her hair, tilting her head back so his eyes could blaze into hers. "I'm going to show you just how right it is. I'm tired of waiting for you to realize it for yourself. This time there is no escape for you, Samantha. You aren't getting out of this room until I've made you mine."

She tried frantically to get away. "I never thought you would resort to rape," she panted.

He gave her a tiger's smile. "I won't have to."

His mouth touched hers, making no attempt to force the defiant lips apart. He placed a butterfly kiss at the very corner of her mouth, his warm lips sliding across her cheek to her earlobe, which he nibbled gently before tracing the curve with the tip of his tongue.

A ripple of excitement started in the pit of Samantha's stomach. She tried to ignore it, twisting her chin away, but his hand cupped the back of her head, holding her so his seductive mouth could continue its quest.

The other hand caressed her throat, stroking the sensitive cord that ran its length. Then he began a downward descent. A long forefinger dipped into the front of her open-neck blouse, making a slow exploration of the little valley between her breasts.

Samantha felt a surge of desire so primitive that it frightened her into redoubling her frantic efforts to escape, but Mike held her easily. His hand continued its devastation, unbuttoning her blouse with an inexorable precision. When it slipped inside to curve around her taut breast, the pleasure was too intense to be denied. Samantha's eyes closed and her breath came out in a little sigh.

His breath mingled with hers as he murmured, "You want me to make love to you, don't you, Samantha?"

How could she deny it? She was like a lost soul, seeking salvation while knowing there was none. "Mike, please don't!" It was an agonized plea for compassion, which he ignored.

She grasped at his hand which only closed more firmly around her breast, his thumb making a sensuous exploration of the hardened peak. The sensation raced through her body, setting it on fire. As Mike sensed a weakening his mouth and tongue took up the seduction, raining burning kisses over her throbbing skin. The tide refused to be stemmed—she was lost in her need for him. Mike had breached her last defense.

In mindless ecstasy, she moved against him. When his mouth descended triumphantly to hers, Samantha parted her lips in total surrender. As he probed the hidden recess she wound her arms around his neck, her fingers twining restlessly through his thick hair. Her hands touched his face and throat, wandering over his muscular back while she pressed her body to his in an effort to satisfy the consuming passion that was turning her to liquid inside.

Mike slipped the blouse from her shoulders and it fell to the floor with a whisper of silk. The bit of lace that was her bra followed it. But when his hand went to the zipper at her waist, Samantha started to tremble. Mike buried her head in his shoulder, gently removing the rest of her clothing. He put her tenderly on the bed before swiftly removing his own clothes.

When he came back to kneel over her, Samantha turned her head away, trying to curl into a little ball. Slipping an arm around her shoulders, he stretched out beside her and cradled her body to his. The contact was like nothing she had even dreamed of. Samantha had never realized that she could have such wanton feelings. She hid her face in his arm so that he wouldn't see the molten passion she knew was in her eyes.

"Don't be ashamed, darling," he murmured into the soft cloud of her hair. "This is the way it's supposed to be."

His mouth found hers, reassuring her with a deep kiss that fanned the flames into a blaze that had to be extinguished. Sliding her body gently beneath his, Mike started her on a journey to uncharted heights, to a place of warm enchantment where the pleasure came in thundering waves. Clutching him tightly, Samantha arched her quivering body against his as she struggled repeatedly to reach some unknown goal. Suddenly they burst through the storm with an explosion that sent her soaring. Her body vibrated with wonderful sensations that slowly ebbed, leaving her to drift down in peaceful spirals, supported by Mike's arms.

He held her close, stroking her gently and kissing her temple. Samantha felt completely drained, but utterly blissful. She had become a woman in the arms of the man she loved. What more could anyone ask?

She drifted off to sleep with her head pillowed on his hair-roughened chest, awakening some time later to find him watching her tenderly. "Why . . . why are you looking at me like that?" she asked.

"Because you're so beautiful." His fingertips trailed over her soft cheek. "Haven't I told you that?"

"Not lately," she murmured shyly.

"Then let me say it again. You're beautiful. You're gorgeous. You're delectable. And you're mine." Each declaration was punctuated by a drugging kiss, and Samantha felt awakening passion cascade once more through her body. Mike murmured endless words of endearment as he skillfully roused her desire to match his own. Once more she was transported to celestial places, coming back to earth totally fulfilled.

Mike slipped into slumber this time, and she was free to look her fill at him. Even in sleep he looked commanding, but Samantha knew the tenderness he was capable of. Her finger gently touched the wide, firm mouth and he smiled in his sleep, drawing her a little closer. Samantha's heart was bursting with love. She touched her lips very lightly to his. Mike was right, she did belong to him—body and soul.

It wasn't until much later that the first doubts began to form like ice crystals around her heart. Mike had said, "You're mine," but he had never said, "I'm yours." He had told her how beautiful she was, but he had never said, "I love you."

Surely she was just splitting hairs. The fact that he had made such tender love to her, introduced her so gently to the joys of her body, must mean that he cared for her. But even as she assured herself Samantha knew that wasn't necessarily true. Mike was a skillful lover and a very sensual man. He could make any woman respond, and enjoy the pleasure they both felt without having any deep emotions involved. Men were different than women. They didn't have to be *in* love to make love.

Was she just another conquest to Mike then? Every fiber in Samantha's being rejected the idea, yet the evidence was there. Mike had said himself that he was tired of waiting for her to give in. He had set about cold-bloodedly to seduce her. Was that the act of a man in love? And if he didn't care, what future was there for her? A few weeks or months until the novelty wore off and he became tired of her inexperience? And then what? Back to the blonde or the redhead—or someone who had the fascination of being entirely new?

Tears welled up in Samantha's eyes. Even though she could feel the warmth of Mike's body and the steady beat of his heart against her breast right now, she knew it was a terribly temporary thing. There would come a time when his eyes wouldn't smolder with desire for her; they would be icy with boredom. She had seen them cold and disinterested; it wasn't something she could bear again. Better to get out now. At least she would have the memory of this one perfect experience, unmarred by what would certainly come after.

Inching herself carefully out of his arms, Samantha held her breath when Mike frowned in his sleep and tightened his grip on her. She waited a heart-stopping moment, then disentangled his fingers, slipping quietly out of his arms.

Gathering her scattered clothes, she tiptoed from the room. In the living room, she hurriedly dressed.

Her suitcase was still standing in the corner. She picked it up, opening the door noiselessly.

The sky was paling, but even the birds hadn't awakened yet. Everything was quiet. Samantha had a bad moment when her car shattered the silence, the motor sounding impossibly loud without any background noises. Nothing could stop her flight now, however. The car picked up speed as she drove through the deserted streets and out the front gate, tears streaming down her pale cheeks.

Chapter Eleven

Samantha unlocked the door of her small apartment with the feeling that she had found a safe haven. It didn't last long. As she walked into the bedroom to put her suitcase away the phone started ringing. A quick glance at the clock showed her it was only a quarter to seven. Who would be calling at this hour except Mike? He had awakened and found her gone.

She stood very still, holding her breath unconsciously until the strident, rhythmic sound ceased. Then with a weary exhalation of breath, she got undressed and went into the bathroom. She stood under the shower for a long time, but she couldn't scrub away the feeling of Mike's seductive hands on her skin. Did she really want to? Samantha hugged her wet body, knowing that he had made an indelible impression no matter what she decided.

She was toweling her hair dry when the telephone

started to ring again. She raised her head like a frightened little doe scenting danger. The phone had an angry sound to it, a harsh cry like a male animal trumpeting his displeasure.

Mike wasn't through with her yet. He had expected to wake up with her in his arms and prove his dominance again in the soft light of morning. Samantha's eyes closed to shut out the tantalizing pictures that presented themselves. She had found the strength to leave him somehow, but she couldn't count on it happening again. He mustn't be allowed to find her or she would become his mindless slave, content with any crumbs of affection he was willing to throw her way. And when even the crumbs weren't forthcoming, she would be an empty shell.

She dressed quickly, knowing that this apartment wasn't a haven after all. As long as Mike knew where to find her, she wasn't safe. He wouldn't hesitate to claim what he knew was his for the taking.

Her fearful eyes went to the clock. She was so nervous that things kept slipping out of her fingers. She couldn't count on the hour and a half it took to drive from Silverado. Mike could be phoning from some place along the way.

Pulling on a pair of cream-colored wool pants and a creamy cashmere sweater, Samantha ran a hasty comb through her hair and picked up her suitcase. Hysteria mounted in her throat as she realized how often she had carried this case without ever unpacking it.

When she had thrown it in the car, Samantha headed for the freeway. Unconsciously she had known all along where she was going. To the only place that was safe—home.

Brooke and her mother were having breakfast

when she arrived. They both looked startled, but Brooke was the one to voice it. "Sammy! What on earth are you doing here on a weekday morning?"

Samantha forced a smile. "Well, I must say that's not much of a greeting."

"What do you expect? You hardly even get here on the weekends! What's up?"

Cecily took a look at her older daughter's white face. "Don't you have a class, Brooke?"

Brooke took a look at her wristwatch. "Holy cow! I'm going to be late again and Professor Reynolds always makes such a big deal out of it." She took a hasty sip of coffee. "I hate to rush off, Sammy, this is such a treat. But I'm on the ragged edge in Psych class already."

"Run along, darling," Cecily said. "I'm sure Samantha will forgive you."

Rational conversation was impossible until Brooke had departed in a whirl of last-minute instructions about phone calls and dresses to be taken to the cleaner. Even after she had rushed out the door, Brooke returned for forgotten articles.

"I suppose I'm a terrible mother," Cecily said with a mischievous smile, "but the day doesn't seem to begin until that child is out of the house."

Samantha looked after her sister with brooding eyes. "She meets life more than halfway doesn't she?"

Cecily's smile faded. "That is what everyone should do, don't you think? Life is so short, it seems a shame to waste a minute of it," she said casually. Before Samantha could answer, she placed a cup and saucer in front of her. "Have some coffee, dear, it's nice and hot."

Samantha sipped it gratefully, trying to think how to begin. They talked in generalities for a while.

Finally she said, "Aren't you going to ask me what I'm doing here?"

Cecily shrugged. "I imagine you will get around to telling me."

There was a short silence. Then Samantha looked at her mother over the rim of her cup. "Do you think I'm pretty?" she asked abruptly.

Cecily laughed. "What kind of mother would I be if I didn't?"

"That's right," Samantha said sadly. "You're the wrong one to ask."

"I was only joking, darling. You are not only pretty, you're beautiful—inside and out."

"I wasn't worried about the part that doesn't show," Samantha said wryly.

"I have been blessed with two outstanding daughters. You and your sister were always the prettiest little girls in town."

"I remember all those long golden curls Brooke had," Samantha said wistfully. "And the way everyone used to stop and make a fuss over her."

"You don't remember, but the same thing happened when you were a toddler. People were always saying extravagant, if trite, things—like those thick eyelashes being put on with a sooty thumb. Once a man even stopped me in a department store, asking to enter you in a beauty contest. Of course I turned him down. That sort of thing is so tacky I think," she said disapprovingly.

"I can't believe I was that eye-catching."

"For heaven's sake, child, don't you ever look in a mirror?" Cecily asked impatiently.

She had looked in a mirror recently—with disastrous results. Samantha could almost feel Mike's sensuous hands gliding over her body as he enumerated her charms. She shivered involuntarily, shaking her head to banish the memory. "I left that sort of thing to Brooke," she said, in answer to her mother's question. "She was your kind of daughter."

Cecily looked at her evenly. "And you were your father's."

"I do look like him, yes."

"It was more than that, Samantha. Even when you were a little girl, you and Rufus had a special bond. You tagged around after him like a puppy and he was terribly pleased. I suppose that's why when Brooke came along, we were very close. Perhaps subconsciously I was trying to make up to her for the fact that you were your father's favorite."

"Dad adored Brooke!" Samantha protested.

"But you were his firstborn, his pride and joy."

The thought that she could have held a place of preference over Brooke in anything was startling. "I . . . I never realized."

"And I never realized that you felt left out when Brooke and I chattered away together with our inconsequential girl talk. I thought you knew that I loved you both equally and I was always here if you needed me," Cecily said sadly.

"Oh, I did, Mother! I did! I was perfectly happy as a child."

"But not now?" Cecily asked quietly.

"Well, I . . ."

"Would you like to talk about it?"

Samantha sighed. "Part of it I have to. I've sold the business," she said without preamble.

For once in her life, she had succeeded in surprising her mother. Cecily blinked, but her only comment was, "I see."

"You don't have to worry," Samantha hastily assured her. "There will be plenty of money. Perhaps more than there was before, after it's invested properly."

"I wasn't concerned about that. It was just a surprise, that's all."

"You're probably thinking that I should have discussed it with you first. I wouldn't blame you if you did."

"You were the one who had the responsibility for running the business, Samantha, so you were the one to make the decisions. I understand that."

"Still, it did concern you and Brooke." Samantha was suffering belated remorse. "It's just that there were . . . were reasons."

"Ones you don't care to talk about?"

"Yes," Samantha said shortly. She was never more grateful for her mother's policy of never prying.

Cecily didn't disappoint her this time. "Well, that's that then. The important thing is, what are you going to do now?"

"I wish I knew." Samantha sighed.

Cecily inspected her daughter's woebegone face. "There isn't any pressing need to make up your mind right away. You have been working terribly hard, dear. Why don't you take a little time off and enjoy yourself?"

Samantha gave her a rueful smile. "I think I've forgotten how."

"That's dreadful! If it's truly the case, I'm happy you got rid of the business. Maybe now you will have time for other things. What happened to that nice young man you brought over?" she asked casually.

"Mike? Forget it, mother. If you're trying to fix me up, you picked the wrong man."

"I thought he was quite charming."

"*All* women do," Samantha said bitterly.

"You sound like you are the exception."

"Oh, he's charming enough, I'll grant you that—when he wants to be, that is. But any woman stupid

234

enough to fall in love with him deserves everything she gets."

"Unfortunately, we are not always given the choice of whom we fall in love with," Cecily murmured. "Why would it be such a disaster?"

"Because Mike likes variety," Samantha answered tersely. "You wouldn't understand, Mother. Things were different in your day—more romantic. People today don't fall in love and live happily after anymore."

Cecily smiled. "I don't think human nature changes that much, my dear. People have fallen in love through the ages."

"Like Romeo and Juliet?" Samantha asked caustically.

"Some," Cecily conceded. "But even in that case, their sad demises were due to a misunderstanding."

"If you are obliquely referring to Mike and me, there was never an *understanding.*"

"Would you like there to be?" her mother asked evenly.

"No! Certainly not!"

"When a woman protests that strongly, Samantha, she usually means just the opposite."

Samantha picked up her cup, going to the stove to pour herself more coffee. "All right, maybe I could let myself fall in love with Mike. Unfortunately he doesn't feel the same way about me."

"Are you sure? He seemed quite interested the day you brought him here."

How could she explain to her mother that Mike was only interested in sleeping with her—and he had already accomplished that! Samantha kept her back turned, afraid that her expressive face would reveal the wonder of last night and the agony of this morning.

"Let's just say that Mike isn't the marrying sort of

man, and I'm not the kind of woman who would be content to share him." She brought her coffee back to the table and sat down, giving her mother a little smile. "You did your work too well."

"I obviously didn't do it well at all," Cecily remarked impatiently. "It is nonsense to say that *any* man is not the marrying kind. I would be very disappointed if you let that defeatist attitude destroy your chance at happiness."

Samantha laughed in spite of herself. "Oh, Mother, it's evident that you never met a man like Mike. He can't be bullied into anything."

"I didn't have bullying in mind," Cecily murmured.

"It wouldn't help to flutter my eyelashes either."

Cecily tilted her head to one side, inspecting her daughter's lovely face speculatively. "It couldn't hurt. I don't mean to criticize, dear, but you are awfully independent. You make it rather difficult for a man to tell you he loves you."

It hadn't been difficult last night! Every word Mike had said to her was engraved on her memory. Just as every one of his tantalizing caresses was imprinted on her throbbing body. Oh, he had whispered *words* of love—things that made her blush and yet glow when she thought of them—but he had never actually said he loved her. And that was the difference. It wasn't anything she could very well tell her mother, though.

Suddenly, Samantha was terribly weary. "If you don't mind, I think I'll go upstairs and take a little nap. I . . . I didn't sleep much last night."

"That's a very good idea, darling. It will be nice and quiet around here. I have a Ladies Guild meeting at noon, and Brooke never comes home until late."

Samantha undressed and climbed into bed gratefully. She wouldn't be able to sleep, but at least it would be nice to lie here and rest. The next minute, she fell fast asleep.

It was late afternoon when she awoke feeling wonderfully refreshed—until memory returned. Then depression settled like a bird of doom on her shoulders.

A shower refreshed her somewhat. The stinging water had brought color to her cheeks, and as she brushed her hair to a dark, glossy sheen Samantha wondered how she could look so vibrant after all that had happened to her.

She was hungry too. It was four o'clock by now and Samantha realized that she hadn't had anything to eat all day. She debated whether she should bother to fix anything, finally deciding that a snack was imperative. There was cold chicken in the refrigerator, and she took a wing and an apple out to the patio. After she had finished eating, she wrapped the bones and the core in a napkin, carefully depositing it in the garbage can. Then she returned to her lounge chair.

It was quiet in the garden except for the birds that were flying back and forth, and the bees that were busily pollinating flowers. A large black and orange butterfly drifted about, content merely to add beauty to the landscape. The intense quiet should have been soothing to Samantha. Instead, it had the opposite effect.

Springing to her feet, she began to pace the flagstone patio. What did people do when they didn't work? Brooke went to college of course, and her mother had her clubs and her charities. But what was she going to do with her life?

Naturally she would get another job, except that it would be a nine-to-five one. Her nights and weekends wouldn't be taken up with crises and deadlines.

A fine dew of perspiration broke out on her forehead as Samantha looked around the deserted patio. There would be ample time for sitting around like this, doing nothing.

No, she was being fanciful. She had to stop that and get hold of herself. There were lots of things she could do, and people she could do them with. She could move back here, for instance, with Mother and Brooke. But they had made their own interests without her. Well, then, she would develop her own. She would start going out again, get back in the swim of things. There was Stan Rasmussen to start with, and there would be other men.

Samantha sank slowly down on the lounge chair. The thought of processions of men was merely depressing. She knew she would always be searching for another Mike, measuring them up against his imposing charms, seeing them all fail the test. But I don't want to go through life alone, she screamed silently.

If only Mike were finally and irrevocably beyond her reach so she couldn't weaken and run back to him as she was tempted to this minute. If only he would get married or something, and put himself forever beyond the pale. Samantha sat very still. Mike would never marry, but she could. Donald had said he would marry her anytime she liked.

The idea was totally repugnant at first, yet gradually it began to make sense. Once she made her vows, Samantha knew she would keep them. Temptation would be forever behind her, and in time the longing would fade. It just had to! The only thing that bothered her was the fact that it was dishonest. She didn't love Donald and never would. She would love Mike until her dying day, but if Donald didn't know about it, then it wasn't cheating.

She would be a good wife to him, Samantha vowed. Donald would never have cause to complain. She would perform her wifely duties more zealously than if it were a marriage for love. For a moment her stomach turned over at the thought of going to bed with him, but she put it out of her mind.

There was more to marriage than that, and Donald had never shown signs of being overly passionate. Perhaps he wouldn't be too demanding. She clenched her teeth. They had had some very pleasant times together before Mike turned her life into a roller coaster that careened between ecstasy and despair. Her marriage to Donald would be more solid for not being based on sexual desire.

With the decision, a kind of resigned calm descended on Samantha. She would call Donald at the office and tell him she had made up her mind. Before she could go inside to phone, Brooke came bouncing onto the patio.

"Oh, good, you're still here, Sammy. I had to dash out so fast this morning that I didn't get to ask you your plans. You will stay to dinner, won't you?"

Their mother appeared in the doorway. "We're in luck. I think Samantha is going to stay longer than that."

"Really? How come? I thought you said it was too far from work," her sister said.

Samantha and her mother exchanged glances. Realizing that Samantha wanted her to be the one, Cecily said casually, "Samantha has sold the business."

"No fooling! Well, I guess you knew what you were doing." Brooke dismissed it as casually as her mother.

Samantha felt a mixture of amusement and irritation, but she didn't know at whom. At herself perhaps, for thinking they would go to pieces if Morgan's went out of the family. Mike was right. It was *her* security blanket, not theirs.

"It will be such fun to have you home again, Sammy. Are you going to give up your apartment?"

"I . . . I don't know." Perhaps Donald would want to move into her place after they were married.

"There is no need for Samantha to rush into anything," Cecily said smoothly.

"If it means she's going to be around here longer, I say super," Brooke said enthusiastically.

"I'll second that." Cecily smiled. "Well, I think I will go in and start dinner. You two girls sit here and chat."

"I have to make a telephone call," Samantha said hesitantly.

"Go ahead, I'll give Mother a hand," Brooke said.

Donald was ecstatic at hearing from her. "I've missed you, darling," he said in a low, throaty voice.

Samantha knew she was supposed to say the same thing, yet the words stuck in her throat. "There has been so much going on."

"I know how hard you work, Sam, but I sometimes feel like that business of yours is a rival," he complained.

"It won't be any longer. I sold out to Sutherland's yesterday, Donald," Samantha said quietly.

"You did? For the amount you mentioned?" There was excitement in his voice. "That's wonderful, darling! You should have told me, though, I could have helped. I hope you had a good attorney."

"Yes, Henry Creighton has been taking care of our affairs for years."

"Sometimes those older men aren't up with the times, though. They can get taken in by a slick-talking young lawyer, and I'm sure Mike Sutherland has plenty of those. You should have let me be there, Samantha."

"It's over and done with. I don't want to talk about it anymore," she said sharply.

"I understand, dear," he soothed. "I know how you felt about that place. But look on the bright side—we'll have more time to spend together. This call does mean that you have decided to forgive me, doesn't it?"

"I've decided more than that." She took a deep breath. "Do you still want to marry me, Donald?"

There was an incredulous intake of breath at the other end of the line. "You mean . . . I . . . we . . ."

"If you've changed your mind just say so," she said crisply, something very like relief rising inside of her.

"Of course I haven't changed my mind! This is the happiest moment of my life! You too, darling?"

"I . . . yes."

"It's just so sudden," he said, too excited to register her lack of enthusiasm. "You were so cold the last time I talked to you. I was really worried. What made you decide?"

"Well, I thought a lot about it," she said flatly. "Mother and Brooke will no longer be a problem, and naturally I'll get a job. We shouldn't have any money worries at all." Samantha listened to her own voice in wonder. She might be discussing a business merger instead of a marriage.

Donald was too delighted to notice. "We'll talk about all that later, sweetheart. The main thing is that you're going to marry me. I can't tell you how that makes me feel."

Samantha's conscience smote her. She had promised herself she would be a good wife, and so far she wasn't even being civil to him. "I'm glad if I have made you happy, Donald," she said gently.

"The only thing that would make me happier is to have you in my arms right now. When am I going to see you, darling?"

Samantha was startled. She hadn't thought past this moment. "I don't know," she said vaguely.

"I have to see you immediately. I'm coming over right now."

"No! I mean I'm not at my apartment. I'm at Mother's."

"Then I'll come out there."

"No, Donald, don't do that. I . . . I'll meet you at my place later tonight—say nine o'clock."

Samantha hung up the phone slowly. Any other newly engaged woman would want her fiancé to come over and share their joy with her family. She couldn't face such a meeting, though. Samantha didn't know how her mother would take the news, but she was only too aware of what Brooke's reaction would be.

"Who did you call?" her sister asked as she walked into the kitchen.

"Brooke! Won't you ever learn about the right to privacy?" Cecily asked.

"It's all right, Mother." Samantha gave her a wan smile. "You might as well know. I called Donald."

"That turkey!" Brooke said indignantly. "I thought you turned over a new leaf."

"I did. I'm going to marry him," Samantha said before she could change her mind.

"What! You must be out of your mind!" Brooke's outrage was immediate and vocal, but even her mother looked concerned.

"Isn't this rather sudden, Samantha?" Cecily asked quietly.

Avoiding her mother's eyes, she said, "Not really.

We've been going together for a long time, remember?"

"I thought when you went out with Stan, it meant you broke up with Donald," Brooke said suspiciously.

"We had a little misunderstanding," Samantha said carefully. "But I thought about it all afternoon, and I decided I'm not getting any younger."

"No, you're just getting dumber," her sister raged.

"Quiet, Brooke." Cecily hesitated. "If this is what you want, Samantha, then I'm very happy for you. I would just like to hear you say that you love him."

Those clear eyes seemed to be burning right into her heart. Samantha realized the futility of trying to lie to her mother. If only it had been Mike she was marrying, there wouldn't have been any need. His beloved face appeared tantalizingly before her, the firm mouth and warm gray eyes thickly fringed with black lashes, sending a shiver down her spine.

The shimmer of tears in her eyes dissolved the image and Samantha blinked desperately. "You will never know how much I love him," she whispered.

Brooke gave a snort of disgust, venting her displeasure while Cecily remained strangely preoccupied.

Finally Samantha put her hands over her ears. "I don't want to hear any more about it," she cried. "If you don't stop, I'm going to leave this very minute." Her face was very pale.

Brooke threw her arms around her. "Don't go, Sammy, I'm sorry. I won't say another word, I promise! I only want you to be happy."

Samantha hugged her back. "I know, baby."

"We won't talk about it anymore. I'll cut class tomorrow and we'll go someplace and just have fun like we used to."

"I'd like that," Samantha said regretfully, "but I won't be here. I'm meeting Donald at my apartment at nine and it will be too late to come back here."

"Couldn't you put it off till tomorrow night?" Brooke asked wistfully.

Samantha shook her head wordlessly. She was committed now, there was no sense in postponing it.

Cecily removed her apron. "Will you two girls carry on for a minute? There is something I have to do."

Dinner wasn't exactly a gala event in spite of their attempts to make it so. Brooke opened a bottle of wine and they all talked animatedly, carefully avoiding the subject of marriage.

Samantha felt a pang as she drove home. They had always been so natural together, enjoying each other's company and never stopping to weigh their words as they had tonight. Was this the opening wedge that would drive her from her family? And was it Donald's fault, or would any man naturally cause a breakup? That was probably it. And yet she remembered Brooke's reaction to Mike and her mother's pleased smile as he kissed her cheek. Why was she tormenting herself? It didn't matter how any of them felt about Mike. It was how *he* felt that mattered.

Samantha didn't notice that Donald's car was parked in front of her building. He got out of it and joined her as she was walking up to the front door.

"Oh, Donald, you startled me! Am I late?"

"No, you're right on time. I was early. Can you guess why I couldn't wait?" he asked jubilantly.

She eluded his outstretched arms. "Not here," she murmured, "people can see us."

"I don't care. They can print our picture on the front page of the paper as far as I'm concerned," he exulted.

Samantha paused in the act of inserting her key. "What has gotten into you, Donald. You were always so reserved."

"That's been the whole trouble. I've been thinking a lot about this, Sam, and I finally realized that what you want is a more assertive man."

"Not . . . not necessarily."

He followed her into the living room. "I know you're too shy to admit it, darling, but you secretly want someone more masterful. And that's exactly what I'm going to be."

He crushed her in his arms, bending her backward and covering her mouth in a kiss that was more punishing than masterful. Samantha could hardly breathe. Suddenly the bright overhead light went on, illuminating them with painful clarity.

"Very touching," Mike said, lounging against the door to the kitchen while he regarded them with hard eyes.

"Where did you come from?" she gasped.

"Who is this man?" Donald demanded simultaneously.

Since Samantha seemed incapable of further speech, Mike introduced himself. "I'm Mike Sutherland," he said, without offering to shake hands.

"Oh, the fellow who bought Sam's business." Donald's truculence disappeared.

"The very same," Mike drawled. "And you must be Donald."

"That's right. Did Sam tell you about me?"

"A little. However, she doesn't tell me very much—not even when she is leaving." Mike's mouth curved sardonically. "Samantha has a habit of walking out when things get beyond her control."

"That doesn't sound like my girl." Donald's arm went around her rigid shoulders. "You just don't know her like I do."

"I have proof that I know her better," Mike said mockingly.

Samantha's cheeks were like wild roses. "How did you get in here?" she asked swiftly.

"You forget, I'm a builder. If I'd known how flimsy your lock was, I would have fixed it long ago."

"I don't want you to do any more for me," she said, flinging her head back and looking at him stormily. "You have already done enough."

Small flames glowed in the depths of his eyes. "Not nearly as much as I plan to."

"You insufferable egotist! Get out of my house!" she cried, forgetting everything except this man who was a torment to her.

"Samantha!" Donald's exclamation was shocked. "How can you talk that way to a man who has treated you so generously?"

Mike's amusement threatened to choke him as Samantha's hands curled into little fists. "Stay out of this, Donald," she snapped. "You don't know what you're talking about. And as for you," she said, turning to Mike, "I meant what I said. Get out of my apartment."

"Excuse us a moment." Donald dragged her to a corner of the room. "Are you crazy, Sam?" he whispered hoarsely. "The papers aren't filed yet. He could back out of the deal!"

"I don't care what he does," she shouted. "Just as long as I never have to see him again!"

Mike sauntered over. "You will have to excuse her. Samantha allowed herself to act like a normal woman for once in her life, and now she is suffering the pangs of remorse." His eyes held hers until she turned away, unable to meet the challenge in them.

"I'm glad you understand that she's a little over-wrought at the moment," Donald said placatingly. "Selling the business was a big step, and I guess getting engaged is a pretty traumatic one for a woman too. Especially when it all comes at once."

Mike's eyebrows rose. "When did all this happen?"

"Just this evening actually." Donald put his arm possessively around Samantha's waist. "I'll bet we're the only couple you know who ever got engaged over the telephone." He laughed.

Mike's eyes went to Samantha. "I wonder how he plans to spend the honeymoon," he murmured.

"Don't you think congratulations would be more in order than a snide remark?" she asked acidly.

"I'm sure Mr. Sutherland wishes us well, Sam. She is very shy," Donald told Mike, as one man of the world to another.

"You have a lot to learn about women," Mike said. "Like, did she tell you that the first baby is likely to be mine?"

"What are you talking about?" Donald demanded before Samantha could do anything but gasp.

"You can't be *that* inexperienced. Surely you know about babies," Mike said derisively.

"Mike, stop! You can't do this!" she cried.

"I ought to knock you into the next county for that," Donald scowled, clenching his fists.

"You could try," Mike agreed, "except that I'd hate to have to hurt you. You're not too bright, but you don't deserve the raw deal Samantha is trying to palm off on you. Ask her where she spent last night—and with whom."

Donald's fists came out flailing, but Mike fended off the blows easily, twisting the other man's arms behind his back and pushing him into a chair. He stood over him, shoving him back when Donald tried to rise.

"Will you tell him the truth, Samantha, before I have to slap him silly?" Mike demanded.

"Leave him alone! Leave both of us alone!" she cried.

"All right, then I'll have to do it myself," Mike said grimly. Samantha and I spent last night together in Silverado. I could prove it conclusively by telling you about a tiny birthmark she has in a very enticing place, except that you have probably never seen it."

The eyes of both men went to her as she unconsciously covered a spot on her left breast. Donald slumped back like a deflated balloon.

"What he's saying is true, isn't it, Sam?" Donald asked.

"Donald, I . . ." She thought of lying for his sake, knowing all the while that Mike wouldn't permit it. "Yes, it's true," she said in a low voice.

"But just this afternoon—you were the one who called me. And all along you knew that last night . . ." Donald's voice trailed off.

"I'm sorry," she murmured.

"Sorry? You damn well should be!" Righteous indignation was flooding Donald, making him ugly. "I wouldn't marry you now if you got down on your knees and begged me! Do you know what you are? You're nothing but—"

Mike took a handful of Donald's jacket, practically picking him up. His eyes were hard as he hustled him out the door. "Shut your filthy mouth or I'll arrange it in a different place." The whole wall shook as he slammed the door.

"Why didn't you let him say it?" Samantha asked wearily. "It's true."

Mike watched her, his face unreadable. "Would you like a drink?"

"I thought the condemned were offered a last cigarette." Her harsh laugh turned into a sob. "Why did you do it, Mike? Why?"

He came over to her then, taking her in his arms. Samantha lashed out wildly, but Mike just held her, crooning soothing words while he stroked her hair. Finally she collapsed against his hard length, crying until there were no tears left, unable to protest when he lifted her in his arms and sat down with her in a chair.

"Are you feeling better now?" he asked when the last hiccuping sob had subsided.

She shook her head, hiding her face in his shoulder even while she knew she should be getting up. Her voice was muffled as she asked, "Was it because I left you in Silverado? Did that make you hate me enough to do what you did tonight?"

He tangled his hand in her hair, pulling her head back so he could look at her. "You know I don't hate you, Samantha."

She caught her quivering lower lip in small, white teeth. "What else would make you destroy me like that? Why did you have to tell Donald about us?"

"I didn't want you to marry him."

His voice was so matter-of-fact that she could almost have laughed if it hadn't been so tragic. "How can you be so selfish? What are a few more weeks of getting what you want compared to the rest of my life?"

"You belong to me, and the sooner you realize it the better off we'll both be," Mike said sternly. "I could just have taken you away from Donald, but he would always have been a threat. Not because you care about him, Lord knows, but because he represents another one of those little safety zones of yours. Something to run to when life gets so exciting that it scares you. Well, we got rid of Donald for good. You really ought to thank me. Marriage to him would have been a terrible bore. He couldn't teach you half the things I can," he teased.

Samantha was suddenly conscious of his hand stroking her arm. It evoked memories powerful enough to make her sit upright, although Mike wouldn't let her escape from his lap. "If you think you're going to keep me tied to you by sex, you're very badly mistaken."

"Strange, I thought you liked it," he mused. His hand cupped her breast, his fingers gently searching for the sensitive tip. "You were a very enthusiastic pupil."

"Mike, don't!" she moaned, trying to fight the embers that were stirring dangerously in her veins.

When his lips touched hers, Samantha knew she was lost. He parted her lips with an urgency that left her trembling. His hand went under her sweater, moving seductively over her back, and she gave up the struggle, winding her arms around his neck as the embers burst into flames.

"Now are you willing to admit that you belong to me?" he murmured against her satin skin.

"Yes, oh, yes! Anytime you want me." She sighed.

"How about all the time?" He chuckled, a low satisfied sound deep in his throat. "I want to go to sleep at night with you in my arms, and wake up the same way."

Samantha became very still. "Are you asking me to live with you?"

"I believe that's customary among married couples."

"Married? You're asking me to marry you?" Samantha was dazed.

"What did you think I was suggesting? No, don't tell me. The minds of young virgins continue to shock me."

It was like a miracle! Mike actually wanted to marry her! Samantha's eyes were like stars as it gradually sank in. Then she kissed his neck, murmuring softly into it, "I'm not a virgin anymore."

He framed her face in his palms, looking at her tenderly. "No, you are my beautiful wife. The license is just a formality." His head blotted out everything as their lips met.

A long time later, Samantha stirred in his embrace, but Mike growled, "You aren't going anywhere this time." He tightened his arms around her. "Oh, my love, you will never know how I felt when I woke and found you gone. Why did you run away?"

She rubbed her cheek back and forth on the crisp hair that covered his broad chest. "I couldn't face the thought that I was just another conquest to you. Rather than wait around for you to tire of me, I decided to keep my memory of that one perfect night."

He lifted her chin and looked at her incredulously. "Didn't you know I was in love with you?"

"You never told me," she said simply.

"My sweet, innocent beauty, everything I did was meant to tell you."

"I know that now," she said humbly.

"I'm not sure you do. Maybe I'd better show you again," Mike said.

"Maybe you'd better because I'm still not sure this is happening," she said, looking up at him dreamily and smoothing his eyebrow with her forefinger. "If you hadn't been angry enough to wait in my apartment tonight, and I hadn't happened to agree to meet Donald here, I would be engaged to him right now."

Mike captured her finger and kissed the tip. "Don't you believe it. In the first place, that is something I never would have permitted. And in the second place, we have someone looking out for us."

"Cupid?" she asked happily.

"In the form of your mother," he agreed. "She phoned and told me what nonsense you were planning."

Samantha's eyes opened wide. "That couldn't be! My mother never interferes."

"There is a first time for everything," Mike said, tracing the line of her lower lip with a seductive finger. "Maybe she prefers me as a son-in-law."

"My mother always did have excellent taste," Samantha said happily, putting her arms around his waist and snuggling close.

If you enjoyed this book...

...you will enjoy a Special Edition Book Club membership even more.

It will bring you each new title, as soon as it is published every month, delivered right to your door.

15-Day Free Trial Offer

We will send you 6 new Silhouette Special Editions to keep for 15 days absolutely free! If you decide not to keep them, send them back to us, you pay nothing. But if you enjoy them as much as we think you will, keep them and pay the invoice enclosed with your trial shipment. You will then automatically become a member of the Special Edition Book Club and receive 6 more romances every month. There is no minimum number of books to buy and you can cancel at any time.

MORE ROMANCE FOR
A SPECIAL WAY TO RELAX

$1.95 each

1 ☐ TERMS OF SURRENDER Dailey

2 ☐ INTIMATE STRANGERS Hastings

3 ☐ MEXICAN RHAPSODY Dixon

4 ☐ VALAQUEZ BRIDE Vitek

5 ☐ PARADISE POSTPONED Converse

6 ☐ SEARCH FOR A NEW DAWN Douglass

7 ☐ SILVER MIST Stanford

8 ☐ KEYS TO DANIEL'S HOUSE Halston

9 ☐ ALL OUR TOMORROWS Baxter

10 ☐ TEXAS ROSE Thiels

11 ☐ LOVE IS SURRENDER Thornton

12 ☐ NEVER GIVE YOUR HEART Sinclair

13 ☐ BITTER VICTORY Beckman

14 ☐ EYE OF THE HURRICANE Keene

15 ☐ DANGEROUS MAGIC James

16 ☐ MAYAN MOON Carr

17 ☐ SO MANY TOMORROWS John

18 ☐ A WOMAN'S PLACE Hamilton

19 ☐ DECEMBER'S WINE Shaw

20 ☐ NORTHERN LIGHTS Musgrave

21 ☐ ROUGH DIAMOND Hastings

22 ☐ ALL THAT GLITTERS Howard

23 ☐ LOVE'S GOLDEN SHADOW Charles

24 ☐ GAMBLE OF DESIRE Dixon

25 ☐ TEARS AND RED ROSES Hardy

26 ☐ A FLIGHT OF SWALLOWS Scott

27 ☐ A MAN WITH DOUBTS Wisdom

28 ☐ THE FLAMING TREE Ripy

29 ☐ YEARNING OF ANGELS Bergen

30 ☐ BRIDE IN BARBADOS Stephens

31 ☐ TEARS OF YESTERDAY Baxter

32 ☐ A TIME TO LOVE Douglass

33 ☐ HEATHER'S SONG Palmer

34 ☐ MIXED BLESSING Sinclair

35 ☐ STORMY CHALLENGE James

36 ☐ FOXFIRE LIGHT Dailey

37 ☐ MAGNOLIA MOON Stanford

38 ☐ WEB OF PASSION John

39 ☐ AUTUMN HARVEST Milan

40 ☐ HEARTSTORM Converse

41 ☐ COLLISION COURSE Halston

42 ☐ PROUD VINTAGE Drummond

43 ☐ ALL SHE EVER WANTED Shaw

44 ☐ SUMMER MAGIC Eden

45 ☐ LOVE'S TENDER TRIAL Charles

46 ☐ AN INDEPENDENT WIFE Howard

47 ☐ PRIDE'S POSSESSION Stephens

48 ☐ LOVE HAS ITS REASONS Ferrell

49 ☐ A MATTER OF TIME Hastings

50 ☐ FINDERS KEEPERS Browning

51 ☐ STORMY AFFAIR Trent

52 ☐ DESIGNED FOR LOVE Sinclair

53 ☐ GODDESS OF THE MOON Thomas

54 ☐ THORNE'S WAY Hohl

MORE ROMANCE FOR
A SPECIAL WAY TO RELAX

55 ☐ SUN LOVER Stanford

56 ☐ SILVER FIRE Wallace

57 ☐ PRIDE'S RECKONING Thornton

58 ☐ KNIGHTLY LOVE Douglass

59 ☐ THE HEART'S VICTORY Roberts

60 ☐ ONCE AND FOREVER Thorne

61 ☐ TENDER DECEPTION Beckman

62 ☐ DEEP WATERS Bright

63 ☐ LOVE WITH A PERFECT STRANGER
Wallace

64 ☐ MIST OF BLOSSOMS Converse

65 ☐ HANDFUL OF SKY Cales

66 ☐ A SPORTING AFFAIR Mikels

67 ☐ AFTER THE RAIN Shaw

68 ☐ CASTLES IN THE AIR Sinclair

69 ☐ SORREL SUNSET Dalton

70 ☐ TRACES OF DREAMS Clare

71 ☐ MOONSTRUCK Skillern

72 ☐ NIGHT MUSIC Belmont

LOOK FOR *AN ACT OF LOVE*
BY BROOKE HASTINGS AVAILABLE IN MARCH AND
ENCHANTED SURRENDER BY PATTI BECKMAN
IN APRIL.

SILHOUETTE SPECIAL EDITION, Department SE/2
1230 Avenue of the Americas
New York, NY 10020

Please send me the books I have checked above. I am enclosing $_____
(please add 50¢ to cover postage and handling. NYS and NYC residents
please add appropriate sales tax). Send check or money order—no cash or
C.O.D.'s please. Allow six weeks for delivery.

NAME _____

ADDRESS _____

CITY _____ STATE/ZIP _____

Silhouette Special Edition

Coming Next Month

Season Of Seduction by Abra Taylor

In keeping her tennis pro sister out of trouble, Michele Haworth ran into a problem of her own: Damon Pierce— and Damon played to win no matter what the game!

Unspoken Past by Linda Wisdom

Unspoken, but not unremembered. How could Anne ever forget the brief hours she had shared with Kyle Harrison—or his anger when he discovered that she wasn't free to love?

Summer Rhapsody by Nancy John

Nina was leery of British tycoon Dexter Rolfe. But gradually she learned that the fire she found in his arms would warm the years ahead and secure their future together.

Tomorrow's Memory by Margaret Ripy

Cole's vengeful tie to Lacey's past held them together. But the passion they found soon melted their anger and had the Kentucky couple racing toward the future.

Prelude To Passion by Fran Bergen

Operatic set designer Nydia Lear was intrigued by world famous maestro Kurt Klausen. But she had a job to do and no time for love—until Kurt taught her otherwise.

Fortune's Play by Eve Gladstone

In the heat of the Arabian desert, Nicki's marriage to Steve had shattered. But now in Montana, Chinook winds swept across the plains to bring them together . . . this time forever.